The Prodigal Father

Hazel Norris

authorHOUSE®

AuthorHouse™
1663 Liberty Drive, Suite 200
Bloomington, IN 47403
www.authorhouse.com
Phone: 1-800-839-8640

First published by AuthorHouse 12/30/2008

ISBN: 978-1-4389-1328-5 (sc)

Library of Congress Control Number: 2008910474

Printed in the United States of America
Bloomington, Indiana

This book is printed on acid-free paper.

I

The tramp rocked back on his heels and wiped the smoke from his eyes. He realized it would do no good to move. The breeze would be blowing the smoke away in a minute. He shifted his weight to spare his bad leg and stared into the fire, deep in thought. The fish he had caught for his breakfast sizzled and sputtered in the frying pan. He stood to get the salt, before he remembered he had used the last of it yesterday. Well, maybe the bacon grease he was using to fry the fish would make it edible, but then he realized that was the last of the bacon grease. The last! Actually, he seemed to have used the last of everything. "Maybe," he thought to himself, "just maybe, it's better that way."

He stepped to the mouth of the cave he had been calling "home" for the past several months and brought out his pack. Slowly he took out the contents one by one and laid them on the flat rock he used for a table. His other shirt, worn threadbare and missing several buttons, but clean; a water jug; an old rag he used for washcloth, towel, dishcloth, and dishtowel; his bar of soap, nearly gone; a well worn map; a small mirror; a stub of a pencil – that was all.

He replaced the things in the pack and emptied his pockets. His gun? He laid it aside. He wouldn't be needing it anymore. His knife? He had had it always. Would it be safe to keep it? He decided it would. No one would remember it. His wallet had gone the way of hard use and had been replaced by an envelope. The envelope contained not a cent of money but several cards, papers, and one picture. He looked them over carefully and returned them to the envelope. The only other things his pockets contained were two papers he had found on his trip to town yesterday. He seldom did trash cans, for this tramp's taste was usually to a higher mode of living, but yesterday he had been *so* hungry and going down an alley he had sniffed the most delicious aroma of frying ham and fresh-baked bread. The next trashcan he came to surely must contain a scrap of something, so he decided to investigate. The first thing he pulled out was a newspaper wrapped wine bottle. The wine bottle was as dry as October's leaves, but his eye caught on the newspaper. A Springfield paper! Away out here! Now how did that – but then he saw something that made him forget everything else.

Funeral Notices

Mary Solomon Bradcox, 38, succumbed, April 20

Funeral at Steeman's Funeral Home, Tuesday 1:00 PM

The tramp had clutched the paper in his hand and stumbled on down the alley. Back at his cave he had carefully cut the notice from the paper and put it into his pocket. Now he looked at it again. Mary! Dear Mary! Dead! He slipped the clipping into the envelope with the other papers and sat holding it a moment. Then carefully he licked the envelope and sealed it. He took the stub of pencil from his pack and wrote on the envelope. ***Pete's identity. Do not open until after Pete's death.*** Then he picked up the one last paper and re-read it. It was only a child's Sunday School paper that had blown across his way. He had picked it up just for something to read. It was the story of the Prodigal Son. Now as he re-read it, the words seemed to catch in his throat and tears formed in his eyes.

I will arise and go to my father and will say unto him, Father, I have sinned against heaven, and before thee, and am no more worthy to be called thy son; make me as one of thy hired servants. (Luke 15:18-19)

He laid the paper on top of the dying fire and ate his breakfast. Then he sat back again, deep in thought. Could he do it? Could he go back home without being recognized? Ten years he had been gone. He had been a handsome man in his youth. He took his little mirror from his pack and stared at his reflection. He had changed a lot in ten years, but had he changed enough? His dark brown hair had fallen out above his forehead and what was left had turned to gray. Strangely enough, as it turned gray, it had become wavy. His nose was much larger, due to a collision with someone's fist in a drunken brawl. He ran his fingers over his three-week growth of beard. He had always hated a beard and had had a shave every time he could beg or steal one. Now, he decided, he would just let it grow. It would cover a lot by the time he reached home.

The tramp had always heard a man was most easily recognized by his voice and his walk. He decided he would practice a lower voice all the way home. By the time he arrived there, it should be a habit. Then, too, he had no intention of spending much time in the company of anyone who would recognize his voice. He was sure his walk wouldn't be a problem, after that accident (or was it an accident?) two years ago when he fell (or was he pushed?) off a cliff. The mountaineer who had picked him up and cared for him had said he would never walk again, but soon he was hobbling around with the aid of two homemade crutches and before two months had gone by he had been able to sneak away in the night, accompanied by a goodly amount of the mountaineer's possessions. Yet, after two years he was certain his walk would scarcely resemble his walk of former days.

He replaced the mirror in his pack and said aloud in his deepest voice, "Might as well get moving. Time doesn't stand still and wait for a man." He picked up the knife and dropped it into his pocket. Then he stood looking at the gun. Should he or shouldn't he? "No," he decided. "If I am going back home I better leave the life of the last ten years out here." He considered leaving it in the cave, but no, it might fall into the wrong hands. He had best just put it in the bottom of the river. He slipped it into his pocket, took his rag of all uses, wiped out his frying pan, and put it into his pack. Then he stood looking around. Not a thing here to let anyone know Pete ever lived here. "It's better that way," he thought. "It's been that way for ten years. Go where I please, but leave no tracks." He slung his pack on his back and started down the trail leading east.

II

The nine Bradcox children huddled in a group in the corner of Pastor Parker's conference room. No one dared sit down even though there were plenty of places available. They all loved Pastor Parker, except Billy Bob, of course. Everything ever to be said of the Bradcox children was said, "except Billy Bob," but their love of Pastor Parker didn't outweigh their anxiety as to why they were here.

Eleven-year-old Darlene pulled on David's sleeve and whispered, "Why are we here, David? Did we do something wrong?"

"I don't know, Honey," was David's reply.

"I suppose he found out about Billy Bob putting the frog in Mr. Peters' mailbox," ventured Nathan.

"No," Rachel answered, "if it had been that he would have called just Billy Bob or Billy Bob and David."

Now Darlene whispered to David, "Billy Bob is meddling in Pastor Parker's desk."

At this David caught the aforementioned Billy Bob by

the shirt collar, and sat him down hard in a chair. "Can't you behave yourself five minutes?" he asked.

"Aw, you leave me alone, I wasn't touching anything. Honest," answered the sullen Billy Bob.

"I wonder why he doesn't want the little ones," Rachel mused.

David answered, "It's probably business. The little ones don't understand business."

"No," Rachel returned, "the triplets don't understand business either and they are here. Actually, if it's business, I don't see why anyone should be here except you and me. I am wondering if—" but no one ever found out what she was wondering, because at that moment the door opened and the quiet voices ceased as Pastor Parker entered the room. David had to help Billy Bob to remember he should be standing, but Pastor Parker didn't appear to notice.

"Good afternoon, everyone!" Pastor Parker said in his friendly booming voice. "Are we all here? Let's see, one, two, three, four, five, six, seven, eight, nine! Yes, I guess that's all of you, isn't it? I always have to count."

"No, this isn't all of us," Letitia said. "The little ones are not here."

"Why didn't you want the little ones, Pastor Parker?" Patricia continued.

"Shh," Darlene said in her ear. "You're not s'posed to talk in here unless he tells you to."

Pastor Parker laughed. "That's all right, Honey," he said. "This is a conference room and in a conference everyone is supposed to have a turn at talking." He turned to the other nine-year-old triplet. "What do you think about it, Honey?" he asked.

Alicia looked first at Letitia and then at Patricia before she answered. "What do I think about what, Pastor Parker? About whether we should talk or whether the little ones should be here? Anyway, I think just whatever Letitia and Patricia do."

The Pastor laughed again. "Well, let's all sit down and be comfortable and then we can talk about some things." He motioned for them to sit down and they sat, David and Rachel being careful to put Billy Bob between them.

"Now to get right to the point of this conference," the pastor began, "I have a question. What are you going to do?"

David looked at Rachel and Rachel looked at David. Finally David spoke. "I don't understand what you mean, Pastor Parker. What are we going to do about what?"

"Why, about everything," the pastor said. "About the way you are living."

Now Rachel spoke. "I didn't realize there was anything wrong with the way we are living. We are all saved except – well, most of us are and we try to live the best we can."

"We are using as our motto 'To be like Jesus,'" David

continued. "We realize we cannot be like Him because He is God, but we try, and we help each other the way Mother always taught us."

"He means me!" Billy Bob spoke up. "Rachel didn't say 'except Billy Bob,' but I know what she meant. But I don't see why Pastor Parker didn't call just me. I'm the little devil in this family and everybody knows it."

"Billy Bob!" exclaimed David. "You *know* we don't use that kind of language."

"Why not?" Billy Bob asked. "You all say 'Hell' when you're talking of the place you think I'm going and I probably am, and I don't care, but when I said the same word in a different way, Mother washed my mouth out with soap and gave me a terrible lecture and cried all afternoon, too. She said it was all right to use it in its place, but not in the wrong place, so isn't the same true of the devil? Ain't I a 'devil,' Pastor Parker?"

The Pastor answered, "No, Billy Bob, I don't think you are a devil at all. You are just a boy that hasn't gotten on the right road yet. I would be glad to discuss that with you sometime when you and I are alone, but right now that is not what I have in mind.

"You children have been left without a Mother," the pastor continued. "Someone is going to have to manage things and bring up the younger ones. What are your plans? Have you thought about it?"

"Oh," David answered, "we mean to go on living just as we are. We'll miss Mother of course. She did just about everything in the way of managing, but we all helped to do the work and we all know how. We may have to all work harder than we have in the past and we may have to do on a little less, but I'm sure our Heavenly Father will help us so we won't go hungry or have to wear rags to church. The house is a good solid house and shouldn't need any repairs for a good ten years except to finish the painting Mother had started and maybe another coat or two in a few years. And it's paid for, Pastor Parker. Everything we have is paid for. We'll get by."

"But how will you *live?*" the pastor asked. "What will you do for money to buy groceries and clothes?"

"Oh, we don't buy many groceries," Rachel answered. "We've always lived off the farm. We don't have a lot of land, but it is enough if we manage well, we can keep two or three cows, a few chickens, and some hogs. We raise our own vegetables. We have fruit trees, too; apples, pears, peaches, plums, and cherries. We also have grapes and strawberries. We can or freeze everything in the summer so we can eat in the winter, and with our own milk, eggs, and meat, we really don't have to buy much except flour, sugar, salt, and things like that. We'll go on living just the way we always have."

"But you'll still need money," Pastor Parker insisted.

"You don't realize what it costs for clothes alone for a family the size of yours."

"Oh, I sew," spoke up Glenda. "I'm fifteen and I love to sew. I started when I was ten and Mother got me a new machine last year. Now I make all the clothes except shoes and socks, and things like that, that we have to buy."

"But money," the pastor continued doggedly. "Where will you get any money?"

David took his turn at answering. "We always sell most of the pigs. Mother always said too much pork isn't good for us so we butcher just one hog each year and most of our meat is beef, chicken, and fish. We catch lots of fish when we have time. Sometimes we sell eggs if we have too many, and some of the fruit. Mother cleaned Mrs. Johnson's house every Friday morning, but she said that was luxury money. We'll have to do without that, but we don't need luxuries, anyway."

The Pastor sighed. He hadn't realized these children were stubborn. They had always seemed so meek and humble. He really didn't know how to get across to them that he couldn't condone a bunch of "kids" living alone. "Haven't you an aunt or an uncle that could come and live with you and help out?" he asked finally. "You children seem to have it all worked out, but you really don't understand the enormity of your undertaking."

"Yes," David spoke quietly, "I think we understand.

Mother understood, too, when she held my hand at the last and said, 'David, you've got to be strong and of good courage. Don't be afraid. God will help you. Keep the children together. They're most of them good kids. They will help. Raise the little ones the way I have raised you. Have family prayer and Bible reading. Don't miss church meetings if it is humanly possible to get there and remember the two basic rules of life. Be as near like Jesus as you humanly can and be happy. If you follow those two rules, life will give you it's best.' Mother left us depending on me to keep the family together and raise the little ones. We have aunts and uncles, but not one who would come into the home and make it a Godly home like Mother did. Rachel and I and the others will do our best to do that."

"But the little ones!" the Pastor exclaimed. "By the 'little ones' do you possible mean the Sparks children? Surely you don't think you can keep them, too! There's no way! It's just too much!"

"Yes, we will keep them," Rachel answered. "Mother brought them home to us from their parents' funeral a year ago. She told us, 'They haven't any mother or father anymore, so they are a part of our family now.' Their mother was our mother's cousin and they were raised almost like sisters, but Mother had no idea when she went to Boston to the funeral that the children had been left to her with a request that she raise them as her own. They do get a small insurance check each month for their support so you need not worry that they are an extra expense. The only way that shows any difference between the little ones and the rest of us is that their name is Sparks and ours is Bradcox. Why, you might as well tell me you were going to take the triplets."

A knock sounded on the door and at Pastor Parker's "Come in" his wife stuck her head in.

"So sorry to interrupt, but aren't you about finished?" she asked. "Sister Leonard called that she couldn't keep those babies any longer. What have you decided to do with them?"

Rachel jumped up. "Oh my!" she said, glancing at her watch. "I didn't realize it was so late. Sister Leonard said she had to leave at 4:30. May I please be excused to go get them?"

"Yes, do go get them, Rachel," Pastor Parker said, "and bring them back here to the back yard of the parsonage. We are having a cookout and you are all invited."

"But you said –" his wife began.

Pastor Parker held up his hand, "Yes I know I said a lot of things, but I didn't realize these children had such determined minds."

"And a Godly mother," Sister Parker added half under her breath.

Pastor Parker rose, "The rest of you children go on

with Sister Parker. Dancy and Franklin will be getting ready for the cookout. You can help them. David, I'd like you to stay so I can have a few more words with you."

"Yes, Sir," David answered, but his eyes were on Billy Bob with a look, which could easily be read, "Please behave yourself."

As the door shut behind the pastor's wife and the children, Pastor Parker stepped through another door where was a small kitchenette. "I think I'll have a cup of coffee while we chat. Do you drink coffee, David?"

"Sometimes," David answered, "but please, Pastor Parker, couldn't you hurry and say what you want to say so I can go keep an eye on Billy Bob?"

"Relax, David," answered the pastor. "Franklin will look after Billy Bob. You and I still have some things to discuss."

David paced the floor uneasily until the pastor returned with two cups of coffee.

"Now, David," he said, "I want to talk to you as man to man. You've got to think things over and realize what you are doing to yourself. How old are you, David? Is it true that you didn't finish high school?"

"I was seventeen last December," David answered. "I quit the public school a year ago so I could be more help to Mother. I studied evenings all winter, but I still lack some of finishing. I am determined, though, that I will do it."

"Have you ever thought of what you are going to do with your life?" was Pastor Parker's next question.

David looked at the pastor, looked at the floor, and finally back at the pastor before he answered. "I've thought quite a lot about it, Pastor Parker," he said, "but I just want to do and be whatever God has planned for me."

"Haven't you ever thought of being a minister?" the pastor asked.

"I've thought about it," David answered, "if that is what God wants."

"Well," the pastor continued, "you know you will have to go to Bible School and who will look after the children then? Our church is getting large enough that we should be sending out a minister from here. I had hoped Franklin would develop an interest in becoming a minister, but he has definitely decided to study to become an electrical engineer. I looked about in the congregation and decided you were probably the next best choice. Can't you see it would be best to let some good Christian couple with no children of their own adopt the Sparks children, and then have one of your aunts move in to oversee the others so you will be free to live your own life?"

"No," David answered, "I don't see that at all. Mother put the family in my care. My brothers and sisters need me. We have no aunt that would love them and bring them up in the nurture and admonition of the Lord the way Mother was doing. Rachel and I are the only ones I know that will try to carry out Mother's wishes for the family."

"But don't you think God has called you to minister?" Pastor Parker argued.

"Yes, I do," David answered slowly. "I think He has called me to minister to the needs of my four younger brothers and seven sisters."

The pastor changed his tactics. "What about Rachel?" he asked. "She is getting to the age she needs to be getting out with other young people, going places and doing things. She soon will be getting interested in young men and before long she will be wanting to marry and have a home of her own. Surely you wouldn't want her to sacrifice her life to be a slave to housework, canning, and gardening, such as she described."

"I can't conceive of Rachel hunting a husband right now when those little children need her so badly," David answered, "but of course I can't speak for her."

David, in his mind was thinking of the impossibility of the idea. He and Rachel had always been close – even before they were left without a Mother. He felt sure if Rachel had any matrimonial ideas, she would have discussed them with him. As far as he could think, she didn't even have a special friend. He thought over all the young men in the church. Martin Green, Carl Sanders,

Donnie Nichols, Greg Thompson, Paul Dobison, Cory Blake.

The pastor interrupted his thoughts, "I may be wrong of course, and maybe I shouldn't say so, but I think I have seen signs of her being interested in our Franklin."

Franklin! Of all the Christian young men David could think of, Franklin Parker would be the very last he'd choose for a brother-in-law, but of course he couldn't say this to Pastor Parker. What he did say was, "Rachel has not discussed her interest in anyone with me. As she is barely sixteen I would suppose she was a little young to be giving the matter any serious thought."

Pastor Parker stood up. "Well, David," he said, "I'm sorry you can't see things my way, but of course you must follow whatever course you feel is God's will for you. If you ever change your mind, there is money in a special fund in the church treasury to send you to Bible School, but as long as you are sure God wants you to stay home and look after the others, then by all means do it. And David," he continued, "I also want you to know I admire you for the stand you are taking. It is a very large undertaking, but nothing is too big if God assigns it to you. If there is ever anything my wife and I can do to help, just let us know."

David felt a love for the pastor he had never had before. "I thank you, Pastor Parker," he said. "There is one thing I'd like for you and Sister Parker to do and that is to pray for Billy Bob. I just don't know what we are going to do with him. He is so different from all the others."

"Yes, I've noticed that. We do pray for him daily. Well, let's go see if those hamburgers are ready to eat."

As Pastor Parker and David approached the back yard of the parsonage, David's eyes began a search for his wayward brother. Franklin and Nathan were by the grill. He noticed Rachel, Dancy, and Sister Parker coming from the house, their hands full of this and that. Glenda had the triplets and the little ones over at the table entertaining them with some kind of story while Darlene, trying to look and act like an adult, looked on, but where, oh where was Billy Bob?

"Where is Billy Bob?" David asked of Rachel as soon as he was close enough to be heard without yelling.

"Why Nathan said he stayed with you," his sister answered.

"Yes," Sister Parker agreed, "He certainly didn't come with the rest of us."

"Nathan," David called sharply, "where is Billy Bob? Why did you tell Rachel he stayed with me?"

"He said he was going to stay," Nathan answered. "At least I thought that's what he meant. When we got up to leave he whispered to me and said, 'I'm not going.' I just supposed he stayed with you."

"You supposed wrong that time. Well, come on,

Brother, we will have to find him. He's probably gone over to Hamiltons or maybe the Stewarts. You folks go ahead and enjoy the cookout without us. Excuse us, Pastor Parker and Sister Parker. We will be back as soon as we can."

Nathan and David checked first with the Stewarts. Evelyn Stewart said Louis was somewhere with Johnny Hamilton, but she hadn't seen Billy Bob. They went to the Hamiltons and found no one at home. Then they tried the homes of all the other boys they could think of that he knew, but no one had seen Billy Bob. Finally David suggested he might have gone on home so it was decided he would go check home while Nathan continued to look in town. After another hour they met again at the parsonage, but still no one had seen Billy Bob.

"Pastor Parker," David said, "do you think we should contact the police." I'm sure something has happened to him because he is very afraid of the dark and it has been dark for a long time now."

"Maybe we should wait a while," the pastor answered. "I'll take Rachel and the other children home. If he comes home, give us a call, Rachel. You, Nathan, and I will look a while longer before we call the police. Billy Bob has been in so many brushes with the police, one more might be just one too many."

III

As the conference room door closed behind Sister Parker and the children, Billy Bob managed to be last in line. He stepped into the first open door and waited until he heard the outside door close. Then he counted to one hundred. Silent as a jewel thief, he crept down the hall and out the door, being careful to look in all directions at once. He turned the opposite way from the parsonage, slipped through a hedge, down an alley, around a corner, through a vacant lot, and then began to run toward the lake. Five minutes later, he was sitting on a pier between Louis Stewart and Johnny Hamilton trying to skip stones on the water.

"However did you get to come today, Billy Bob?" questioned Johnny.

"Oh, I managed!" Billy Bob answered nonchalantly. "No one knows where I am and I won't be missed for about an hour. With luck I'll make it back at the right moment so I won't ever be missed. Come on, I haven't much time.

Let's do something."

The boys jumped up. "Like what?" asked Louis.

"Follow the leader. That's always fun," suggested Johnny.

"All right," Louis agreed. "Let Billy Bob lead. He always thinks of more fun things to do."

Now follow the leader to some children means walking one behind the other, putting your hand to your head just like the leader, stooping over to pluck a blade of grass at the same place, and such like. To these three friends it meant walking bridge banisters, hanging by your feet from the old oak tree, walking on your hands through a blackberry patch, and any other outrageous thing they could think of.

The boys got in line one behind the other. Billy Bob went up a tree, swung across to another tree and slid down it to the ground. The other boys followed. Billy Bob walked out into a busy street and for half a block walked down the center line with cars zipping by on both sides. Johnny and Louis followed. Billy Bob went through an empty warehouse, climbed on top a roof and walked around the edge. Johnny and Louis were right behind him. Finally when he thought his time was about up, he turned back toward the parsonage beside the church where his family had attended for the past several years. It was then he saw the culvert and an idea struck him. He was the smallest of the three boys. Just maybe he could crawl through the culvert and the other boys couldn't. For a moment he wondered what the act would do to his clothes, but he looked down at himself and decided the damage couldn't be much worse. He had a passing wonder as to what Rachel would say before he got down on his stomach and crawled into the dry culvert.

Once inside the culvert he felt it was a little smaller, or else he was a little bigger than he had supposed. He was almost too big. Yet he managed to pull himself through a few inches at a time. With one arm stretched out in front of him, the other by his side he would bend his knees the least bit, then straighten his legs to move forward. He heard Louis and Johnny behind him admitting to each other that they couldn't do it.

He smiled to himself as he watched the light gradually coming closer to him from the other end of the culvert. All at once he was having trouble. There seemed to be a slight bend in the culvert. He bent his knees ever so slightly, and straightened them again but he hadn't moved his shoulders. He tried to back up, but he couldn't. Suddenly he realized he was stuck. "Johnny! Louis!" he screamed, "I'm stuck." He heard the sound of running footsteps, then all was quiet."

"They've gone for help," Billy Bob thought to himself. "I'll just lie quietly until they come back." He waited what he thought would be about five minutes, but no one came, ten minutes, fifteen. Suddenly he panicked and began to scream. The sound seemed to come right back to him. Cars continued to run on the street above him, but none stopped. After a while he became calmer. "I'm going to die," he thought to himself. "My friends have gone off and left me and I'm going to die; alone."

Into his mind flashed a thought of a Bible verse he had once had to learn, something about a friend sticking closer than a brother. Well he knew these friends hadn't. David or Nathan would not have deserted him like that, but then the Bible verse, if he remembered right was speaking of God, and he and God were not friends. Just how was it that verse went? Oh! Now he remembered, *A man that hath friends must shew himself friendly: And there is a friend that sticketh closer than a brother.* (Proverbs 18:24). There! That was the trouble. He hadn't been a friend to God! God probably wouldn't hear him if he asked Him for help. He remembered just a few short hours ago that he had said he was going to Hell and he didn't care. Well, now death was staring him in the face and Hell couldn't be very far behind death, and he found he did care – very much!

"I wonder if God would help me," he thought to himself. "I'm going to die and it isn't going to cost anything to try." He closed his eyes and began. "Oh God," he prayed, "I know I've been bad, and I haven't done anything the way I should, but I'm not ready to die. Won't you please help me out of this? Amen." He opened his eyes and another verse he had been compelled to learn came into his mind. *And whatsoever ye do in word or deed, do all in the name of the Lord Jesus, giving thanks to God and the Father by him.* (Col 3:17). "Oh," he thought, "David always asks in Jesus name and I've got to give thanks to Him, too." He closed his eyes again and prayed. "Jesus, I'm sorry I forgot to say in Jesus name. Please help me get out of here in Jesus name and I do give you thanks in advance. Amen again."

Billy Bob lay still. He was still stuck, but he was no longer so frightened. "I've got to try again," he said to himself. "I wasn't too big to get in here, so I'm surely not too big to get out. Having missed my supper, I couldn't have grown any." He pushed backward with all his might and felt himself move a fraction of an inch. He lay still and tried again. Again he felt himself move ever so slightly. Slowly he worked himself backward, a quarter of an inch or so at a time. It grew dark. Billy Bob lay quiet and rested. Then he worked some more. Finally he was clear of the bend and the going grew easier. Not long after that he felt the toes of his shoes hook over the end of the culvert and soon he was out.

"Thank you, Lord, for helping me," Billy Bob said, "but I guess I mostly did it myself. I guess a person can usually do it himself if he really tries, but anyway I think you helped me get calm, and if I hadn't got calm I couldn't have done it."

Pastor Parker, David, and Nathan met in front of the church. None of them had gotten a clue. "I suppose we had better go ahead and contact the police," Pastor Parker said.

"I suppose so," David answered.

They went into the house and Pastor Parker reached for the phone, but just as he touched it, it rang. It was Rachel. "Billy Bob is home," she said. "He just came swaggering in and wanted to know if there was anything to eat. He said he was as hungry as a bear after hibernation."

IV

The Bradcox home was a large two and a half-story house with full basement, set in the middle of the front edge of forty acres. The house had been built by the children's maternal grandfather, Chester Solomon, when Mary Solomon Bradcox was a small girl. Chester Solomon spared no expense in having the house exactly as Mary's mother, Emily Solomon, wished it. It was built with the idea in mind that many more children would be added to the family after Mary, but alas, no more children arrived and Mary grew up in a home where several bedrooms were entered only twice a year to be cleaned and aired. Chester Solomon put all his savings into the home, and soon after it was built, his health began to deteriorate, so that it was all he could do to get by without mortgaging it.

When Chester Solomon left this earth a year or so after his daughter, Mary, had married William Bradcox, he left Mary the home – debt free, and the furnishings, but very little money. Mary loved her home and every one of her nine children shared her feelings for it.

There were rooms enough in the house to allow Glenda to have a sewing room, the children to have a playroom, and, except for the triplets, have no more than two children to a room. There was a living room, a parlor, a kitchen large enough to eat in, and a big sun porch. Off to the side of the kitchen was a small room Mary Bradcox had always called the office. Here she had a desk and here she kept the necessary records for income tax purposes and such like.

On the door of the office was a small bulletin board where notices of all family dates of importance were posted. All school meetings, dentist appointments, special church services, etc., were posted there so each member of the family would be informed. On this bulletin board Rachel had just posted a notice which read, Family conference night, Saturday after supper. Work distribution and other business. Be prepared with all suggestions and complaints.

Rachel went back to her cookie making. Family conference night had always been a gay affair, complete with refreshments and plenty of fun. Whenever any decisions were to be made, or a serious subject to be discussed, Mother had called a family conference. Other family conferences were scheduled between times just to give the children a chance to air their grievances and make suggestions.

Just as Rachel slid the first pan of cookies into the oven, she heard David taking off his shoes at the door. He had been helping a neighbor make hay in exchange for the neighbor helping him. She marveled again at the thoughtfulness of David. If ever there were a dirty footprint on the floor, it wouldn't be David's.

She was dishing up the food she had been keeping hot for him as he came through the door.

"Hmm! Smells Good! Just let me wash off a little of the grime and I'll be right there." David disappeared into the bathroom and Rachel heard the sound of running water. The cookies were sending out a pleasant aroma as David returned.

"Cookies?" David asked.

"Yes," Rachel answered, "for Saturday night conference, but I'll let you have a couple for dessert."

"No need for you to worry about me spoiling my appetite, hungry as I am, but I'll wait. This other food looks mighty good, too."

David sat down and Rachel bowed her head as David prayed. Then he continued, "It sure has been a long time since noon. I don't know when I've been so hungry."

"If there isn't enough there," Rachel teased, "I suppose I *could* let you have three cookies, but you will have to eat all of your spinach first."

After a time of silence, David spoke. "It's going to seem strange, this first family conference without Mother. It seems there ought to be some other way."

"I know," Rachel agreed, "but we did agree to keep everything as nearly as possible as it was before. Glenda was, 'shocked speechless,' her words, when I said I was going to bake cookies. She said, how could we have a party without mother?"

"Everyone in bed except you?" David asked.

"And you," Rachel answered. "David, do you know it's almost eleven o'clock? Couldn't you have gotten off earlier?"

"Not really," David answered. "It looks like rain and we couldn't afford to let the hay get wet. We did get it all in."

"You could have kept Nathan longer. He was really upset because you sent him home. He tries so hard to be like you."

"I know," David sighed, "but he was so tired. He's only thirteen, Rachel. I kept thinking Mother would be taking better care of him. Nathan's a good chap. Too bad Billy Bob isn't more like him."

"Now David," Rachel reproved, "you know Mother never liked us to compare. Why don't you take Billy Bob with you more? He's only fourteen months younger than Nathan, and he's a good worker."

"That he is," David agreed. "Fact is, he's stronger than Nathan, but what Nathan lacks in strength he makes up in effort. The trouble with Billy Bob isn't that he won't work, it's that I never know if he's going to be putting mice in somebody's lunch box or a snake under their tractor seat. Did you ever find out what he was doing or where he was the other night?"

Rachel shook her head. "He just won't talk about it to me. He told Brad that a couple of little purple men caught him and put him in a UFO and took him to the moon."

David sighed, "Honestly, Rachel, what are we going to do with him? He sure can make up some wild ones, but he told Pastor Parker that he didn't do anything wrong except run off in the first place, and he really intended to be back before he was missed. He said the rest of it wasn't his fault and he couldn't tell because it would get somebody else in trouble."

"Well, I guess there's no way to find out," Rachel said. "I can't think what Mother would do."

"I believe he would have told her the truth," David said. "Somehow I have the feeling he tells me the truth, when he tells me anything, but all I've been able to get out of him about this is that he is sorry, it wasn't intentional, and he doesn't want to talk about it. Did he do the chores tonight?"

"Yes, he did them all, except I milked. He hates to

milk, and the cows generally end up kicking the bucket over when he has to do it. We just can't afford to have that happen."

"You should not be doing that kind of work," David said. "Mother never had you do it."

"Now David," Rachel answered, "you know Mother had all of us learn to milk, even the triplets. She said it was good to know how; we might need to sometime. Why did she say that if she didn't want us to do it when there was a need? Besides, she did it!"

David sighed, "Yes, I know. I sometimes think if she hadn't had to work so hard, we might have kept her longer. I want to do the best I can to keep you from having to work so hard."

Rachel took the last pan of cookies from the oven and set them to cool, then she sat down beside David. "David," she said, "you're working too hard yourself. Can't you figure out some way to get more rest? If you break down where will we all be?"

"I won't break down," David answered. "Men don't."

Rachel sighed. "Much as I hate to, I'm going to say something. You like to consider yourself a man, and I like to consider myself a woman, but we both are still just kids. We have to take the place of adults, and we're both doing our best, but that doesn't change the fact that I am only sixteen and you are seventeen. Now I suggest as soon as

I get these cookies under cover we both go to bed and, David, Nathan said for you to sleep as long as you could in the morning, that he and Billy Bob would take care of everything that has to be done."

David nodded. "Good old Nate!" he said. "All right, I think I'll take him up on it this time, but there is a question I've been wanting to ask you for several days, and I haven't been brave enough."

"How ridiculous!" Rachel exclaimed. "As if I'd ever hesitate to answer anything you would ask. I keep no secrets from you. What is the question?"

"Are you interested in any young man, or boy, you'd probably say?"

Rachel turned and stared at him for several seconds before she answered. "Why, yes, come to think of it, I am interested in three of them – you, Nathan, and Billy Bob, and if you are talking of little boys, add Brad and Greg. Why?"

"You know what I mean, Rachel," David said. "Don't evade. Is there a special young man at church or anywhere?"

Rachel answered. "Wherever did you get an idea like that? Are you wanting to start dating Stacey Crowlman and was just fishing to find out if I thought we were old enough? I saw her making eyes at you the other night."

David laughed. "I intend to remain unattached until

Sue Ellen is at least eighteen," he said. "If my mathematics isn't faulty I will be about thirty four by then. By that time, at the rate Stacey is working she will probably have grandchildren and just for your information, Dear Sister, in my opinion, Stacey Crowlman is the least desirable of all the unmarried females in our church. Now quit changing the subject. Are you or are you not romantically interested in a certain young fellow in our church?"

"I am not!" Rachel stated. "What has Sis. Nosenevets started now?"

"I'm not sure that dear lady is to blame for this," David answered, "but will you answer me one more question?"

"Of course, David."

"If you wanted to get married and could have your choice of all the fellows in the church, which one would you take?"

"Well, in the first place, I don't want to get married. If you will be almost thirty four when Sue Ellen is eighteen, then I won't be much farther from thirty-three. By that time there wouldn't be much choice. As for who – I really haven't given it a thought. Let's see – I suppose Donnie Nichols or maybe Paul Dobison. I suppose Paul Dobison would be the best choice. Now *why*? Who said what and about whom did they say it?"

"I can't very well tell you that," David said. "If I did you would be self-conscious every time you were around them, but you sure have taken a load off my mind. Now let's get to bed. It's almost tomorrow."

David quietly made his way upstairs and down the hall toward his room. Just as he passed the room Nathan and Billy Bob shared, he thought he heard a sob. He stopped and listened. He heard another sob and someone turned over. He knocked gently on the door, but no one answered. He opened the door a crack and whispered, "May I come in?"

"Yes," said a voice from Billy Bob's bed.

The sounds from the other bed assured David that Nathan was sound asleep. He sat down on the edge of Billy Bob's bed and asked gently. "What's wrong, Billy Bob?"

Billy Bob answered gruffly, "Go away! I don't want to talk about it."

David stood up and started toward the door, but Billy Bob's voice stopped him. "No, stay here. I've got to talk."

David sat down again. "Is there any way I can help you, Billy Bob?" he asked.

"No. Yes. I don't know. I'm just so miserable and I know Mother said not to grieve for her, but I can't help it. I promised her I'd obey you and Rachel and be good, and I don't want to be good, and sometimes I hate you and Rachel for trying to make me be good. One part of me wants me to be my own boss. I'm tired of being bossed.

You're only five years older than I am and Rachel is only four years older. Why should I have to obey you? But yet another part of me wants to obey and be good, because Mother wanted me to. I – sometimes I just hate myself."

David sent forth a quick petition to God for wisdom and said, "Billy Bob, your biggest problem is that you want to run your own life. If you would just turn your life over to God –"

"I don't want to hear about God," Billy Bob interrupted. "That's all life is around here. God, Church, and be good. I think I'll run away."

"Well, that's up to you," David returned. "I'm not going to tie any ropes on you to keep you here, but remember you are only twelve and you are not of legal age to do as you please. Also remember that the last time you were taken up for shop-lifting the judge said the next time you got into trouble he would send you to the reform school."

"I remember," Billy Bob answered. "I *don't* steal anymore and that's the truth. I've heard enough from Mike Jenning's older brother to know I want to stay away from that place."

"Well, the judge didn't say 'stealing,' he said the next time you got into trouble. I'm afraid he would consider running away as trouble."

"Oh, I know. I'm not going to run away. But nobody around here cares anything about me since Mother is gone. You don't want me. You only want Nathan. Nathan is good. Nathan was born good. I *hate* Nathan!"

David sighed. Right now he was wishing Mother back as much as Billy Bob was. This was her job. He didn't know how to cope with it.

"God help me," he said under his breath. Then he had an inspiration. "Billy Bob, have you done something wrong that you need to tell me about?"

Billy Bob shook his head and a fresh supply of tears came forth. "I haven't done anything, only I can't sleep much at night since I got stuck in the culvert."

"Stuck in the culvert!" exclaimed David.

Then Billy Bob poured forth the story of where he had been the night of Pastor Parker's cookout. "I didn't really mean to do anything wrong, only I can't stand that Franklin Parker and I thought I could slip away and come back about the time you got there and maybe not be missed."

"Why wouldn't you tell us before?" David asked. "We wouldn't have been as upset as we were by not knowing."

"Because Louis and Johnny left me and their moms would skin them alive if they knew. You won't tell on them will you?"

"I won't tell their mothers," said David, "but I am going to have a talk with Louis and Johnny. They need to learn a few facts about being their brother's keeper. Billy Bob, why did you tell Brad that line about the purple men putting you in a UFO and all that?"

Billy Bob chuckled. "Brad believes anything I tell him. It's so much fun to see his eyes get big —"

"Actually, though," David said, "if you had told him the truth it would have seemed about as wild as what you did tell him, but Billy Bob, don't you understand that Brad believes you because he, himself is truthful? What you are really doing is teaching him to lie."

"I never thought about that," Billy Bob answered.

David yawned and got up. "Do you think you can sleep now, Brother?" he asked.

"Sure," Billy Bob answered. "I could probably sleep 'til noon, but Nathan will see that I don't."

"I'm just about dead on my feet," David said. "It's after one o'clock and I've got a lot to do tomorrow, so I really must get to bed. Goodnight, Billy Bob."

"Goodnight, David," Billy Bob answered. "I love you."

V

Darlene carried the last of the dirty dishes to the sink where Glenda was washing them. Letitia and Alicia had dishtowels and were hurrying to dry them while Patricia placed them in their places in the cabinet. Darlene wiped the table and Rachel placed a pencil and piece of paper at each place. Then the girls came back to their places at the table. Rachel lifted Sue Ellen down from her high chair to run around in the room while the others were busy.

"You little boys can get down too, if you'd like," David said.

Bradley answered promptly, "I'm six years old and I've been to school and I've got to help to take care of my family. I'm going to work, too."

"All right with me," David said as Nathan helped Gregory down from the height of a catalog and dictionary on his chair. "We'll do work distribution first. Each one of you write down what you want your share of the work to be now that school is out. Think hard. There is garden work, milking, chickens to tend, pigs to feed, and then the housework, dusting, sweeping, cooking, dishes, taking care of the little ones. Put down about three jobs that you wouldn't mind if they were assigned to you and then at the bottom put down any jobs you particularly hate. We won't promise to give you just what you want and that you won't have to do any of the ones you hate, but we will do the best we can. Now, I'll give you about ten minutes and then you can have ice cream and cookies while Rachel and I do the best we can with your work division. Each one of you write on your own paper. Don't look at each other's papers and don't talk among yourselves."

The children wrote quietly, not talking or even whispering.

As each one finished, he brought his paper to David and Rachel. When they were all finished, David read them aloud while Rachel recorded them on a big sheet of paper.

Glenda wrote that she wanted to continue to do the family sewing, that she was willing to help with the canning and garden work or wherever she was needed, but that she thought the dishes and housework should be done by turns as it had been all winter. She hoped she wouldn't have to cook.

Nathan was next. He wanted to help David however he was needed, and he didn't want to cook.

Billy Bob said he wanted to go fishing, rake the leaves, (in May) shovel the snow, and drive the tractor. He didn't want to do housework or cooking.

Darlene wanted to take piano lessons, learn to sew, learn to cook, help with the canning, take care of Sue Ellen, and whatever else Rachel needed her to do.

Then David picked up Letitia's paper. It said simply, "I want to help with whatever Patricia and Alicia do."

Alicia's was next. David read it. "I want to help Patricia and Letitia do whatever they want to do."

Patricia's paper said, "I want to do whatever Alicia and Letitia do, but I hope they don't feed the pigs." Patricia could still remember the time when she was small and had climbed into the pigpen to get a better look at the baby pigs. If David hadn't been close, there would probably have been only twins left instead of triplets.

"Those three didn't help us much," David commented. "All we know is not to assign them the care of the pigs. Why, where is Brad's paper?"

"I'm not quite done," said the little boy. "Can you wait a minute? I'm 'most done."

David waited until Bradley had brought the paper. It said, "I want to take kare ov the chikens, feed the pigs, lern to milk the cows, drive the trakter, werk in the gardon, pik the straberys and chaires, help with the diches, take kare of Greg and Sue Ellen, and enyting els is needed. I don't want to tell lis or be bad enymor."

"Whew!" David said, "If Brad gets all that done, none of the rest of us need worry about being overworked. Do you really think you can do all that, Brad?"

"Yes, if Billy Bob will help me," the little boy answered.

"Don't you want to have any time to play?" David asked.

"No," Brad shook his head. "I'm too big to play and I've got to help take care of my family now that Mother is gone." Big tears formed in his eyes as he added, "Why did Mother die? Didn't Jesus know we needed her?"

David's voice choked as he answered. "Yes, Brad, He knew. He knows everything. Maybe it was that we depended too much on her and He thought we needed to learn to take care of ourselves, or maybe we need to learn to depend on God instead of Mother."

"Well, I sure miss her," said Brad. "My other mother died, too. I'd just be ever so good if God would let one of them come back to us."

"They can't come back to us," David said, "but we can all go to them."

"Oh, I guess I don't want to do that. I'd have to die, wouldn't I? I don't want to die."

Rachel put her arm around the little boy and pulled him to her. "Of course you don't want to die, yet. We don't want you to die either. You've got to stay here and help us take care of Gregory and Sue Ellen." Rachel had seen tears forming in the eyes of the other children and she knew if she didn't do something to prevent it, the whole family would soon be weeping. "What was it Mother told us all to do?" she asked. "Everybody together now, say it."

As one voice the children answered, "Try to be like Jesus, and be happy!"

"We must not forget the 'be happy' part. Now Glenda, you and the little girls dish up the ice cream and pass the cookies while David and I try to untangle these work assignments."

The work was assigned to everyone's satisfaction and the refreshments nearly gone when David announced question and complaint time.

Billy Bob spoke first. "Tim Tanner is having a birthday Saturday. His Mother said he could invite his friends to go to the show Saturday afternoon and then have cake and ice cream afterward at his home. I want to go."

A sudden stillness settled on the room. David looked at Rachel and Rachel looked at David. Finally David spoke, "You know, Billy Bob, that we don't go to shows. Why don't you explain that to your friend and see if it would be all right for you to meet the others after the show?"

"I didn't ask *you* to go to the show. I said *I* want to go. It's a good show – not a thing wrong with it. *Why* can't I go?"

David took his time about answering and Rachel knew he was asking God for wisdom just as she was doing. "Shows are worldly and the Bible says we are to be separate from the world." David answered.

"The Bible! That's all I can hear around here. The Bible! God! Church! Be good! I'm sick of it. I'm not interested in what the Bible says." Billy Bob was shouting now. "I can't do *anything* I want to do. I just want to be like the other boys and do the things they do. I'm ashamed to hold my head up. I'm so tied down I'm afraid I'll kick my nose when I walk. You guys are all Christians. That's fine for you if that's what you like, but I'm not a Christian and I don't want to be one and I don't want to be stuck with your silly rules of do's and don'ts!"

Suddenly, the usually quiet Nathan, stood up. "That is enough of that, Billy Bob," he said. "I don't want to *ever* hear another word of that kind spoken in this house. Like Joshua said, '*As for me and my house, we will serve the Lord.*' (Joshua 24:15) As long as you live here you abide by the rules. If you don't like it, just put up with it, but hold your tongue, especially in the presence of your younger brothers and sisters."

"Says who?" Billy Bob sneered.

"Says I!" Nathan answered.

"I'd like to see you do anything about it."

"All right, I know you are stronger than I am, but you are *not* stronger than God and me. If I hear one more word against God, the Bible, the Church, or the rules of this household, I *will* mash your mouth." Then turning to David, Nathan said, "Sorry to have to make a disturbance. Please go ahead with the next business."

Billy Bob sat quiet and sullen while the others discussed the need of a car, which they couldn't afford, the possibility of getting a puppy, and Darlene's desire to learn to sew, cook and take piano lessons.

Not until someone suggested popping some corn did Billy Bob again become a part of the family group and by the next day, he and Nathan were as good pals as before, but from then on Billy Bob was very careful of his words.

VI

It was just the next day as the Bradcox children were filing out of church that Pastor Parker laid his hand on David's shoulder and said, "David, I need to talk with you a little while in my office. Can you wait for me a few minutes?"

David followed Pastor Parker to his office. The rest of the family left him and went on home.

Pastor Parker went straight to the point. "David," he said, "I'm afraid I have some bad news. I heard this morning by way of the church gossip channels that someone has reported you children to the county welfare department. Do you know what that likely means?"

David nodded, "Sis. Nosenevets, I suppose."

"What! – Who?"

David stammered, "I – I didn't mean to say that, I'm sorry! Really! Forget I said that, will you?"

"David, what *do* you mean?" The pastor asked.

"Oh, I didn't mean any harm, really, Pastor Parker.

I didn't mean to be disrespectful. It's just that one time a long time ago, Rachel and I were playing around and writing everyone's name backward. We happened to write Stevenson and it came out Nosnevets. It seemed so fitting to just slip an extra 'e' in there and call it 'Nosenevets'. It's been a long time since I have called Rachel, Lehcar, or she has called me Divad, but we've called Sis. Stevenson, Sis. Nosenevets ever since. I didn't mean to say it to anyone else though. I'm really sorry."

The pastor tried to keep a straight face, but he couldn't hold back a grin. I can see how a thing like that would catch on. I suppose some kind of reprimand is due you, but I still have enough of the child in me to see the funny side. Do be careful though. It would be disastrous if you were to call her that to her face. Now let's see, what do you call me? Pastor Rekrap, or do you say Rotsap Rekrap?"

"Oh," David moaned, "I've never called you anything like that. Honest!"

"All right, David, let's forget it and go on home to dinner. You're right, though. I'm afraid it was your dear friend, Sis. Nosenevets. What good she gets out of things like that I don't see, but be prepared for a visit from the welfare department. If God doesn't intervene, they will likely put the Sparks children in foster homes and maybe even the triplets and Darlene."

"Oh, they can't do that, can they? Don't they have to

prove we are mean to them or something?"

The pastor shook his head. "I'm afraid not, David. There have been many cases where they just picked the children up and took them with hardly any reason at all. They usually just take the younger ones though. It's harder to find homes for older children. They almost never take them over twelve unless there is proof of actual abuse, or the children themselves want to go."

"What can we do, Pastor Parker?" David asked.

"There isn't much you can do but pray. If I were you though, I'd see an attorney if there is any way you can handle the expense. He might be able to advise you better than I can."

"I can see the attorney. There is one, Mr. Clarke, that Mother had when – well years ago. When it came time to pay him, he told Mother he wanted his pay in fresh fruits and vegetables. She told him he could have all he wanted. He said in return she could have free legal services as long as she raised a garden. I met him the day after Mother's funeral and he said if the garden were still open to him, the free legal services would still be open to the family. I'll go see him first thing in the morning."

Later at home David told only Rachel about the talk with the pastor.

"Oh, David," Rachel cried. "What are we going to do? What would Mother do?"

"This is one thing we are going to have to face without questioning, what would Mother do?" David answered. "This wouldn't have happened if Mother were still with us. All we can ask is, what would Jesus have us do?"

"Well," Rachel said, "I'm very sure he wants us to keep these children together and raise them for Him. I can't understand why He would make us go through this right at the start this way, but I am very sure it will all come out right, because He is always in charge. Let's just tell Glenda and Nathan, so they can help us pray, but not Darlene and the triplets, because they would worry."

"Then you don't think I should go ask advice of Mr. Clarke?"

"Yes, definitely! That's why God gave us free legal advise, so we could find out what to do. But don't worry, David, God will take care of us. We're doing our best and it will all come out right."

As it happened, David didn't have a chance to consult Mr. Clarke, nor much time to worry. Quite early Monday morning it was discovered that the hogs were out, and by the time they were rounded up, put in, and the fence fixed, it was getting quite late. Glenda and Darlene were just finishing the breakfast dishes. Rachel and the triplets were upstairs gathering up the laundry. David was giving Nathan and Billy Bob instructions as to what they should do while he was gone when someone knocked. Brad being free at the moment and closest to the door, opened it to admit Mrs. O'Conner of the County Welfare Department.

Mrs. O'Conner was a pleasant mannered lady with a ready smile and a way of putting those around her at ease. She introduced herself and asked to see the children that were to be placed in foster homes.

"We have no children to place in foster homes," David said.

"Oh," Mrs. O'Conner said. "Why I was told there were several children here, left without parents and that they needed homes where they could have proper care."

"Well," David answered, "I can't understand why anyone would tell you that. All of the children here are our brothers and sisters. It is true that we have been left without parents, but we older ones are taking care of the little ones. We have all we need. The children are not neglected, nor abused. There are twelve of us. Mother said before she left us that we were to stay together and Rachel and I were to take care of the others. You are welcome to look around and see if everything isn't up to a fine standard, but if you want to put any of us in a foster home, I guess you will have to find a big foster home, because there are twelve of us and we can't be separated."

Mrs. O'Conner laughed. "I'm afraid I don't have a foster home to meet those specifications. I guess I've been mis-informed. I will have to look in to this and see just what is going on. I was told that there were three babies here that don't belong to the family, and that maybe you wouldn't be able to keep the younger ones that do belong to the family."

"Mrs. O'Conner," Rachel said, "the three youngest in this family are not our blood brothers and sister. They are the children of our Mother's cousin. They are six, three, and eighteen months, and Mother had full custody of them. She told us they are our brothers and sister and to keep them and raise them. They are part of the family."

"Well, you give me the names and ages of all the children and I will take the matter under advisement and see what is to be done."

When the door had closed behind Mrs. O'Conner, David said, "Rachel, I don't think you should have told her that about the little ones not being our blood brothers and sister."

"Everyone knows it. It's no secret. She would have found it out anyway, and then she would have considered us liars," Rachel answered.

David sighed, "Yes, I suppose you are right. I think I'll go on and see Mr. Clarke. I have a feeling we haven't seen the last of that lady."

Suddenly all the children were talking at once. "Who is she?" "What is she trying to do?" "Did she mean she was wanting to take the little ones away?" "And the triplets?"

"Can she do that?" "What are we going to do?"

David held up his hand for silence. "I can't answer your questions because I don't know the answers. I'll tell you what. I'm going in to see our attorney, Mr. Clarke. I've got some other business in town, so I'll probably be late to dinner. I know we had a family conference Saturday night, but I think we should have another one tonight. I'll get some ice cream if I can find a ride home, but otherwise we can have cookies and lemonade. Rachel, does anyone have time to bake some cookies or should I buy some?"

"Darlene has a recipe for a cake she's been begging me to let her make. Why don't we have that?"

"That is fine with me. Don't wait dinner for me and don't worry. God is in control."

Rachel was picking strawberries that afternoon when she saw David coming. She could tell by the dejected way he walked that something was wrong. She hurried in to set out his food and had pasted a smile on her face when he came through the door, but one look at his face and her smile was gone.

"David, what's wrong?" she asked.

For answer David asked a question. "Rachel, do you have any money?"

"Money," Rachel said alarmed. "Not much, maybe two or three dollars. Why? Is Mr. Clarke going to charge you for advice after saying he wouldn't."

"No," David answered. "It isn't that. Mr. Clarke wouldn't do that, but he didn't give me much hope of keeping the little ones. He said the welfare in this state is hard to whip and if they decide to take a child they generally do it. He did say though, that he would fight for us every way possible. Rachel, I paid Dr. Gillard and Steemans Funeral Home. I closed out both the savings accounts and depleted the checking account and I have exactly thirty-seven cents left in my pocket. Needless to say, I didn't get any ice cream even though I rode home with Mr. Smith. I don't know what we are going to do."

"That's all right," Rachel said. "We will have strawberries and whipped cream to go with the cake Darlene made." Then she laid her hand on his bowed head. "Don't worry, David," she said. "God is taking care of us. We will make it somehow."

"I know, Rachel," David said, "but I don't know how. We won't have any pigs to sell until the last of September, and school starts before then. How are we to get school supplies, shoes, and clothing?"

"The children won't need much. We have the little ones' check every month. Let's see, this is May. If we are careful –"

"But, Rachel, the taxes are due in August."

Rachel dropped into a chair. The taxes! The taxes *must* be paid. Mother always said the taxes should be paid even if they didn't have shoes. She said a person could always grow food if they had land, but if they let the taxes go, they wouldn't have anything. If Mother had been well, the taxes would already have been paid. Rachel knew if she saved every penny of the little ones' check, it wouldn't be enough to cover the taxes, and Brad needed new shoes now. Mother had said the check was to take care of the little ones. She said it was all right to put the money from the little ones' check into the family budget as long as the little ones had everything they needed, but Rachel well realized she couldn't save the little ones' money for taxes and let Brad go to church with a hole in the bottom of his shoe.

Rachel suddenly realized David hadn't eaten his dinner, the strawberries needed picking, and life must go on.

"David," she said. "We are forgetting. We still have a home, *all* the children, plenty to eat, and clothes to wear. We should be thanking God there was enough money in the bank to cover the doctor bill and funeral bill. You did pay it all, didn't you?"

David nodded.

"Now, I'm going back to the strawberry patch. You eat your dinner and put your smile back on."

"Getting bossy, aren't you!" David said, but he smiled as he said it.

Rachel was hurrying from kitchen to dining room and

back again and again as David came into the kitchen that evening. "Where is your helper?" he asked. "I thought you were assigned a helper for each meal."

Rachel sighed, "Glenda is supposed to be helping me, but I sent her to her room. David, I don't know how to cope with her."

"You aren't supposed to be having to cope with her," said David. "She's supposed to be helping you cope with the others. What happened?"

"You know Darlene has been begging to learn to cook and sew. I have been letting her help in the kitchen and teaching her as much as I had the time, but I told Glenda she should be teaching her to sew and she had a purple fit. She said she doesn't want any of the children touching her sewing machine. David, she acted terrible."

"Somebody took the time and trouble to teach her, didn't they?" was David's reply.

"Yes, but David, it isn't that she won't take the time and trouble to teach her, it is that old selfish streak of hers showing up. She doesn't want anyone to touch her things. Of course I know how she feels about the sewing machine. It was her sixteenth birthday present from Mother. She got it early because she wanted it and needed it."

"It seems to me I heard her playing the piano the other evening, and if my memory hasn't failed me, I think that was your sixteenth birthday present."

"Yes, but I said when I got it I wanted it to be for the family. Being used doesn't wear a piano like it does a sewing machine."

"But David, actually I never even suggested Darlene use the machine. Glenda and I both learned to sew on Mother's machine. It is still good. It just won't do all the things Glenda's machine does. It is plenty good enough to learn on and I intend Darlene and the triplets shall all learn on it, but Glenda just blew up before I had a chance to explain that. I told her I thought she needed to go to her room and ask God if He approved of her attitude."

"That is fine," said David. "That was about the only thing you could do." He reached for a bowl of potatoes.

"No, you don't!" Rachel objected. "As long as you insist I don't help with the chores then you don't help in the kitchen."

"I'll help!" Glenda said as she came through the door. "Hi, David. I'm sorry, Rachel, for the way I acted. You were right, God didn't approve. I'll teach Darlene to sew. Somebody took the time to teach me."

David looked at her tearstained face and said, "Good girl! As long as you keep in mind to do what Jesus wants, you'll make it."

"We will talk more about it later," Rachel added. "David, who was that came in?"

"One of the thirds," David answered.

"Tell her to call the other kids to supper."

"Hey, One Third," David said, "go find your other two thirds and come to supper. Call the boys, too. They have Greg and Brad with them and Darlene is just coming with Sue Ellen."

When supper was over and the dishes washed, the children were once again assembled for family conference.

"Where do we begin?" asked David.

"I just want to know if that Mrs. O'Conner is going to try to take me and Greg and Sue Ellen away," said Brad. "I thought that's what she said."

"Yes, Brad, that's what she said," David answered, "but I don't believe God is going to let that happen. At least if He does it will be just for a little while."

"I don't want us to go away even for a little while. Mother said we could live here always and this is my family."

"I guess you'll just have to tell Mrs. O'Conner that," said David.

"She wouldn't pay no 'tention to me. But I'm telling you we are not going to live anywhere else," stated Brad firmly.

"May God grant that you are right," commented David.

"Did she say us, too?" questioned Letitia.

"Yes, One Third, you and your other two thirds, and

56

maybe Darlene," David said.

"Oh, what are we going to do?" wailed Glenda.

"Nothing," Rachel answered. "There is just nothing we can do. We are just going to leave it to God because there is plenty He can do. Now I see worry on about eight faces. Did worry ever solve a problem for any of you?"

No one answered.

"Glenda," Rachel asked, "did worry ever solve a problem for you?"

"No," Glenda answered, "but that doesn't keep me from worrying."

"All right, now," David said. "We all know what the score is. None of you children want to leave this home, and none of us want you to leave. Worrying won't change anything. God will. So now, let's remember what Mother told us. Let's say it, all together now."

"Try to be like Jesus and be happy."

"Can you all do that, girls?" He looked at Darlene and the triplets.

"I can if I pray enough," Darlene answered.

The triplets looked at each other, wiped away a tear apiece, and nodded.

"Brad?"

"She's not gonna get me, Greg, and Sue Ellen!" Brad stated.

"Well, now we have something else to discuss that

isn't good news," said David. "Mother always did very well managing the money. She always managed to keep something in savings for emergencies, in case of an accident or sickness. Now we have had sickness and a funeral bill and all of our money has been spent."

"Even our savings?" questioned Nathan.

"Yes, even our savings," answered David. "Not only that, but the taxes are about due and we have nothing to pay them with."

"What are we going to do?" asked Darlene.

"Couldn't David use some of his savings to pay the taxes and then get it back when we sell the next pigs?" asked Glenda. "That wouldn't be quite the same as going in debt, would it?"

"That would be a fine idea, Glenda," David answered, "except that I already used that to pay Mother's funeral bill."

"May I be excused?" asked Brad.

"Yes," David answered.

Brad slipped out of his chair and clumped upstairs.

"Now where is he going?" David asked.

"I don't know," Rachel answered. "I supposed he was going to the bathroom, but it sounds like he went to his room."

"Maybe he is going to pack his clothes," ventured Billy Bob. "Maybe he figured if we were out of money a foster home would be a better bet."

Nathan jabbed his elbow in Billy Bob's ribs. "Not funny!" he said.

Brad came back downstairs, took his place at the table and pushed his bank across to David. "There's not much money there, David," he said. "A couple of dollars I think, but it will be a start, and if everyone else gives all they've got, I thought maybe it would help."

"I've got an idea," Nathan said. "I heard Sister Blake tell Sister Parker that she wished she knew where she could get some strawberries and I heard Rachel say she wished the patch would quit bearing, that she has all she wants and she's sick of seeing them. I think Sister Blake would buy some."

"They would still have to be picked," moaned Rachel.

"Couldn't I do that, David," asked Nathan. Wouldn't you be able to spare me some time tomorrow?"

"The alfalfa has got to be cut first thing after the dew is off," said David. "We are several days late with it now, and as if we haven't already had enough bad news, I just found out today that Mr. Johnson has sprained his ankle so he won't be able to help us put it up. That means we do it with just the three of us."

"Couldn't I help?" Brad asked.

"Maybe. We will see," David answered. "Back to the subject of money – why don't we see if we can think of answers? Brad, you take your money and keep it until time to pay the taxes. All of us will save what we can and when tax time comes we will put it together and pay the taxes. Nathan, I can cut the hay alone. You can have the morning to pick strawberries if you can sell them. You keep the money as your project. Any other ideas?"

"Sister Stortle asked me if I could baby-sit Jennifer for her this summer," said Darlene, "but I didn't suppose you would let me."

"I think you are a little young to be going away to work," said David. "I don't think Mother would approve of that. We don't want to do anything we wouldn't do if Mother were with us."

"I agree," said Rachel, "but wouldn't it be all right if Sister Stortle brings Jennifer here?" I think she only needs someone afternoons."

"If Sister Stortle is willing for that, I won't object."

"May I go call her now?" Darlene asked.

"As soon as Nathan is off the phone," Rachel answered. "I believe he is calling Sister Blake about strawberries just now."

"Oh," cried Darlene, tears forming in her eyes. "Mother promised me I could start my music lessons this summer. Now there won't be money for it." A tear ran down her face and another threatened to follow.

"I've been thinking," Rachel said. "A penny saved is a

penny earned. I really am pushed for time, but if Nathan sells the strawberries that will help some. Do you think, Darlene, that it would be all right if I give you music lessons? You'd have to practice just like with a regular teacher and you couldn't always be calling me to come help you. I'd just give you an hour a week like a regular teacher or probably it would be better a half hour twice a week."

"Oh! That would be dandy!" Darlene cried. "I'd rather have you than another teacher anyway."

"Does 'a penny saved is a penny earned' mean that if we don't spend some money it's the same as if we earned some?" asked Brad.

"Yes, Brad," said David.

"Well," Brad went on, "I don't know how to earn any money, but I know how to save some. I heard Rachel say I have to have new shoes this week, and I found some the girls outgrew that look as much like boy shoes as girl shoes. There are three pairs of them. We could polish up the best pair for church and I could wear the worst ones for every day. Then we could save the others for Greg in case we still don't have money then."

"He's right," Rachel said. "I know what shoes he means. They do look like boy shoes. I thought so when the triplets wore them."

"All right, that takes care of the shoes," David said, "Let's have refreshments. It's getting late and we have a big day tomorrow."

"I'll call Sister Stewart first thing in the morning," Rachel said. "She's been wanting me to give Evelyn music lessons, but I thought I was too busy. I might as well do her and Darlene together if that is all right with Sister Stewart." Then she looked at Glenda. "Why, whatever is the matter, Glenda?" she cried.

"Oh, I feel so little. Just about the right size to sit on the edge of a sheet of paper and swing my legs. Here I have not wanted anyone to use my sewing machine, and David has spent *all* his birthday money to pay the funeral bill. I've been intending to ask for money for material to make myself a dress." Glenda laid her head on the table and sobbed. "I'm just so awful selfish!"

VII

The Tramp stood in the loft door of the Bradcox barn. He had arrived late last night. Before ascending to the barn loft he had gathered the facts that the family didn't have a dog, that they didn't own a car, that the strawberries were ripe and a good crop of cherries would soon follow, that there were three cows, one with a calf, two young steers, four brood sows, a good sized flock of chickens, and a big garden. He also knew that the alfalfa needed to be cut, the potato patch was in bad need of a hoe, and that the house was only half painted.

He watched the house closely. As soon as he saw a light appear in an upstairs room, he picked up his pack, slipped from the loft, rounded the corner of the barn, walked through a grove of trees, and sat down on a stump a quarter of a mile away. There he sat for what he judged to be two hours, the time he estimated it would take for the chores to be done and the family to be eating breakfast. Then he made his way out to the road and walked toward the Bradcox house. As he walked he said to himself. "I will arise and go to my children and will say unto them, 'Children, I have sinned against heaven and before thee, and am no more worthy to be called thy father. Make me as one of thy hired servants.'"

The children were all seated at the table except Nathan when he came in.

"You're late," accused Billy Bob, "and we're starving."

"Sorry to delay you. David, could I have a word with you alone?"

"Now, what have I done wrong?" asked Billy Bob.

Nathan turned as he followed David through the office door and said, "I give you my word of honor, Billy Bob, that I'm not going to say anything about the sandburs you put in my bed."

Billy Bob squirmed as the family waited, but in less than five minutes Nathan and David were again seated at the table. David asked the blessing and they all started to enjoy the oatmeal, eggs and biscuits.

"Timothy Fletcher came past this morning as I was feeding the chickens," Billy Bob commented between mouthfuls. "He said he saw an old tramp go past his house late last night."

David and Nathan's eyes met across the table.

"Aw, Billy Bob," Glenda said, "You know you can't believe anything Timothy says. There are no tramps anymore."

"I believe Glenda is right," went on Rachel. "Mother said when she was a little girl that tramps came by real often. She said they would knock on the door and ask for food and sometimes offer to pay for the food by working, but I don't believe there are tramps around anymore."

"Don't be too sure," David said. "If Timothy said he saw one, it might be well not to let the little girls go too far from the house for a few days until we're sure he is no longer in the neighborhood."

"I think it would be neat to be a tramp," Billy Bob said. "I think I'll be one when I grow up."

"If Billy Bob is going to be a tramp, I think I'll be one, too," Brad said. "I like to do things with Billy Bob."

"I think you boys could both set your goals a little higher," said David.

"What's goals?" inquired Brad.

"Goals are your aims and ambitions, what you mean to do in life, what you are going to make of yourself. I hope all of you spend a little thought on your goals occasionally."

"What are your goals, David," asked Brad.

"My goals? I suppose the only earthly goal I have is to get my eleven brothers and sisters raised to be good solid citizens and God fearing Christians."

"Well, thanks a lot," retorted Rachel. "I rather had the idea that I was already nearly as grown up as you."

At that moment the tramp knocked at the door. All the children looked up to see who had knocked and simultaneously drew in their breaths.

"I told you," Billy Bob whispered.

David arose and went to the door.

"I've walked all night and I'm awfully tired and hungry," the tramp began. "Can you spare me a little bite of food, and let me sit and rest a spell before I go on?"

"Rachel, could you fix a plate of food and hand it out to me?" asked David. Then he went out and unfolded two lawn chairs beside a little table in the yard. He and the tramp sat down. "Going far?" he asked.

"I really don't know," the tramp answered. "I'm out of work and I can't seem to find any. I hate to beg, but when a body gets so hungry there isn't much else to do. You don't know where I might get a job, do you?"

"Not off-hand," David said. "Jobs are not scarce around here right now. You should be able to find something if you want to stay in these parts. What kind of work do you do?"

"That's it," the tramp said, "I used to be a good farm worker, but I had a tractor turn over with me and now I've got a bad leg so I'm not worth much. No farmer would hire me anymore."

Rachel came to the door with a plate of food and as David took it she said, "David, you didn't finish your own breakfast, and it's getting cold."

"Hand it out and I'll eat out here with him." David took the tramp's food to him and then returned for his own. As they ate he noticed the tramp had reasonably good eating habits.

"This is mighty good food," the tramp said. "Your wife is a good cook."

"My sister," David corrected him.

"Oh, then you still live at home. Is your father at home?"

"My father is dead. I'm the man of the house here."

"Oh, I'm sorry to hear that. Those others all your brothers and sisters?"

David nodded.

"Say, your mom's really got her hands full, hasn't she?"

David didn't answer.

"Well, you tell your sister I'm much obliged for the food, will you? I was real hungry. This is the first real meal I've had for many months. You wouldn't be having any work I could do, would you?"

"No," David answered thoughtfully, "there's no work for you here, but Mr. Johnson on the next farm down has sprained his ankle and he might be able to use you for a few days. Would you like me to call him?"

"I guess so but I'd really rather work for you. You seem so pleasant I think you would be nice to work for."

"Thanks for the kind words, but we really cannot afford a hired man. I have two brothers that help me."

A phone call to Mr. Johnson revealed that his younger brother had come to help him out for a few days until his ankle should improve.

"Well, I guess you got work to do. I'd best be getting on my way and quit bothering you. Thanks again for the food." The tramp took a few steps and turned back. "Say, Mister," he said, "I used to be a pretty good painter in my younger days and I see your house is only half painted. If you have the paint I'd be glad to finish it in exchange for supper tonight, a place to sleep, and breakfast tomorrow. I think I could finish it by noon tomorrow."

David did some quick thinking. He sure needed help. Nathan and Billy Bob were good workers, but they were just boys yet and there was so much to do.

"Sit down again and let's talk," David said. "First let's introduce ourselves. I'm David Bradcox."

"Pleased to meet you, Mr. Bradcox," the tramp said, extending his hand to David. "I'm Pete."

"No last name?" David asked.

"No last name," the tramp answered.

"All right, Mr. Pete," said David. "I'll tell you just how things are. My mother and father are both dead. I live here with my eleven brothers and sisters. I'm trying to be a man before my time I guess, but someone has to be the man of the house. My sister, Rachel, is making a pretty good attempt at taking a mother's place. Some of the other children are old enough to be good help. We are doing all right, but the work has piled up. Right now I need to be cutting the alfalfa, spraying the fruit trees, cleaning out the potato patch, and patching the roof on the barn. As you say, the house isn't but half painted, but that can wait. The problem is we don't have any money to hire help."

"I don't need any money," said the tramp. "All I need is my meals and a place to sleep, but I must tell you I'm not as good a worker as I used to be because of my bad leg, but I think I can get enough done to earn my board. What do you want me to do first? I can do any of the things you mentioned."

"You can drive a tractor?" David asked.

"I used to years ago. I'm sure I can pick it up again."

"Do you smoke?" was David's next question.

The tramp shook his head.

"Drink?"

"No."

"Well, I've got my little brothers and sisters that I am responsible for, Mr. Pete," David said. "I've got to be careful what kind of person I bring around them and I know nothing about you – not even your name."

"I won't bother your little brothers and sisters," the tramp said. "What's that little shed? Couldn't we fix up a place for me to sleep in it?"

"We might," David said. "If you are going to stay here and work for your keep it will have to be understood that you will be truthful with me."

"All right," the tramp said.

"Care to shake on that?" David asked.

The tramp stuck out his hand and David took it.

"Now," David asked, "where did you sleep last night?"

The tramp hesitated, then answered, "In your barn."

David took a pocketknife from his pocket and held it out to the tramp.

"My knife!" the tramp exclaimed.

"Yes, Nathan found it where you lost it when you slid out of the barn loft this morning."

"I've carried that knife about twenty years," said the tramp, "and I've never lost it before."

"Now," David inquired, "wouldn't it be better if I knew your name? Do you have a name you're ashamed of, Mr. Pete?"

The tramp stood and gazed off at the distance, then he brought his eyes back to David's face.

"No, Mr. Bradcox," he said, "I don't have a name that I'm ashamed of. I rather think I have a name that is ashamed of me."

By that evening the alfalfa had been cut and raked, the fruit trees had been sprayed, the barn roof had been repaired, and the little shed that had held garden tools, bicycle parts, and miscellaneous junk had been cleaned out and an old cot brought down from the attic and put in the shed. But the next morning Pete didn't show up to help with the chores. When Billy Bob took his breakfast out to the shed there was no answer to his knock. He called for David. David knocked and called; finally he opened the door and looked in. The bed had been made and the room was tidy.

"He hasn't gone," David observed. "His pack is still here."

Brad came running up. "Why are you looking in Mr. Pete's house?" he asked.

"He didn't answer our knock," David answered. "I wanted to see if he was all right. I don't know where he is."

"Oh, he's in the potato patch," said Brad. "He was there when I first looked out my window this morning."

VIII

Glenda came into the kitchen where Rachel was canning cherries with the help of Darlene and the hindrances of Sue Ellen and Jennifer Stortle. "Do you need my help?" she asked.

"I could sure use it. I'd like for Darlene to take her two little girls and put them down for naps. They will probably sleep an hour or two."

"I don't want a nap," declared two year old Jennifer.

"Don't want nap," echoed Sue Ellen.

"It seems to me I hear that once each day," said Rachel to Jennifer, "but your mother said take a nap, so you take a nap."

"Mommy say take nap?" questioned Sue Ellen.

"Jennifer's mommy said to take a nap, so you take a nap, too."

"Me take nap, too," stated Sue Ellen.

Darlene led the two little girls away and Glenda sat down in her chair to help pit the cherries.

"The triplets will soon be in with more," Rachel said. "They wanted to pick, so I told them they could pick the lower limbs as long as they don't climb higher than the third step on the ladders. Alicia brought these in a few minutes ago and said they were almost done."

"Do you want me to go pick the higher ones?" Glenda asked.

"No, Nathan and Billy Bob are going to get them after they finish weeding the carrots. Are you tired of sewing or are you all done?"

"I don't think I would ever get tired of sewing," answered Glenda. "The mending is all done, and I don't have anything started. I wanted you to come up to the sewing room and help me make some decisions when you have time. I don't have any pretty material. I know I can sometimes make a pretty dress from ugly material when I get inspired, but right now I don't know how to get inspired. Rachel isn't there going to be any money at all for material for school clothes? How is the tax fund coming?"

"Fairly well. Nathan made thirty dollars on strawberries. Well, I should say Nathan and Billy Bob. They have pooled their resources and are working together. We've been selling some eggs. We will have enough now to pay the taxes if we use the little ones checks, but we still have to bring in enough to buy everything the children need. You know we can't spend their money for taxes and neglect their needs, especially with the welfare threat hanging over us the way it is."

"It's been nearly a month now. Maybe Mrs. O'Conner isn't coming back," Glenda said.

"I wish I could believe that."

"Well, what are we going to do about school clothes?" Glenda asked.

"We will just have to wait until we sell the pigs. The children have enough to start with."

"I know, but it's so much easier if I can get the sewing done in the summer rather than have to mix it in with homework and everything. Besides, Nina's Fabrics have their basement sale in three weeks and that's when Mother always bought material. Is it all right if I drop out of choir?"

"That was a quick change of subject. Why would you want to drop out of choir?"

"It wasn't really a change of subject, and I'm really not being selfish. It's just that all the girls want dresses alike for when we – they go to Lakeland to the conference. The teen choir is supposed to sing. I know I can't get one and I'd just rather drop out than spoil it for the rest. Pastor Parker wouldn't let them dress alike if he knew it would make me drop out and every other girl would offer to buy my dress and I wouldn't want that. I'd rather just drop out without saying anything."

"I really hate for you to drop out, Glenda," Rachel said. "David and I had to because we didn't have time for practice, but it's about all the outside activity you and Nathan have. I'll talk to David about it and see if there is any way we can work it out, but don't hold your breath. I don't see as there is anything we can do."

David came in with a bucket of cherries. "I saw One-Third lugging them in and thought I'd carry them for her. Rachel do you know what Two-Thirds are doing?"

Rachel went to the window and looked out. As it happened, the cherry tree was in line with the kitchen window. There was a triplet standing obediently on the third step of the ladder, but two legs of the ladder were sitting on a big box and the other two legs were in the little red wagon.

Rachel couldn't help but laugh. "What are we going to do with them?"

"Oh, keep them and love them and raise them. They're pretty nice to have around," David said. "I don't see how any family can get along without a set of thirds."

"I guess you'd better call them in," Rachel said.

"The boys are there now," David answered. "The thirds will have to quit anyway. How is Darlene doing on her sewing lessons, Glenda?"

"Pretty well. Rachel said I should start her in mending,

sewing on buttons and things like that. She's doing all right, but now the triplets are starting to say they want to learn, too. I told them to wait until next year and now I dread next year. Imagine! Trying to teach three to sew!"

"Glenda, do you have any material on hand," asked David, "that you could use to make Uncle Pete a shirt?" (The children had changed the mister to uncle at Pete's request.) "I've been asking him to go to church with us and he says he doesn't have suitable clothes. I don't know, maybe he is just using that for an excuse not to go. I told him God doesn't care about clothes and we don't either, but I can understand how he feels. He really doesn't have much."

"I might have," answered Glenda.

"David, do you think it would be all right to see if there is anything in that old trunk of clothes that belonged to our dad that he could wear?" asked Rachel. "Mother kept them when Dad left. I think until he died that she always hoped some day he would come back. After he died, she just didn't know what to do with them, so they are still in a trunk in the attic. I don't see any reason to keep them, do you?"

"Not really," David answered. "There is no sentimental value in them to me. Uncle Pete may as well get some use out of them if there is anything he can wear. I'll ask him if he minds. They are probably ten years out of style, but men's styles don't change much. If I remember right, though, our Dad was a bigger man than Uncle Pete."

"I wouldn't mind to alter some of them if they are not too much to big," said Glenda. "We can't afford to pay him money, but he sure does enough around here to warrant some consideration."

"My feelings exactly," David agreed. "This is the first time in ten years I have sat down in a chair in the daytime without feeling I should be doing something. I just can't think of a thing that needs to be done."

"What is Uncle Pete doing now?" asked Rachel.

"He's supposed to be resting, but I doubt if he is." Then looking out the window, he continued. "He's helping the boys pick the cherries. I might have known he'd find something to be doing. I hate it that we can't pay him, but when I mentioned it to him, he said, 'I'm eating good meals and I have a shed to call home. That's enough for me.' I feel God sent Pete here and I feel while he is doing so much for us, we should be helping him to find God."

Rachel nodded. "You know, David, that first night he was here I don't think I slept at all. I guess I reviewed all the murders and robberies I had ever heard of in my life. Now I don't even think about it anymore."

"You too? I thought I was the only one lying awake that night. I guess I did more praying than I had ever done before in one night. Well, I think I'll amble out and see if I can pry him away from the work long enough to talk about clothes."

"Speaking of clothes again," said Glenda as the door closed behind David, "do you think it would be all right if I could find a way to earn my dress for choir without buying it? That wouldn't be the same as spending money for it."

"However could you earn a dress?" asked Rachel.

"Oh, I just had an idea. May I go and call Dancy?"

"All right," Rachel said, "I think I hear Darlene coming back to help me. As soon as we get the cherries done, I'll find some time to come to the sewing room."

It was that night at the supper table that Glenda again brought up the subject. "David," she said, "the girls in the teen choir want dresses alike for when the choir sings at the conference in Lakeland. Is it all right if I make them?"

"I don't believe Mother would approve of you taking in sewing," said David. "She would want you to take better care of your eyes. It seems to me you were in the sewing room awfully late last night without taking on any more."

"It was only ten – something when I turned off the light."

"What? Ten fifty-nine?"

Glenda giggled. "No, actually it was only ten fifty-six. I was trying to get Sue Ellen a new dress made. Did you happen to notice how short her dress was last Sunday?"

"I noticed! Really, Glenda, you are to be commended

for the sewing you do, but God gave you only one pair of eyes. When you wear them out, they're gone."

"But David," Glenda argued, "it isn't like it was when Grandma taught Mother to sew. She didn't even have a sewing machine then. Grandma made her lace by hand, crocheted it with sewing thread. Remember that baby dress she made for mother, yards and yards of lace all made by hand and sewn on by hand. Every stitch of that dress was done by hand. Then Mother got a sewing machine, but it only sewed straight seams. She still had to work her buttonholes, put in hems, do her gathering, and I don't know what all, by hand. Now I've got a machine that does it all. I hardly know what a needle and thimble is. Of course I don't make lace, we buy that, but the machine sews it on, puts in the hems, makes the buttonholes, and even sews on some of the buttons. Sewing isn't as hard on your eyes now days as – reading."

"Is that straight?" David asked of Rachel.

"Quite straight. I don't see anything wrong with her making the dresses if she wants to, but David, I'm afraid she's going to have to quit choir, because we can't get her a dress."

"Don't worry about that," said Glenda, "I have a very bright idea. If you will let me make the other girls dresses, I'll get mine. They are going to give me three dollars each and the scraps."

"You are going to buy your material with the money you get for making the others?" asked David.

"Absolutely not!" declared Glenda. "All money made at this stage of the game goes for taxes. If the money I make is not needed to pay the taxes, I'd like to use it to buy material for school clothes when Nina's fabrics have their basement sale, but not one cent of it will be spent on me, unless Rachel thinks I need a new school dress. Now, do I have permission to make the girls dresses?"

"How many?"

"Eight, besides mine."

"Only on the condition there will be no more sewing after ten P.M."

"Done. Now may I be excused to go call Dancy?"

As Glenda left the table, Rachel said, "I sure can't understand how she is going to get her dress out of that, but if she has it figured out, I'll just let her go her own pace."

"We're going to make it with the taxes," said David. "If her scheme doesn't work we'll figure out some way to get her dress. If she makes the others, she certainly ought to be able to buy her own out of the money."

It was mid-morning of the next day when Rachel entered the sewing room. Glenda had laid out all of the cloth she had on hand. "First of all," Rachel said, "I'd like the triplets to have some new dresses for every day. They're just about destitute."

"I know," Glenda agreed. "Those brown prints are in the mending every week and the green stripes are too short, but I don't have anything big enough for the three of them."

"You can make them different. Those triplets are too much alike. They are not developing any individuality. Mother worried about that when she was alive."

"I think they are cute that way. I like the way they all want the same thing, do just alike, and even think alike. Remember when the school separated them in the first grade?"

"I remember!"

The school officials had insisted they be placed in three separate rooms. The triplets had laid their heads on their desks and cried all day. By the third day, all three had a fever and were unable to attend school. Doctor Gillard had been called and after he had heard the story, he went straight to the superintendent of the school and ordered him to see that the triplets were placed in the same room and that they should never again be separated until such time as the mother requested it, or the triplets themselves desired to be separated.

Glenda's voice brought Rachel's mind back to the present. "I don't think it will work. They won't wear them."

"They will have to wear them. They used to wear different dresses for every day before they grew up to so near Darlene's size. Now they can't wear her outgrown clothes anymore, so they are always dressed alike."

"That has been a long time," said Glenda. "I don't think it will work, but I'll make them and if you can't get them to wear them, I suppose Darlene can wear them."

"Don't make them too different. What do you have?"

Glenda thought a moment, then turned to the stack of material and brought out three pieces. "What about these?" she asked. "There is about the same amount of each. I wanted to use them together to make a dress for Mother, but I never did quite figure out how to do it." She laid the three pieces of material in front of Rachel. One was plain blue, one was blue and white stripe, and the other was the same stripe with the addition of pink roses scattered over it. The three pieces did look as if they belonged together.

"Super!" Rachel said. "Since the material is different, why don't you make them exactly alike. Then maybe they won't object so much. Just make them real simple so it won't take so much time."

"I'll have Darlene help with these when she comes for her lesson tomorrow. I like that idea you had of just having her in for an hour each day. That way I don't become impatient. She is doing well – really well."

The next evening just before supper Glenda brought the finished dresses in to show Rachel. "I'm glad I got them finished," she said. "The girls are supposed to bring the material and patterns for the choir dresses tomorrow."

"Glenda, how do you figure to get your dress?" asked Rachel.

"Why, I'm going to make it out of the scraps of theirs."

"You can't do that! It will be all pieced up. You will look awful and be ashamed to be seen in it."

"Just wait, Dear Sister, I'll do it and you will be proud of me."

"I hope not," said David coming in the door at that moment. 'Pride goest before destruction'. I think the word you mean is 'pleased' isn't it?"

"I suppose so. The Bible meaning of pride just isn't the way it's meant now-a-days. I should have said 'pleased.'"

"What's this?" David asked, looking at the dresses in Glenda's hands. "Aren't our thirds going to be thirds anymore?"

"Oh, they're just some for everyday wear," answered Rachel. "Call the girls and see if they like them."

The girls did not like them. Tears came into their eyes as they looked at the dresses and each other. They took the dresses to their room and appeared at the supper table quiet and subdued. They pushed the food around on their plates, but could not eat. It was a sad meal until suddenly Patricia looked at Letitia and then at Alicia, her eyes bright. Both the other triplets' faces brightened. "Are the dresses really ours?" asked Patricia.

"Of course," answered Rachel.

"Can we have them for our own and not just to wear?"

"They're really yours, but you do have to wear them. You can't throw them in the trash or anything."

"We will wear them. May we be excused?"

"After you have eaten," said David.

The three hurriedly cleaned their plates and left the table and the room.

Rachel and Darlene did the dishes and cleaned up the kitchen. It was time for family devotions and the triplets had not yet come back into the scene.

"I wonder what they're doing," pondered David.

"They're up in their room," answered Rachel. "I'll just have to go see." As she went up the stairs and down the hall, she could hear the triplets' chatter and laughter. "They certainly have gotten over being sad about the dresses," Rachel thought. She pushed open the door of the triplets' room. There, hanging on a hanger on a knob of the chest of drawers was the blue striped dress with the roses. The triplets were seated in chairs at their little study table with a box of crayons industriously coloring white strips and

84

pink roses on the other two dresses.

After devotions were over, Glenda sat with her head in her hands. Finally she sat up straight and said, "Well, it's my turn to do the hardest job of the day."

"What's that?" asked Rachel.

"Putting Sue Ellen to bed."

"Why? I didn't realize that was such a hard job for you."

"Oh, she always cries for Mother, and I generally end up crying with her."

"Do you want me to do it?" asked Darlene. "I don't mind. Honest."

"Would you? Oh, I would do anything in exchange – dishes or whatever."

Darlene picked up Sue Ellen. "Want Sister to get you ready for bed, Honey?" she asked.

"Mommy tant tum night?"

Fifteen minutes later Darlene was back in the living room. Did she cry?" asked Glenda.

"No, she never does," answered Darlene.

"She always cries for me. If she cried just because she didn't want to go to bed, I could take that, but it's Mother she cries for. Poor kid, she's lost two mothers. I think that's more than any baby's share. Anyway, Darlene, how do you do it?"

"You know that monkey Mother bought her that she

can put in the bath tub with her? We call him Choco. Well, when Sue Ellen says, 'I want Mommy,' I say, 'Mommy can't come tonight. Choco is going to get you ready for bed.' So whatever I do, I do with Choco in my hands. Choco unfastens her dress and takes off her clothes. Then he gets into the bathtub and washes her. After he gets her dressed and helps me put her in bed, he gives her her doll and then we both kiss her good night. Choco turns out the light and she goes right to sleep. Did you hear what she said when I asked her if she wanted me to get her ready for bed?"

"I didn't notice."

"She said, 'Mommy tant tum night?' because that is what I always say."

"You're a wonder, Darlene," said Glenda. "I wish I were wise like that."

"No, I'm no wonder," said Darlene. "I'm just one of the family. God gave us all a place in the family and made us able to do our part. That's just one of the things he gave me wisdom for, but you have just as important a place in the family as anyone else. Where would we all be if you couldn't sew? I will never learn to sew like you can."

IX

It was a quiet afternoon that Rachel decided to straighten up the playroom that trouble paid another visit to the family.

Greg had a new piece of chalk and was putting all his efforts into drawing a picture on the little blackboard when Rachel noticed him with the chalk between his first two fingers. He carried it to his face and stuck the end of it in his mouth. Rachel's heart did a flip-flop and she almost cried out, but she steadied herself and waited to be sure. Presently he again took the chalk between his fingers and held it out away from him while he curled his little lips into a circle and blew his breath out.

"What are you doing, Greg?" asked Rachel quietly.

"Mokin," came the reply.

"Why are you smoking?" asked Rachel. "No one in this family smokes. Why do you want to smoke?"

"Bwad does, and Billy Bob."

Rachel's anxiety was mounting. Oh, if they should

have this problem added to all they already had, how could they handle it? She managed to control her tension and keep her voice steady as she continued. "When do Brad and Billy Bob smoke, and where?"

"They moked one day out ahind the chicken house, they did."

"Well, Gregory," Rachel said, keeping her voice low and controlled. "They shouldn't have done that. They were not being good boys when they did that. Jesus does not want his children to smoke. David doesn't smoke, nor Nathan. David and Nathan are living for Jesus. You always say you want to be like Jesus, so you shouldn't copy Billy Bob and Brad when they do bad things."

"Is mokin bad?" asked Greg.

"Yes, Gregory, smoking is very bad."

"Oh, I not know that. Is Bwad and Billy Bob gonna get panked?"

"I don't know yet. We will have to see when we talk to them, but Gregory, I don't want you to play that you are smoking anymore. If I see you do that again, I will have to spank you."

"I not do it no more," Greg shook his head until the brown curls bounced. "I wanta do like Jesus."

Rachel met Alicia as she left the three year old in the playroom. "Do you know where Bradley is?" she asked.

"I think he's somewhere with Billy Bob. He's always

with Billy Bob."

"You find him and tell him I want to see him in the kitchen."

When Brad came through the kitchen door, Rachel took him by the arm and led him into the office. She sat down on a chair, turned Brad toward her, looked into his eyes and asked. Bradley, have you been smoking?"

"Sure!" Brad answered. "Billy Bob said I was a baby if I didn't. He said all men smoke and I want to be a man so I can take care of my family."

"All men do not smoke, Bradley. Did you ever see David smoke, or Pastor Parker?"

"No," answered Brad.

"Jesus didn't smoke when he was on earth. I thought you wanted to be like Jesus."

"My Daddy smoked."

Rachel hesitated before she answered. She knew she had to be very careful. She must not teach Brad to dishonor his father, yet she knew she must teach him that smoking was evil.

"Your Daddy did not know Jesus, Bradley. His mother never taught him to use Jesus for his example the way our Mother taught us. Maybe she didn't even know it was a sin to smoke."

Bradley's eyes got big and round. "Is it a sin to smoke, Rachel?"

"Yes, it is, Brad."

"You never told me that before. If you had told me that, I wouldn't have done it. I didn't like it anyway. It choked me and Billy Bob laughed."

Rachel never mentioned the matter to Billy Bob, but when David came in she told him what had happened. Then she said, "I'm afraid I don't know what to do about Billy Bob, David. I'd like for you to handle the matter. I know Mother would have given him some 'woodshed psychology,' but I know that isn't the answer for me and I rather doubt it is for you."

"No," David said, "it wouldn't do any good. Most of the time he resents my authority, although in his better moments he admits Mother told him to obey you and me. Remember the night Nathan threatened to mash his mouth?"

"I do."

"I talked to Nathan about it and he told me that once when Billy Bob was mad he said if I ever laid a finger on him he'd have me arrested. Nathan said he figured that being so near Billy Bob's age the law wouldn't do anything to him, so that is why he said what he did. Well, call Billy Bob and tell him I want him in the office, and then *pray*."

"Billy Bob and David were in the office a full half hour. David's voice was low and controlled, but Billy Bob's went from quiet to loud and angry, then to crying, and gradually to quiet again before the two emerged from the office. Billy Bob went straight to Rachel and said. "I'm sorry, Rachel. I know I did wrong, and I want you to forgive me, especially for getting Brad to do something wrong." Then he ran crying up to his room.

"Rachel," David said, "Billy Bob isn't to be with Uncle Pete, Brad, or Gregory without being in the presence of you, Nathan or me."

"Why Nathan? Do you think that's wise? He's only a boy, too."

"Yes, but Nathan has a good brain in his head. I would not have included Nathan if it hadn't been Billy Bob requested it. He loves to take Brad fishing and he knew the only chance to be able to do that would be with Nathan. It's the only thing Nathan ever does for pleasure."

"Why Uncle Pete?"

"I'm not sure. I like Uncle Pete in a way, but Billy Bob has been spending a lot of time with him, and I'm afraid he's a bad influence. He keeps telling me he's going to be a tramp like Uncle Pete. Billy Bob is genuinely ashamed. I don't remember to have ever seen him so sorry for any of his wrongs."

Nathan took Pete his supper that night and the next morning David took him his breakfast.

"Where's Billy Bob?" Pete asked.

"Oh, he's in the house."

"Is he sick?"

"No."

"Well, is something wrong? I mean – well – he always brings me my meals and I enjoy talking with him. It's just that if there's some reason –"

"Billy Bob is being punished. He did something he knew he shouldn't and he won't be coming with your meals."

Pete pushed the door wide open. "David, would you come in and sit down?" he said. "I'd like to talk to you."

David remembered that breakfast would be waiting in about five minutes, but for all the weeks since Pete had been here, he had never seemed to want to talk. David felt he couldn't pass up an opportunity like this. He entered Pete's little home and sat in the chair Pete offered.

"I don't know what Billy Bob has done," said Pete, "and it isn't my business to ask, so I won't, but I do think you should tell me if you feel I am to blame for what he has done."

"No," answered David, "I don't mind to tell you what he has done. He has been out behind the chicken house smoking. That is bad enough in itself, although I realize most boys who are not Christians, try it sometime in their lives. What really has me upset is that he had Brad out there getting him to smoke, telling him he wasn't a man if he didn't."

"I see," Pete said meditatively. "Billy Bob is a problem to the family, isn't he?"

"I don't like to consider him a problem, it's just that he is so different from all the rest. Yes, I guess I have to say he is a problem. It's just not a problem without a solution. God is the solution, but –"

"Billy Bob doesn't want God. Right?"

"Right! I don't feel you are directly to blame for what he has done, yet I know you are his idol. He wants to be like you, he has no goal in life but to be an old tramp, like Uncle Pete."

"I see, but I told you I don't smoke. David, I want you to listen to me, and then think about what I have to say. I was a boy like Billy Bob. I grew up wanting my own way. I married a lovely girl and had a darling baby boy. I felt fenced in. I wanted freedom. I left my wife and little boy and struck out to have a good time. My good time didn't last. I will spare you the details, but I went from bad to worse, until I was in the condition you first saw me. My life is ruined. I can't do anything about that. At that, I'm happier right now than I've been in many years."

"God can straighten out your life, Uncle Pete."

"I'm working on that, David. I don't understand your religion. I was raised in another kind of church, but even as a boy, when I thought I was a Christian, I didn't have the peace within that shows without like yours does. But even if I do get that peace, I can not have my family again."

"Why not, Uncle Pete?" asked David. "Couldn't you go back? Wouldn't your wife forgive you?"

"It's too late, David. My wife remarried. My little boy grew up knowing another man as his father. I can't turn back the clock."

This time it was David's turn to say, "I see."

"Well, now I suppose they are waiting breakfast on you, so I won't delay you, but I just want to say this; I don't have much happiness left. You have given me a place where I can work enough for a roof over my head and three good, mighty good, meals a day. Now I have clothes so I can go to church and maybe get things worked out so God and I will be on speaking terms again, but I wish you wouldn't punish me by keeping Billy Bob away. The others are all mannerly to me, but they act like they are afraid of me. They never stay around where I am. Billy Bob acts like he cares about me as a person, and I care about Billy Bob. Give me a chance, David, I promise you I would never encourage him in anything you would not approve of, and if he gets any worse by being with me, then by all means tell me and keep him away. Being as I have traveled the road he's going, I think I might be able to make him see that there is a better road."

David stuck out his hand to Pete. "All right," he said, "I'll think it over and make a decision. You will know what that decision is by whether Billy Bob brings you your lunch."

Then David hurried back to the waiting breakfast and his anxious brothers and sisters.

X

Billy Bob took Pete his lunch, his supper, and his breakfast. In fact as the days went by, Billy Bob spent more and more of his time with Pete. When David first told Rachel of his conversation with Pete, she was apprehensive.

"That means Billy Bob won't really be punished at all. Because of Nathan he is allowed to be with Brad and now if you let him visit Uncle Pete —"

"Is it really punishment we want Billy Bob to have?" asked David. "I believe Uncle Pete is genuinely interested in Billy Bob. I believe he will be an influence for good."

"He is not even a Christian, David," Rachel argued.

"I rather doubt the donkey that spoke to Balaam was a Christian."

Rachel said no more. David was head of the house.

In a few minutes Glenda came in to show off her new dress. It had a high neckline, full puffed sleeves, and a bouffant skirt.

"It's beautiful!" exclaimed Rachel. "How ever did you do it?"

Glenda's eyes danced. "I told you I was making it out of the scraps of the others. That's exactly what I did!"

"Well, I don't know much about sewing," said David, "but I do have sense enough to know that dress isn't made of scraps. What's the story?"

"Well, I didn't buy the material, and I didn't steal it."

"We know that."

"All right, since you two are so curious, I'll tell you my secret. Rachel knows that when you buy a pattern and a piece of material the size the pattern says, you always have plenty. The girls all bought just the amount the pattern said, and they all bought off the same bolt. I made Dancy's dress first. By rearranging the placement of the pattern on the material, I had enough left to get the collar and sash of Laura's dress. Then of course when I cut Laura's, because I already had the collar and sash, I had twice as big a piece left so I cut the back and the sleeves of Kathy's out of what was left of Laura's. By the time I had all eight of them made –"

"I get the picture," said Rachel.

"Yes," David added, "I believe we have a genius in the family. Rachel and I are both immensely pleased with you. How are you going to get to the conference?"

"Oh, Brother Dobison is going to take us in the Sunday

School Bus."

"I suppose Nathan is going, too. Does he need anything new?"

"I don't think so, but you might ask Nathan. He would never speak up on his own."

A chat with Nathan disclosed that he considered his wardrobe adequate for the outing.

"If it wasn't I'd stay home," declared Nathan. "The taxes have to be paid!"

"We are going to make it on the taxes without using Glenda's sewing money, so I promised that that should go for school clothes, but if you need anything –"

"No, I'm fine."

The next night Billy Bob was sitting on the floor of Pete's cabin listening to him tell a tale of being out on a mountain at night with a panther when Pete suddenly changed the subject.

"What are you going to be when you grow up, Billy Bob?"

"I don't know. I haven't really spent much time thinking about it: a cowboy maybe, or a sea captain. I want to be something that I can be free. I hate the feeling of bondage, of being tied, or fenced in."

Pete nodded, "Just the way I felt at your age."

"Really? I like you, Uncle Pete. I'd like to be like you. I've really thought of being a tramp, but Timothy Fletcher says tramps always steal and one thing I've made up my mind, I won't steal anymore."

"Why?"

"Well, I got caught three times and the judge said one more time and I go to reform school. Mike Jennings' older brother has been there and he told me enough stories about it that I know I don't want to go there. Do you steal, Uncle Pete?"

"No," Pete said, "but I'm not a tramp anymore, remember? I used to steal. In fact I used to do a lot of things I am ashamed of, but I don't do them any more."

"Tell me more about yourself," said Billy Bob. "Tell me all about everything in your life. I think you are the nicest person I ever met, and I want to be just like you."

"All right, but first I want to ask you a question. How old do you think I am?"

Billy Bob stood up and studied Pete thoughtfully. He squinted one eye, turned his head sidewise, and then said, "About sixty-five, I guess. How far did I miss it?"

"That will have to wait. You wanted the story of my life. I'm going to tell you, but I promise you it isn't a pretty story. I was born into a good Christian family. We weren't rich, but we weren't poor. We had everything we needed and most everything we wanted. I guess I was spoiled. At a young age I developed a case of thinking more of myself than of anyone else. When I was ten, the other boys and girls were giving their hearts to God and joining the church. Oh, it wasn't salvation as your family knows salvation, but it was the best we knew. I guess at first I did it because the others were doing it. I wanted to be a Christian, but I didn't want to give all of me to God. I wanted to be free. As they would say it today, I wanted to do my own thing. I went on that way for about four years, calling myself a Christian but doing lots of things I knew were not pleasing to God. Then when I was fourteen, a strange minister came to our church to preach one night. He really got to me. I decided to re-dedicate my life to God. I went up to the altar that night and something happened to me. The presence of God seemed to come to me and I knew God wanted to use me in a special way. He wanted me to go somewhere as a missionary, I'm not sure where. I think somewhere in South America." Tears came into Pete's eyes as he continued. "If I had said 'Yes' to God that night, everything that happened afterward would not have happened, but I didn't. I said, 'No!' God kept trying to talk to me and I kept saying, 'No' and, 'I won't.' There were things I wanted to do. I had my life all planned. I made up my mind I was going to carry out my plans."

Pete paused and wiped his eyes and Billy Bob spoke. "If the church you were in wasn't right, why would God want you to be a missionary in it?"

"I'm sure He didn't, Billy Bob. I didn't realize then

that the church I was in didn't have the truth. I have only known that since listening to David and the few times I've been to church with your family. I am sure if I had said, 'Yes' to God He would have led me into more truth. I was only fourteen remember? You can't go as a missionary to a foreign country at fourteen. He wanted me to get ready to be a missionary. I left that church that night determined not to have anything more to do with God. I wouldn't have gone back to church any more except in that church was a beautiful Christian girl that I liked. I will call her 'Susie'. I had already made up my mind that I was going to marry Susie. For that reason I kept going to church and pretending I was a Christian. It took me eight years to win Susie. In the meantime I lived a pretty wild life, but somehow managed to keep Susie deceived. Well, I made a real big mistake when I married Susie. She was a real Christian. I thought as soon as we were married that I could lead Susie to my way of thinking and we could have a wild carefree life together, but Susie wouldn't change. Right away we started quarreling. I wanted to go to the show, Susie wanted to go to church. I wanted to go to a dance, Susie wanted to spend a quiet evening at home. I said we quarreled, but really we didn't. Susie would not quarrel. I shouted and stomped and raved, but Susie would just quietly let her tears fall and say nothing, or she would say 'I love you B – Pete, but I love Jesus more and He does not want me to do those things.' She was a wonderful little woman, Billy Bob, but I still wanted my own way.

"I had that feeling of bondage you spoke of, the feeling of being tied or fenced in. I couldn't stand it. I had to break loose, to be free, so I left my wife. I have never seen her since. I went my own way. At first I thought I was having fun. I went to shows and dances to my heart's content. No, that's just a saying. My heart wasn't content. I started drinking. I smoked three packs of cigarettes a day. I didn't want to work and my parents wouldn't help me any more, so I started stealing. I got in with a stealing ring that robbed stores and came awfully near getting caught. I won't tell you all I did. It is enough to say if I had been caught I would be in prison yet, but I hopped a freight train and got out of that state. I went away out west and got a job as a cowboy on a ranch, but the wages weren't enough to buy all I wanted to smoke and drink, so I started rustling cattle. Why I didn't get shot or hung I don't know. Some of my buddies did, but I guess God still had something ahead for me. The two nights and a day I spent in the top of a tree while they looked for me all over the county was when I made up my mind I'd had enough of that. When I finally got out of the tree, I went to live in a cave. I had to quit smoking and drinking because I had no money for tobacco and liquor. I stole what I could and begged what I could. That's the way I lived until I came here. I told your brother a lot of lies when he knew some of them were lies. Then he told me if I were to stay here and work for my board I would have to be truthful. I promised him I would tell the truth and I have."

"How old is Pastor Parker, Billy Bob? Do you know?"

"Yes, I know. We had a birthday party for him in the fellowship hall back in the winter. He's forty two."

"How old does he look to you, Billy Bob? Does he look like an old man?"

"No, he looks about his age, I guess, but what's that got to do with you?"

"Pastor Parker's a good man, Billy Bob. He's lived a good life. He chose the right road. He is forty-two and he looks forty-two. I'm just forty and I look sixty-five. Billy Bob, I'm no good. I couldn't do a man's work if my life depended on it. My leg is messed up because of the life I lived. My lungs are messed up because of too many cigarettes. I can't run because I can't get my breath. My heart's no good. I've made a mess of life. Is this really what you want to do with your life?"

A door closing at the house brought Billy Bob's mind back home. He jumped up. "What time is it?" he asked.

"Twenty five minutes till ten."

"Oh, my. David told me to be home at 8:30 for devotions."

Billy Bob was out the door in a bound, running to the house, but just before he reached the door of his own home he met David. He stopped short in front of him. "I'm sorry, David," he said, "I didn't mean to."

David swiftly walked toward the house with Billy Bob following. When they were in the kitchen David spoke. "You do realize you are over an hour late?"

"Yes."

"You do realize you will have to be punished?"

"Yes."

"Why are you late?"

"I didn't notice the time. I wasn't even thinking of time."

"What were you doing that caused you to forget time?"

"We were talking. Pete was telling me about himself."

"Billy Bob, what do you think I should do about this?"

"Well," Billy Bob shifted his weight from his right foot to his left, then back to his right. He rubbed his hand across his forehead and blurted. "I hope you don't do it but I know you are supposed to use a belt on me."

"I think there ought to be a better way than resorting to the belt. If Mother were alive I know she would do it that way, or if you had a father he probably would do it, but we are brothers. I'd like to have you learn some responsibility. We had to go ahead with devotions. It was the little ones bedtime. We couldn't wait or they would have gone to sleep. We studied Colossians 3:1-10. What do you think about studying it and writing a report on it?"

"I think that's just about right. I know I should have watched the time. I should be more dependable and I know I have to be punished, but I honestly believe I got more good teaching out of tonight than I would have if I had been in here for devotions. I wouldn't have missed it if I'd had to write half a dozen reports, and David, I've decided I'm not going to be a tramp."

"What are you going to be?"

"Oh, a doctor, maybe, or a farmer, or," Billy Bob dropped his voice to a whisper, "whatever God wants."

David put his hand on Billy Bob's shoulder and looked into his eyes. He noticed he didn't have to look very far down to look into Billy Bob's eyes. You go ahead and study those verses, Billy Bob, and then you get to bed. You can forget about writing that report."

XI

"Meow!" Rachel stopped in the middle of her jelly-making to listen. "Meow, meow."

"Bradley!" she called, "Bradley, do come and get this kitten!"

Brad came running into the kitchen and grabbed the kitten who was at that time sharpening its claws on the leg of a chair.

"Bradley, we have a rule here, no pets in the house. In general cats belong at the barn. I know you have made a pet of that one, but if you don't keep it out of the kitchen, we are going to have to get rid of it."

"I'll try, Rachel. I really will."

Brad took the kitten outside, sat down on the back steps, and tried to reason with it. "Now, you listen to me, Kitty Cat. Rachel doesn't want you in the house. If you don't stay out of the house you're going to have to get adopted to somewhere else. Maybe that's what they call going to a foster home. Please don't go in the house

106

anymore, because I want to keep you." He set the kitten down and went back inside.

"Rachel," said he, "can I have some milk to feed Kitty Cat?"

"May I, Brad," Rachel corrected.

"May I?"

"Yes, you may have some milk, but please feed her outside and away from the house. Feeding her at the house is what is causing her to hang around the house."

Brad got a cup from the cabinet and set it on the table. He then got the pitcher of milk from the refrigerator and filled the cup with milk. As he went back to the refrigerator with the milk, Rachel took her pan of jelly off the stove and Greg came running through the door and into the kitchen. Rachel screamed! Greg stopped short just in time to keep from colliding with the jelly pan, but not soon enough to keep Rachel from spilling some of the hot liquid on her hand and a goodly amount on the kitchen floor. She quickly set the pan down and put her hand under the faucet to wash off the jelly. No one noticed the cat had slipped in with Greg until she was climbing the tablecloth and had succeeded in pulling off the cup of milk, adding it to the jelly. Greg made a dive for the cat and slipped and fell in the mess. Rachel picked him up and administered one good sharp whack on his sitting down place, saying, "I told you to stay out of the kitchen this morning."

At that moment Mrs. O'Conner spoke at the door. "Well, if you have lost control to the place where you have to start beating the babies, I should say it was about time I came after them."

Rachel's scream had brought the other girls from the four corners of the house. Nathan and Billy Bob noticed the car drive up and came from where they were mending the chicken pen fence. Suddenly the kitchen was full of people.

Glenda took command. She picked up the cup, which miraculously hadn't broken and said, "Alicia, get me the ungentine and some bandage material from the hall closet. Darlene, you take Mrs. O'Conner into the parlor and wait there until Rachel can come and talk to her. Letitia, get the bucket and mop and clean up this mess. Patricia, take Greg to the bathroom and wash him up and get him some clean clothes."

By the time Glenda had finished talking, she had poured what was left of the jelly into the glasses Rachel had lined up for it. Brad had taken the kitten outside and Nathan had disappeared. Billy Bob followed Mrs. O'Conner and Darlene to the parlor.

"There's no use wasting the time," Mrs. O'Conner said. "I have come for the babies. I'm in a hurry this morning, as I have a long way to go. Couldn't you gather up their things and be ready by the time Rachel comes?"

"I could *not*!" declared Darlene. "Here, Mrs. O'Conner, would you like to look at our family album? I'm sorry I don't have a magazine to offer you. We used to have a subscription to a magazine, but no one had time to read it so we let it drop."

Mrs. O'Conner looked around her. This room was beautiful! The house, what she had seen of it, was very nice. One certainly couldn't complain of the living conditions of the children.

It was only a few minutes before Rachel and Glenda appeared, and the triplets not very many minutes behind.

"I'm sorry, Mrs. O'Conner, but I was delayed," Rachel said just as if Mrs. O'Conner hadn't been at the door and seen it all. "Greg ran in front of me when I was taking the jelly off the stove and I burned my hand. It does hurt fiercely."

"I have come for the babies," Mrs. O'Conner repeated. "I have very nice homes waiting for them where they will be well cared for."

The girls sat quietly, each one praying in her mind and heart.

"Well," Mrs. O'Conner said, "can't you get their things? I'm in a hurry. I'm working on a home for the triplets and Darlene, but I haven't found a place willing to take three, and it seems a shame to separate the triplets. I will be back for them, probably next week."

"You mean to separate the little ones?" asked Rachel.

"Of course. No one can handle three babies."

"The children have a nice home here where they can all be together. They are well cared for. There is no reason for taking them from this home."

"There is every reason to take them from this home. Children must have parents to love them and oversee them. You are nothing but a child yourself. Children can't properly care for children. Our foster homes are the best in the state. They don't beat children as I saw you do."

Billy Bob brought himself up to his full 5ft. 7in. "Now you listen to me, Mrs. O'Conner. Rachel doesn't beat the children. It is true we don't have parents, but Rachel and David are not children. Marsha Renfrow down the road is married and has a baby of her own, and she is two months younger than Rachel. I suppose you'll take her baby because she's a child. I'll tell you something, I'm a problem to this family – always have been – probably always will be. If you want to take me to a foster home, I'll go. It's probably what I deserve."

"I don't think I could find one that would take you. You deserve the reform-school."

"You are probably right about that, but it's the only thing you are right about. We had the best Mother in the state. She raised the rest of the kids to be the best kids in the state so far as she raised them. David and Rachel are doing their best to carry out Mother's wishes. If you want kids, there are plenty of kids being neglected and abused. I go to school with one boy, comes to school with welts and bruises all the time from being beaten. His old man gets drunk and comes home to beat his wife. The boy interferes and takes the beating. The little kids hide under the bed. David has never gotten drunk in his life and none of the kids hide when they see him coming. They run to meet him."

"Who's that? What's his name?"

"Think I'm gonna tell you that? You got another think comin'! He's my friend! I wouldn't betray him into your hands to be put in one of your precious foster homes. He's talked to me. I know how he feels. He loves his mother and his mother loves him. It would kill his mother to have her little ones taken away."

Billy Bob was angry, his face red. The longer he talked the faster and louder he talked.

"Then there is another family. The father is sick and the mother has seven little kids, too little to help much. They have hardly any clothes, and almost nothing to eat. Or you could go on down the road to Mrs. Society. She's gone all day to her club meetings and who knows what else. Her two darling well-dressed imps run around the country and get into more trouble than I do. Why don't you go put them in your precious foster home?"

"Oh, yes, I know about your foster homes, too! I go to school with boys from two of them! I don't mind mentioning their names. Carl and Velma Thompson have a little princess of their own. They didn't have as much money as they wanted, so they started taking in foster kids. Their foster kids come to school in the plainest of clothes, while darling little Veronica is in ruffles and frills. Dick told me she even has different food from the rest, because she's sickly, they say, but Dick said he didn't see why a sick kid should have a candy bar more than a well one. Then there's the Couliers. They took the two boys to do the work. They get up at 4:30 each morning and fix breakfast for their foster parents. Then they have to wash the dishes, clean up the house, feed the chickens, and milk the cow before they go to school. Mrs. Coulier says they should be grateful, because the Couliers are giving them a home. I suppose you took them out of a good home like this one, though I don't believe there are any as good as this one. Well, I'm telling you something, Mrs. O'Conner, if you take these kids from this home, God is going to punish you for it."

Billy Bob turned to the door, angry tears running down his face and almost collided with David who stood in the doorway listening, Nathan right behind him.

"Mrs. O'Conner isn't going to take any of our children, Billy Bob."

"Oh, but I am! I have come for the Sparks children and I will be back for Darlene and the triplets."

"Do you have any court custody papers giving you a right to take the children?"

"N-no."

"Well, I have the court custody papers made out to my mother and I also have a legal paper that states my mother left everything to me, so unless you go to court and the court puts the care of these children into your hands, you will be arrested for kidnapping if you take one of them out of this home. Now I suggest you be about your other business. Nathan, see Mrs. O'Conner to her car."

"All right, you young smart-aleck. You have it your own way. I'll see you in court," and Mrs. O'Conner swept out of the room and out of the house.

"Oh, David," breathed Rachel, "I was so scared."

"There wouldn't have been one thing I could have done if she had taken them, but that's what Mr. Clarke suggested, so I tried it and it worked, temporarily at least."

"Oh, I don't know what is going to become of us all," said Rachel.

David took her hand. "God is taking care of us, remember? We'll take it one day at a time. Today we still have our little ones. By the way, where are they?" The children looked from one to the other.

"Alicia," Rachel said, "aren't you supposed to be

watching Sue Ellen today?"

"Y-yes. I had her with me until Glenda sent me for the stuff to bandage your hand and when I came back she was gone. I supposed she went with Darlene. She goes with Darlene every chance she gets." Alicia, tears running down her cheeks, ran from the room in search of Sue Ellen.

"Where is Greg?" David asked. "And Brad?"

"I left Brad helping Greg dress," said Patricia. "Oh, maybe Mrs. O'Conner took them."

"Mrs. O'Conner did not take them," said Nathan. "I saw her get into her car and I watched her drive away."

"But where are they?" cried Rachel.

"They are around somewhere," assured David. "Let's get calm and organized and look for them. Where did the other third go?"

"Alicia went to look for Sue Ellen. She had charge of her this morning."

"Call her."

Alicia came in crying. "I can't find Sue Ellen anywhere."

"Greg is probably still with Brad. Does anyone know where Brad is?" David looked around at the others.

Alicia wiped her eyes. "I don't know where Brad is, but he said when you want him to tell you to hammer on the iron skillet with the big spoon like you do when they've gone fishing and you want them."

Billy Bob ran to the kitchen for the skillet and big spoon, and made enough noise calling Brad to arouse the neighbors half a mile away.

"That's enough, Billy Bob. If Brad hasn't left the farm he can surely hear that."

They waited a few minutes. Presently they saw the top of a head bob around the corner of the house. Then Brad appeared. "Is she gone?" he asked.

"Yes, she's gone. Brad, do you know where Greg and Sue Ellen are?" asked Rachel.

"Yes, I've got them hid! I had to come and see if she was gone before I brought them home." Then he hung his head. "Rachel, I guess you got to spank me. I disobeyed. I went off the farm. I really couldn't help it. We don't have a culvert and there was a nice one across the road in front of that old house. I looked real good before I crossed the road."

"A culvert?"

"Brad looked at Billy Bob and said, "Yes, I thought a culvert was the best place to hide. I thought she'd never find us there. I'll go get them."

"It does seem to me," said Billy Bob looking at David, that someone has been telling tales."

"I told him," said Nathan. He was so scared of little purple men that he couldn't be left alone for a minute."

"Who told you?"

115

"Well, actually, Billy Bob, you and I sleep in the same room, and –"

"And you were awake and listening. Couldn't you have let it be known?"

"There's something about a person's name that gets through to them even when they are asleep. I guess I was pretty tired that night, but when you spoke my name I woke up just in time to hear you kill me. What was I supposed to do, say 'I am awake,' get up and black your eye, or just lie there and pray for you? I decided on the latter."

"What do you mean, kill you? I never said anything about killing you. You're still alive, aren't you?"

"Well, I John 3:15 says, *Whosoever hateth his brother is a murderer*: and I seem to remember hearing you say you hated me."

Brad came up the driveway pulling the wagon with Sue Ellen asleep on a blanket, with her Teddy Bear in her arms. At her feet was a big bag of what proved to be food. Greg walked behind.

"I had to take some things, Rachel," said Brad. "I didn't know how long we might have to stay. Sue Ellen walks too slowly and she's 'bout too big for me to carry so I took the wagon. I pulled it right into the culvert and it made a nice bed for her. We could have stayed a month if we had to. Are you gonna spank me, Rachel? I couldn't let Mrs. O'Conner get Sue Ellen and Greg."

Rachel shook her head and put out her arms to Brad. She had a very real sense that if she tried to speak she would cry.

XII

David entered the kitchen and dropped heavily into a chair. "I thought I'd find you here, Rachel. I believe you spend fourteen hours a day in this kitchen."

"I probably do now that you men are doing so much of the garden work. I hardly go outside at all unless my work is all done and I go out to enjoy the flowers."

"Which very seldom happens. I think if you didn't have any work you'd make some."

"I don't want to get behind, David. I've got to keep up or I'll never catch up. Things are a lot easier for me now though. Without the garden work I have a lot more spare time."

"We didn't have time for the garden work before Uncle Pete came. He sure has made it a lot easier on all of us."

"Well, what bad news did you bring from town?"

David sighed. "I don't know how you can tell, but yes, it's bad news. The man I was depending on to fix the tractor says he can't get to it for at least a week and we need it like yesterday."

"What's wrong with it."

"I haven't the faintest idea. I know less than nothing about mechanics. I do wish I could have picked up a little know-how somewhere, but there just wasn't anywhere to pick it up. Mother didn't have any and everything I know I learned from Mother except what I learned in school. They don't teach mechanics in Oakland High School."

"Maybe they will this year, but of course that won't do you any good. Kathy Martin came out for a little while the other afternoon and she said they are offering several new classes this year. David, did you know Glenda wants to quit school?"

"Glenda, too? I knew Nathan does. He says he's needed at home."

"Nathan can't quit. He is just going to be fourteen."

"I know, but he has finished eighth grade, and that is all that is required by law in this state. I don't want him to quit, but I won't force him to go. It's a little hard sometimes for a Christian to fight everything the school puts on them. I sure wouldn't want to be the cause of Nathan backing up."

"I don't think we need fear for Nathan. I wish I could feel as confident of Glenda. Glenda's reason for wanting to quit is she feels it detracts from her walk with God. Oh, I wish we had a Christian school here."

"Pastor Parker plans to have one in a few years, but that doesn't help for now. Well, I will check on the courses offered this year. If a mechanics course is offered I can use that to persuade Nathan to go, but I won't force him. He knows how strong he is better than we do and the same goes for Glenda, but I do hope they will both go back. It would be just one more bone for Mrs. O'Conner to chew if they don't. Now, I guess I'll go out and see what Uncle Pete is up to. I imagine the tractor being down hasn't stopped him from finding something to do."

David found Pete driving nails in some loose boards in the barn. "Uncle Pete," he said, "don't you ever rest?"

"Sure!" Pete answered. "Every night. Did you get somebody to look at the tractor?"

"Not for at least a week."

"Want me to give it a look?"

"Do you think – can you – I mean? I didn't know you knew anything about machinery."

"Know a little; owned a tractor somewhat like that one in my younger days."

"Go ahead, Uncle Pete. Why didn't you say so yesterday?"

"I didn't want to push in."

"I think you've earned the right to push in around here. While we are on the subject of your abilities, tell me. Do you know anything about plumbing?"

"Not much, but some. I can fix a leaky drainpipe or a broken water pipe. Why? You got a problem?"

"No, it's just that I found some used bathroom fixtures in town. The guy said he would hold them for me until I sell the pigs. I think there is room in that shed of yours, no more belongings than you have, to install a bathroom. Think you can do it?"

Pete nodded, not trusting his voice to speak. He cleared his throat twice and then said. "You're being mighty good to me, David."

"I can't see that at all," David answered. "You earn many times what little we do for you. I don't know what would have become of us if you hadn't come."

"Thank you, David. I'm mighty glad I came. I don't know what would have become of me if I hadn't."

David had to make another trip to town for a couple of spark plugs, but before night the tractor was running smoothly.

During the next few weeks Pete spent all his spare time working on his house, enclosing a little corner to be ready for the fixtures when the pigs should be sold.

Billy Bob spent every available moment helping Pete. David and even Nathan were seen occasionally helping out. Not only were they preparing for the bathroom, but also winter weather; patching cracks, and making the little shed as tight as possible. Billy Bob produced all the old paint he could find in the basement and by mixing several cans, came up with enough paint to paint the shed inside a not so beautiful gray. Pete laughingly said gray was almost his favorite color, being surpassed only by all the other colors. Moreover, he said he didn't want to hear anyone ever again speak of Pete's shed. From now on it would be known as "Pete's Palace."

Oh, they had a good time, in those days, but all the time hanging over them like a bomb ready to drop was the threat of Mrs. O'Conner and the welfare. When would the bomb drop?

XIII

"Somebody's coming!" Billy Bob, standing at the kitchen window one September evening watched the car drive in. "It looks like Pastor Parker." Rachel looked out the window, whisked off her apron, smoothed her hair, and was in the front hall by the time David had admitted Pastor and Sis. Parker. She attempted to usher them into the parlor, but Sister Parker objected.

"Can't we sit in the living room? The parlor is so formal and this is a friendly visit, not a formal one." When they were seated in the living room, Sister Parker said, "I fear we are a little early. Have you finished your supper?"

"Just finished," said David. "The thirds are doing the dishes."

"The official reason for our un-official visit," said Pastor Parker, "is to see if we can get you and Rachel back as active members of the youth group."

"Oh, I don't think we can," began Rachel.

"Why? We are ready to put up some good arguments

as to why you should, so if you really don't want to you had better have some really good arguments as to why you shouldn't. How is everything going anyway, David?"

"Pretty well, Sir. We had some real financial problems this summer, but by working together we've made it."

"What was the problem?"

"Well, you see, the doctor bill and the funeral bill took all our savings and the taxes weren't paid."

"Oh, I didn't know! I'm so sorry! Why didn't you come to me? The church would have helped."

"Frankly, Sir, I never thought of it. I came home and presented the problem to the family and everyone pitched in to help. That was when Nathan started selling strawberries, Darlene started taking care of Jennifer Stortle, and Rachel started giving Evelyn Stewart music lessons. Oh, we scrimped and saved, but we all had fun doing it. Glenda made those dresses for the teen choirgirls. Did she ever tell you how she got hers?"

"She told Dancy and Dancy told us. We thought it was perfectly fabulous."

"Well, we got the taxes paid, Glenda had enough money for a reasonable amount of cloth when Nina's Fabrics had their sale, and we had enough to get all the necessary school supplies, though no extra's."

"How are things now?" asked Pastor Parker.

David laughed. "If you mean do we have any money

the answer is 'no'. We spent it all last week on school supplies, but we will be selling a litter of pigs in a short while. I want to get a little put back in savings as soon as we can, but we can't save any out of this litter. We're doing some necessary repairs to Uncle Pete's Palace, as we have been ordered to call it. He couldn't live in it over winter the way it was."

"Do you really think it is wise letting Pete live here?" asked the Pastor. "I understand you don't know anything about him. The women at the auxiliary meeting the other night were expressing concern about his influence on the little boys and the safety of the little girls."

"Led by Sis. Stevenson, I suppose," David remarked.

The pastor looked embarrassed. "Well – a – I think she maybe was the one that brought it up, but several of the others agreed with her."

"I've always heard anyone could get a following of some sort, no matter what outlandish idea they came up with," Rachel said.

"Wouldn't you think," David commented, "Sis. Stevenson had caused enough trouble sicking the welfare on us? Really, Pastor Parker, I believe Uncle Pete was an answer to prayer. I knew all the time it was a tremendous undertaking to carry out Mother's wishes, and I am afraid we weren't doing so well alone. I'm sure we would have managed. We were all so determined to make a go of it.

The only thing is, Rachel was working herself to death, and I wasn't far behind. Uncle Pete has really taken a load off us."

"Oh!" exclaimed Sister Parker, "Does Pete help Rachel, too? Do you let him be in the house when you are out, David?"

"Uncle Pete has never been in this house. Rachel seldom sees him close enough to speak to. The other girls stay as far away from him as possible. Rachel was doing a lot of garden work, which she doesn't do any more. The other girls still work in the garden, but never at the same time Uncle Pete does."

"Pastor Parker," David went on, "would you think there was any cause to worry if we lived in a house in town and had a neighbor like Uncle Pete?"

"No, I don't suppose so," Pastor Parker answered.

"Well, Uncle Pete lives in his 'Palace.' He works hard and we feed him. There isn't much we can do for him but he appreciates every little thing we do. He says life is so much better than before. Why can't people like Sis. Stevenson just leave us alone, or better yet, spend a little time praying for us? We sure do need some prayer help in the matter of Uncle Pete. We would like to see him saved."

"I noticed he has been coming to church."

"Right! You *noticed* that. I doubt you have had an opportunity to talk with him. He manages to get there ten seconds late and slip out ten seconds before it is over, and he won't talk about it at all anymore except with Billy Bob, and I don't have much faith in Billy Bob helping him any. I've tried to talk with him about God several times lately. He listens, but makes no comments. I just don't know the answer."

"Don't push him, I believe he's doing some deep thinking. I'd like to talk with him, but to tell the truth, you're right. I haven't even managed an opportunity to speak to him. He acts like he is afraid."

"If you want to know what I really think," said David, "I think he doesn't want anyone to ask him any questions."

"You mean he's covering up something?"

"Could be. For my part, I don't care. It's his present and his future I'm concerned about, not his past."

"Did you find out anything at all when he came?" asked the pastor.

David shook his head. "He agreed to be truthful and not do anything to cause problems with the children and I've been careful not to question him about his past. I know he has told Billy Bob a lot of things, but I don't question him about it either."

"Aren't you afraid he will be a bad influence on Billy Bob?" asked the Pastor.

"I was at first, but now I think he's helping him more than any of us. I haven't been able to do him any good at all."

Darlene came in then with sparkling glasses of lemonade, with plenty of ice and some cookies she herself had made that afternoon. It was a warm evening and the lemonade was especially welcome. When they had finished their refreshments, David suggested they bring the children in and let Pastor Parker lead in devotions. Billy Bob thought as long as Pastor and Sister Parker were there they ought to ask Uncle Pete, too.

"He wouldn't come," was David's opinion.

"He will come," said Billy Bob.

"Why not try?" asked the Pastor. "I'd like you to ask him."

"If you think it's wise, Pastor Parker," said David. "As I said before, he hasn't been inside the house."

Five minutes later Pete was among them. He spoke pleasantly to Pastor Parker, telling him how much he had been enjoying his sermons, greeted Sister Parker kindly, and was introduced to Rachel, Glenda, Darlene, the triplets, and the little ones. He told Pastor Parker what a good cook Rachel was, and how much he appreciated his palace. He sat quietly and attentively during Bible reading, and bowed his head while they all prayed. After the children left the room, Pastor Parker said, "Are you a Christian, Pete?"

"Ah, no, I guess not," answered Pete. "I guess I had

better be going now. It was nice meeting you, Pastor Parker and Sister Parker. Thank you, David, for inviting me," and he was gone before the four left in the room realized what was happening.

"Well," said Pastor Parker, "that was quickly done. I suppose we should be thinking about going also, but first I'd like to get back to what we came for. Just why can't you two be an active part of the youth group again? By your own admission you are not as busy as you were. If Pete is good for anything, he should be worth enough to allow you to be off one evening a week, or even two when there are special events."

"Uncle Pete is worth a lot for work and I do trust him, but I would not go off and leave the responsibility of these children to him. Glenda and Nathan are both in the youth group and teen choir. If Rachel and I were to go, there would be no one at home to look after things. Billy Bob isn't dependable and anyway he is a couple months short of thirteen. Darlene is dependable, but she is only eleven. They are just too young to leave alone, and there is no one to leave with them. It is just out of the question."

"Why couldn't you take turns, Rachel go one time and you the next?" Sister Parker turned to Rachel. "You wouldn't be afraid, would you, if David were gone."

"No, I wouldn't mind him being gone."

It was finally decided they would give it a trial period

and see how it worked out. Then Pastor Parker brought up the youth retreat, which would be three days in December. He said he wanted them both to go, that their fee had already been paid, as well as Glenda's and Nathan's. "We would like all our young folks from the church to go. The ages are fourteen through twenty-one. There are four of you in that group aren't there?" asked the Pastor.

"Yes, Nathan was fourteen last week, but I don't see any way possible for the four of us to be gone three days."

"We have a list of names of ladies in the auxiliary group who have offered to come here and stay with the younger children while you are gone. There are seven names on the list. You are to choose one and if you don't trust any of them, then Sister Parker and I will come ourselves."

"Now we must be going. You take the list and study it and make a decision. Then you can tell us Sunday what you have decided. Really, David, I want you both to go. What you and Rachel are doing for the family is fine, but you need this for yourselves. If you just keep giving and giving and giving while you receive nothing, soon you will be all used up."

"What do you think about it, Rachel?"

"Let me see the list."

Sister Parker handed the list to Rachel, and then waited eagerly for her reaction. She was not disappointed. The first name on the list was that of Sister Wilma Stevenson.

XIV

Sheriff Gilliland sat down in his chair, leaned back and propped both feet on his desk. Only nine thirty in the morning and he was tired. A domestic quarrel at two thirty; fine time of night to be quarreling. Folks with any consideration would save their quarrel until office hours if they had to have one worthy of calling in the sheriff. He hadn't gotten back to sleep after that before someone called in about a horse loose on the highway south of town. By the time he had routed the owner of the horse out of bed and got him to retrieve his property, there was an accident out on Tucker Road. After that he didn't even try again to nap on the cot he kept in the back of the office for when he worked nights. He was too old to work nights anyway. Why had he let himself be talked into running for another term? When this term was up, he would be sixty-four. He should have quit after the last term. Well, When Blevins got in he would go off duty, go home, and get some much-needed rest.

His secretary stuck her head in the door. "Mrs. O'Conner from the county welfare department to see you, Sheriff."

"Send her in," Sheriff Gilliland sat as he was while the lady entered. He realized it was not exactly proper conduct, but he was tired.

"I have some papers for you to serve, Sheriff," said Mrs. O'Conner.

"Who they for?"

"David and Rachel Bradcox."

The Sheriff chuckled, "Poor kids. What's Billy Bob been up to now?"

"Billy Bob? Well, nothing that I know of, more than being disrespectful and smarting off his mouth."

"And you're gonna take him to court for that?"

"Billy Bob? No, we aren't taking him to court. Though goodness knows something needs to be done with him. We're going to put the younger children in foster homes."

"You're gonna **WHAT**?" The sheriff's feet came down from his desk and landed on the floor with a thud.

Mrs. O'Conner took two steps backward and her expression changed to bewilderment. Then she regained her composure and replied. "There are seven little children in that home without parents that are too young to look after themselves. We're going to put them in foster homes where they will be taken care of and loved. The older children kicked up a fuss so we have to go to court and get custody of them. I have the papers here for you to serve on them to appear in court."

"Serve papers on Mary Solomon's kids? Never! You'll just have to get someone else to serve your papers if you want them served."

"Haven't you got any deputies?"

"Yup! There are a few around, but I don't think there are any would serve papers on the Bradcox kids unless it's Collins. He might do it. He's new!"

"Collins!" called the sheriff to a deputy he knew had just come in to the next room.

"Yes, Sheriff," said a tall young man, appearing in the doorway.

"I have some papers here to be served," said Mrs. O'Conner, looking at Collins and entirely missing Sheriff Gilliland's wink.

"Sheriff won't serve them?" asked Collins.

"No, he said maybe you would."

"No," said Collins, looking at Sheriff Gilliland. "I told you when I took this here job I'd work aside of you wherever you went, but if you won't do a job, don't try to push it off on me. My life is just as valuable as yours." And Collins disappeared the way he had come.

"Well, there you are, Mrs. O'Conner," said the sheriff.

Two angry red spots appeared in Mrs. O'Conner's

face. I'll have your job for this!" she cried.

"Well, have it," said the sheriff. "I don't much want it anymore anyway. I'm too old and tired, but I think it might be a little harder than you think for you to get it. I'll tell you something, Mrs. O'Conner. I am an elected official of this county and I think it will take someone with a little more power than you to un-elect me. Furthermore, I was an elected official of this town when you was still suckin' a baby bottle. I knew Mary Solomon when she was a little girl. Fact is, I went to school with Mary Solomon's mother. A nicer girl never lived in this county. She and Chester raised Mary to be just like her. Only mistake Mary Solomon ever made in her life was when she married William Bradcox. Mary raised her kids just like Chester and Emily raised Mary, except for Billy Bob, who obviously took after his Dad. There are not any better kids in this state than Mary Solomon's kids. They have a good home, they eat well, they dress well, and they take care of each other. If you try to take those kids out of that home you're a bigger fool than I knew this county possessed."

"Perhaps you do not know that the older girls go out evenings and leave those helpless little girls in the care of that teenage boy. No telling what goes on."

Sheriff Gilliland brought himself out of his chair and up to his full six foot two. "Now let me tell you something, Lady, if you can call yourself a lady. I don't care for your insinuations. One more word like that and you will be in court for slander. I have a three-year old granddaughter. I'd trust David Bradcox with her anywhere at any time. I'd rather trust David Bradcox with her than any other man I know and a lot of women, you included! Now GET OUT OF MY OFFICE!"

Mrs. O'Conner took her way back to her own office and after reconnoitering with the other members of the staff, decided there was not a reason in the world that the Bradcox papers couldn't be mailed.

XV

Rachel stumbled as she came down the steps of the county courthouse and would have fallen had it not been for David who caught her and balanced her on her feet again. "Steady girl," he said.

"Oh, David," sobbed Rachel, "it looks so hopeless."

"It is not hopeless, Rachel. God has taken care of this so far, and He doesn't quit in the middle of a job like we do. We've just got to trust Him. We still have the children. Let's just thank God we still have them and trust Him for tomorrow. He will not let us down."

By the time they had collected Greg and Sue Ellen from Sister Leonard and walked home it was almost time for the others to come from school.

Pete stood leaning on the gatepost watching for them.

"How did it go?" he asked.

"Not at all good," said David. "Mrs. O'Conner had more reasons why we couldn't keep those children than it seems possible one woman could think up. She must have quite a staff of helpers."

"And Judge Gardner was in a terrible mood," Rachel went on. "He must have had indigestion or a bad toothache. Mrs. O'Conner said she saw me beating Greg, (I gave him one swat with my hand) and some other woman I didn't even know said she saw me pull Brad's hair in the grocery store and that never happened."

"There were some speaking for us, too." David took up the conversation. "Miss Floyd, the elementary school principal, said that except for Billy Bob, the children were among the best-behaved in the school; that they seemed to be well-adjusted, healthy and happy; did their work well; and made good grades."

"So, what did they decide?" asked Pete.

"Nothing yet. Judge Gardner heard the evidence, said he would review the matter and we would be notified by mail of the decision. He sure didn't sound very hopeful. Well, Rachel, here come the children. Put on your best smile and assure them everything is going to be all right."

"If Mother could have known everything that was going to happen, I don't see how she could have told us to be happy. Sis. Nosenev – pardon me, I mean Sis. Stevenson sure stirred up a good one that time with her long tongue. After what happened before we're going to have to break ourselves of saying Sister Nosenevets."

Sunday morning came. When Billy Bob took Pete

his breakfast Pete casually mentioned that he wouldn't be going to church with them, that he had decided to try out another church.

Seeing Billy Bob's crestfallen look, he continued. "It is just for this Sunday morning, Billy Bob. Tonight I think I can go with you, but this morning I can't make it."

"Oh, all right," said Billy Bob, as if the sun wouldn't be shining that day.

` Pete seldom left the farm except to go to church with the children. Only once had he been to town since the day he came. That was after they sold the first litter of pigs and David had insisted Pete get a new pair of shoes.

Now Pete dressed carefully and took his way to a larger church uptown, fifteen minutes behind the Bradcox children.

He was careful to arrive late and spent much time looking around the church bulletin boards and reading notices. Finally an usher handed him a church bulletin. He took a back seat in the church and sat with bowed head during the service. He left early and arrived home well ahead of the Bradcox children.

Early Tuesday morning Pete met David at the barn. "David," he asked, "do you have anything important to do today?"

"Why, Uncle Pete, don't you feel well?"

"Oh, yes, I'm feeling fine. I'd just like to have some bit

of time off."

"Of course, Uncle Pete. There's nothing pushing. You take as much time as you want."

Some time later in the morning David saw Pete leave his palace and walk down the road toward town, with his pack on his back and dressed in the clothes he had worn when he arrived.

"Well, that's that," he said to himself. "It was nice having him here. Maybe if we could have paid him he would have stayed. I do wish we could have led him to God. He sure helped us over some rough places, but now he's gone and I'm thinking he won't be back."

Judge Gardner was sitting in his den at home when he saw the tramp go past his window toward the back door. He was home alone, his wife having gone to a ladies breakfast at a town twenty-five miles away with other ladies of his church. The judge had been reviewing the arguments he had heard last week concerning the Bradcox children. It was up to him to make a decision and as yet he didn't know what the decision would be. He knew they were good children, lived in a nice home, and were well fed and clothed, but Judge Gardner had had a grouch on concerning the family for seven years, ever since Mary Bradcox had taken her family from the large uptown church where he attended and attached themselves to that insignificant bunch of nobodies that attended that new little church with the big name at the edge of town. Well, Judge Gardner called them just old Holy Rollers and he had no use for them at all.

Now, as the tramp passed the window, he had a thought that had fleeted through his mind when he had met the Bradcox's hired man with them in the shoe store. That this tramp was the same hired man he had not a shred of doubt.

The judge waited until the second ring of the doorbell before he moved from his chair and took his leisurely way to the door. As he opened it the tramp spoke. "Could you spare a bit of food for a poor hungry tramp?"

"Why? Don't the Bradcox children feed you?" the judge asked.

"Ah – a – well," the tramp stammered, then he looked steadily at the judge, "I want to talk to you."

The judge looked intently into the tramps eyes for a full minute. Then he swung the door open wide. "Come on in, Bill," he said. "Tell me what it's all about. Why are you doing what you are doing? I suppose you have come to talk about the children."

"Well," the tramp answered, "I'm aware that you cannot legally discuss the case with a member of the family or you would be disqualified as a judge, so it's best we don't mention it. I've been thinking you knew me the day we met in the shoe store and I thought you should know a few facts."

"I was pretty sure it was you, but I realized David didn't know, so I decided to keep out and let you go your own pace. What's the idea anyway? I want to hear where you have been and why. The last I heard of you, you had stowed away on a ship and jumped off into the Atlantic Ocean."

"I think Vic Dunberry started that one because he was interested in Mary. I understand Mary had me legally declared dead, but then Mary would not look at Vic, so he got no reward for his efforts."

"Well, why did you go away and why are you playing this tramp game now? Why do you not tell the children the truth? Have a chair, Bill, and let's have it."

Pete took the chair Judge Gardner offered and repeated the story he had told Billy Bob, adding the part about finding the notice of the death of Mary Bradcox in the paper and deciding to come home to the children.

"But why didn't you just come home and tell them the truth about yourself?" the judge asked.

"Can't you see they would have hated me? I left their mother when she needed me the most. I didn't love them then and they wouldn't be able to understand how much I love them now. As it is, I can help them a lot. They don't resent me and some of them even love me a little. It's so much better this way. If they were to find out who I really am, there isn't any doubt in my mind that they would tell me they had gotten along without me for ten years and they don't need me now. As it is, they tell me daily how much they appreciate me. I suppose it's the need of every human to want to feel important and even with all evidence to the contrary, I *am* human."

"How are the children doing – really? I haven't seen much of them since they've changed churches. I can't see why Mary wanted to get messed up with that bunch anyway."

"They are good kids, Joe, really good kids. That church really has something we never had in the one we all went to before. Have you ever been there?"

The judge shook his head.

"You ought to go once. You've probably heard a lot of things that are not true about them. I've been going regularly and it's really getting to me."

The judge changed the subject. "What about the Sparks children? Aren't they a burden? Don't you resent it?"

"No," the tramp answered. "Oh, at first I did, but then I realized I have no right to. They are part of the family. Mary would be very angry to have it otherwise."

Pete stood up – obviously preparing to leave. "Well, Joe," he said, "you and I grew up good friends. You made something of yourself. I made nothing of myself. I went the wrong road. I've made a mess of everything. My health is bad now and I'm not going to be around a whole lot longer, but what little time God does allow me here I'm going to spend doing my best to make what amends I can for the wrongs I have done. I have been legally declared dead, but I don't think it would be very hard to prove I am alive. I don't need to go to court to get custody of the kids. Custody has not been taken from me. Mary's death leaves me the full responsibility of them. I'm doing my best, Joe. I know the Sparks kids aren't mine, but I know what Mary would want, and I believe you do too. I'll leave you now. I'm going to face God pretty soon. You'll probably be around a few years longer, but eventually you will go the same route and have to face the same God. Think about it, Joe. Think about it!"

Just before noon, David saw Pete entering his palace. When he took his dinner to him, Pete was dressed in his usual work clothes and asked about what they were going to do in the afternoon.

Pete said nothing of where he had gone or why, and David, wisely, didn't ask.

Three days later a letter came from Judge Gardner. Rachel opened it with shaking hands. It was so full of big words and high-sounding phrases that Rachel was bewildered. She sat down in the lawn chair to better study it. "Oh, if David were only here," she thought. "He's good on high-class words and I'm so ignorant."

Just then Pete came around the house and spoke to her. "David said to tell you he'd be about a half hour late for lunch."

"Oh, I was hoping he'd come in early. We've heard from the judge."

"Oh, really? May I ask the outcome?"

Rachel was embarrassed. She hated to admit that she couldn't understand the letter. Finally she looked up at Pete. "I'm just no good on words. I don't have what you would call a 'legal mind.' I can't understand it."

Pete reached out his hand. "I can maybe read it if you wish," he said.

Rachel gave him the letter and he hurriedly scanned it. "Why, it's good news!" he said. "The welfare is barred from bothering you in any way unless the case is re-entered in court and the court proves beyond a doubt that there has been actual physical abuse or neglect. I don't think you need worry about that anymore."

"Praise the Lord!" exclaimed Rachel.

"Do you think the Lord had anything to do with the judge's decision?" asked Pete.

"I certainly do!" declared Rachel.

"Why?"

"Why? Because we prayed! Because we asked Him

to do it."

"But I thought – oh never mind." Pete turned around and left the way he had come.

That night the Bradcox children had no trouble keeping the "be happy" part of their mother's instructions. Such a lot of merriment had not been heard since their mother's death six months before, and the next day would be Sue Ellen's second birthday.

XVI

Out between the orchard and the cow pasture was about a half acre, fenced, brushy, and useless. It had been a goat pen several years back, but Mother Bradcox had decided goats were more trouble than they were worth, so in spite of the tears of some of the children who loved the goats, they were sold. Because Mother and David had never found the time to remove the fence as they had intended the little pen had been left idle, growing up in weeds, briars, and bushes; its only use being a place for David to occasionally find a rabbit to supplement the meat supply.

It was a cool day the first part of November, when David suggested to Pete that they take out the fence. For the first time since Pete had come, David met with opposition from him.

"David," Pete said, "do you really think there is anything in that pen for the cows worth the trouble of taking out the fence?"

David whirled suddenly and looked at Pete. "Are you sick or something?" He asked. "You don't need to help. Nathan can help me with it after school."

"If the fence has to come out, I'll help. It's just that I've had my eye on that pen and I can't help making plans though I haven't an idea in my head as to how to get the money to carry out my plans. I wanted to think of a way to finance the project before I mentioned it to you."

"How much money would it take, Uncle Pete? Why don't you just share your idea so we can talk it over? We have a little money left from the last litter of pigs and the next litter should be ready to sell by the first of December. If it isn't too much money you're talking about maybe we can manage."

"I really have no right to try to manage your affairs, David, but I know stretching the income from this little farm to meet the needs of thirteen people isn't easy and I thought we could get that little pen producing a money crop," Pete stopped and dropped his head.

"By thirteen people I suppose you are including yourself. Precious little you benefit from any of it, but go on. What is your idea?"

"I eat, don't I? Three good meals a day. Besides, look how you've fixed up my palace and all the clothes I have. But to answer your question – peaches! They do well here. The trees you have produce all the family can use, so if you planted that in peach trees you could market the whole crop. There really isn't a lot of work to peaches. You see, David, I'm worried about how you're going to make it when I'm gone."

"Are you planning to leave us, Uncle Pete? I was hoping you would stay. Rachel and I were talking the other night, planning that in the spring we can start paying you, treating you like a real hired man."

"I don't want any pay – ever. I like to feel – to pretend that you are my family." Pete hung his head. His voice was hardly above a whisper. "It's a harmless pastime. I just pretend we are related and that you children love me a little bit. I wouldn't ever take any advantage of the idea. It's just something I think on to make me feel I belong."

David's voice was husky as he answered Pete. "We do love you, Uncle Pete, some of us. We all appreciate you, but I wouldn't say the girls love you. If you feel that way, though, why are you planning to leave us?"

"I won't be leaving unless you drive me out as long as there is breath in my body, but David, I'm not going to be here always. This condition in my lungs is serious. I've been a heavy smoker. I've had this cough for the last few years. About a week before I came here, I stopped at a house in Kansas overnight. My cough had gotten so bad I was coughing up blood. The good man of the house took me to one of those clinics where poor people don't have

148

to pay. They examined me from hair to toes, and the long and short of it seemed to be that I could live anywhere from six months to five years. Well, I've already made the six months, but I rather doubt I'll make the five years. I'm not squawking none. I brought it on myself with the way I lived, but I'd just like to see you kids a little better fixed financially before I go."

"Uncle Pete, haven't you any family at all? Isn't there anyone besides us to care?" asked David.

Pete shook his head. "I left my family, my wife remarried, the kids consider another man their father. I would only cause problems for them."

"But wouldn't you want them notified?"

"Only after I'm gone."

"But how would I – I mean – I wouldn't know who or where."

Pete reached into his shirt pocket and brought out an envelope. It was worn through on the corners and the corner of a picture was sticking out through the edge, but across the front of it could still be determined to read "Pete's identity. Do not open until after Pete's death."

"It's all in here, David. This tells who I am and who my people are. I always carry it with me, but I do need a new envelope. This one is pretty much worn out."

"I'll bring you a new envelope – half a dozen of them – but you should have a safer place for your important papers. Say, did you ever think of laminating them?"

"Never heard of the word."

"It's a new process they're using – enclosing important things in plastic. Usually they just do them so you can read them right through the plastic, but I think you could have the whole envelope done. There's a place in town that does it. It makes them waterproof and everything."

"Sounds good to me, but I could use a new envelope first, two of them if you don't mind. I've got a use for another one."

"All right, now about this goat pen, we'll do this your way. You figure how many trees you will need and I'll check up on prices and see if we can swing the money end; if we can't, we can buy some and add more next year. Now, we may as well take out the fence between the pen and the orchard. That will make it easier to get into it to spray and take care of. It's going to be a heap of work to get that ready to plant trees, but you are right, of course. It will be far more valuable planted to peach trees than as cow pasture. Uncle Pete, did I tell you Nathan and I are both going to be gone three days the end of next month?"

"No. May I ask where you are going?"

"Springfield, to a youth retreat."

"The girls going?"

"Yes, Rachel and Glenda. Darlene isn't old enough. Neither is Billy Bob. I don't suppose he would go if he was."

"Who is going to be in charge here?"

"We're getting Mother's best friend, Gladys Cook. She lives in St. Louis now with her daughter since Bro. Cook died, but likes to come back here occasionally for a visit with old friends. She said she would be delighted to do it and she's the only one we can think of that we could have and not worry. She's only in charge of the house, though. Do you think you and Billy Bob can take care of the chores?"

"Sure! If there isn't anything else to do we can handle the chores and feel like we're on vacation."

XVII

Billy Bob held the envelope in his hand. One part of him wanted to lay it back in the open dresser drawer, but another part of him felt he just *had* to open it. He was sure he had time. Uncle Pete was far away in the back of the pasture with a new mother cow. The problem was how could he seal it back so Uncle Pete wouldn't know he had opened it. He turned the envelope over and read again. "Pete's identity – Do not open until after Pete's death." Above everything else, Billy Bob felt he just had to know everything possible about Uncle Pete. He took out his knife and slipped the blade under the flap of the envelope. To his surprise, he found it was hardly sealed. It wouldn't be hard at all to re-seal it. There was plenty of unused glue. He carefully worked the envelope open, unfolded a single sheet of paper and began to read.

Dear Billy Bob,

Billy Bob gave a start and looked around him. Why, what was this? A letter to himself in an envelope marked "Pete's identity"? He brought his eyes back to the paper and read on.

> *I am very sorry that you are reading this letter. I had hoped that I could trust you, that you loved me enough to have some respect for my privacy and me.*
>
> *Billy Bob, do you not know that snooping is a form of stealing? When you go through other folk's things and open sealed envelopes you are getting or taking information that doesn't belong to you. Really, I'm ashamed of you.*

Billy Bob let the letter fall from his fingers and sat down. What had he done? He had destroyed Uncle Pete's confidence in him, but no, Uncle Pete did not have any confidence in him or he wouldn't have written the letter in the first place.

Fifteen minutes later Pete came in and found Billy Bob sitting at the table with his head on his arms. The letter still lay where it had dropped on the floor.

"Hey, Boy!" Pete said. "Isn't it supper time? I thought Mrs. Cook said for you to be after our food promptly at 5:00."

Billy Bob shuffled to his feet, his eyes on the floor. "Maybe you'd rather I m-moved back – a – home." He said. "Mmaybe it would be better if – if – if – I didn't stay here while David is gone."

"Why?" Pete asked cheerfully.

Billy Bob tried to swallow the lump in his throat. He picked up the letter and handed it to Pete. "I read that," he said simply.

"Oh, that?" Pete crumpled the letter into a wad and tossed it toward the wastebasket. "It's trash now," he said. "Go get our supper. I'm hungry."

Pete kept up a cheerful one-sided conversation while they ate, but Billy Bob answered only when asked a direct question. When Billy Bob picked up the empty plates to return them to the house, Pete said, "Billy Bob, I'd like you to come straight back. I think we need to talk."

Sitting on the foot of Pete's bed, with his eyes on the floor, Billy Bob waited for Pete to open the conversation. To his surprise, Pete asked, "What's wrong, Billy Bob?"

What's wrong? Couldn't anybody with half good sense see what was wrong? Billy Bob sniffed and then blurted, "You said it was stealing! You said you were ashamed of me! You practically called me a thief!"

"Well, isn't it stealing?" Pete asked.

Billy Bob nodded. "I – I guess so."

"And shouldn't I be ashamed of you? Aren't you ashamed of yourself?"

Again Billy Bob nodded.

"All right now," Pete continued, "you said the word

thief, I didn't. But if you steal, then I guess that is the right word."

Billy Bob cringed as if Pete's words were blows, but Pete continued.

"You already knew you were a thief. I already knew you were a thief. The only thing that has changed is that now you know that I know you are a thief. I think it is good for friends to thoroughly understand each other."

"I didn't really think it was stealing. I made up my mind about a year ago I wouldn't steal anymore."

"Well, maybe you'd best tighten your rules a might – get a little better idea of what stealing really is. Now to change the subject, what do you think about God?"

"God? Oh, I donno."

"Aw, come on. You can do better than that."

"Oh, I suppose you think if I'd ask God, he'd help me to be good. That sounds like David and Rachel."

"That wasn't quite what I had in mind, but it might help. Let me ask another way. Do you believe there is a Heaven?"

"I suppose there is."

"Do you believe there is a Hell?"

"Yeah, I guess so."

"Do you believe that when you die you go to one or the other of those places?"

"Probably."

"Well, do you suppose any of us are going to escape death?"

"Now wait a minute. I can see where this is leading. I thought you were my friend. I always liked to come here because I didn't have to hear about God all the time and be preached at. This is getting as bad as home. Besides, Mother always said the kettle shouldn't call the pot black. Have *you* made *your* preparations to die? You're older than I am."

"I can't really see where age has much to do with it. Seems to me the last time I read the obituaries they were passing out at about all ages. I think the Hargrave girl was about three, wasn't she? But really, Billy Bob, if you'd raise your boiling point a few degrees, I might have a chance to get to the point. That remark about the kettle and the pot – well – that's what I was getting to. If you don't care whether you go to Heaven or Hell – well that's up to you, of course, but seeing as you've been raised in church I thought maybe you might be able to help me out in a few points. I've been doing a lot of thinking lately."

"Maybe you should talk to Pastor Parker."

Pete shook his head. "I'd rather work this out just between God and me, with what help you could give me, but if you're not interested, then I guess it's just God and me. I'm not going to live forever, Billy Bob. My physical condition is such that I could go any time. Regardless of how *you* feel, I have a desire to see my Maker, to know He has forgiven me for all my wrongs."

Pete stood up, walked to the window and looked out into the darkness. "I believe it is going to snow. Hope those kids don't get stranded in Springfield."

"Uh – Uncle Pete."

"Yeah, what?"

"How was it you wanted me to help you? I – I'll help you however I can, if there is anything I can do, but you got to be baptized and I can't do that. Pastor Parker has to do that."

"Yes, I know. That's one thing that worries me. He baptized that Tom Clayton Sunday night. I especially noticed as I've noticed ever since I've been going to church there. He said, 'Thomas Clayton, I now baptize you in the name of the Lord Jesus Christ for the remission of your sins.'"

"Well, isn't that the way it's supposed to be done?"

"Yeah, but – well, I don't know. There's something – well, I can't tell you about it."

"Aw, come on. I won't tell, honest!"

"No, Billy Bob, I won't tell you so there's no use to beg. I left that letter as a sort of test to see if I should. I shouldn't! Someday you'll understand, but until then let's just forget it. One thing I would like to know is, how's a guy supposed to be baptized when he doesn't have a name?

157

Pete Nobody, I now baptize you, etc?"

"Oh, does he always say the name of the person he's baptizing?"

"Every time I ever saw him baptize anybody."

"Why don't you ask Pastor Parker, Uncle Pete? Talk it over with him. You can trust him, honest. He doesn't steal."

"I know! I know! It's just that – well, Oh forget it. I'll just have to talk to God. I know I can trust Him! Do you need to go home for devotions?"

"David said I didn't need to if I'd study a chapter here."

"Fine, any particular place?"

"No, just open the Bible anywhere. That's what I always do. Sometimes it's boring, but sometimes I hit on something actually interesting."

Pete took the Bible and handed it to Billy Bob. Billy Bob sensed that Uncle Pete was not his usual self. He was more – more what? Sober? Serious? Grave? Billy Bob didn't seem to be able to pick an appropriate word, yet there was no doubt in his mind that he was different.

Billy Bob sat holding the Bible as if he were afraid to open it. "Well, here goes," he said. "Do you want to read or shall I?"

"Go ahead," Pete answered.

Billy Bob opened the Bible to Luke, chapter 15 and

began to read. *"Then drew near unto him all the publicans and sinners for to hear him. And the Pharisees and scribes murmured, saying, This man receiveth sinners, and eateth with them. And he spake this parable unto them, saying, What man of you, having an hundred sheep, if he lose one of them, doth not leave the ninety and nine in the wilderness, and go after that which is lost, until he find it? And when he hath found it, he layeth it on his shoulders, rejoicing. and when he cometh home, he calleth together his friends and neighbours, saying unto them, Rejoice with me; for I have found my sheep which was lost. I say unto you, that likewise joy shall be in heaven over one sinner that repenteth, more than over ninety and nine just persons, which need no repentance."*

Billy Bob read on to the end of the chapter and closed the Bible. He looked at Uncle Pete and saw tears raining down his face. He jumped up, "Oh, Uncle Pete!" he exclaimed, "What's wrong?"

Pete took out his handkerchief, wiped his eyes, blew his nose, and answered in a husky voice. "Oh, nothing, really, I was just thinking."

Billy Bob thought a moment and then spoke timidly, "Uncle Pete?"

"Yeah?"

"Were you maybe being reminded of when you left? Were you maybe thinking how maybe you should go back to your family? I would sure hate to have you leave, but I so often think of your little boy, how he must long for you to come back. You said once I reminded you of him. Ever since then I have thought how I would feel if it were me."

Pete shook his head. "No, Billy Bob, I've told you I can't go back. My wife married again. My little boy took her new husband as his father. I can't go back and that's final. Tonight, I'm not really thinking so much about the family I left, I'm thinking of the God I left. He hasn't forgotten about me or he wouldn't have led me here where I could get to know you kids and learn the truth. Pastor Parker says the book of Acts tells us how to be saved. I've read the book through five times. I've memorized Acts 2:38. I know how to be saved. I just haven't done anything about it. If I die tonight, I'll go straight to Hell, and you know whose fault it will be? Mine!"

Silence fell over the little room as Pete and Billy Bob both studied the toes of their shoes. Finally Billy Bob spoke in a small voice, "that's true for me too. I've lived in a good Christian home for thirteen years. I've been taught from the time I was a baby how to be saved. I've just been too stubborn." Then suddenly his voice became stronger, more normal. "Let's do it, Uncle Pete," he said. "Let's do it together, now, while the others are gone to the youth retreat. Won't they be surprised when they get back?"

Pete started to shake his head, but Billy Bob spoke again. "C'mon, Uncle Pete. You said you wanted my help.

Let's go talk to Pastor Parker, or – say Uncle Pete, why don't I go up to the house and call Pastor Parker and ask him to come out here and talk?"

"Here to my shed?"

"Your *shed*? I should say not! Your *palace*, remember? I'm going up to call him now. OK?"

Pete never answered. Billy Bob took his silence as consent and started for the door. Pete held up his hand. "One thing, Billy Bob. Would you, could you, do you think it would be all right if you would ask him to come alone?"

"Sure!" Billy Bob left on the run.

Fifteen minutes later Billy Bob opened the door to admit Pastor Parker. He took his coat and gave him the palace's only chair. Then Pastor Parker turned to Pete. "Billy Bob said you wanted to see me," he said.

Pete nodded, but said nothing.

"We want to be baptized," Billy Bob blurted out. "Uncle Pete and I. We want to be baptized!"

"Baptized?" Pastor Parker said dazedly. "Why I, well, I guess so, but are you sure? Have you repented? Have you repented, Billy Bob?"

"Repent means to be sorry for what you've done, right? Yes, I guess I've had to repent every day of my life."

A twinkle showed in Pastor Parker's eyes, but he kept his face straight. "I don't believe you have the whole idea, Billy Bob," he said. "Repent means a little bit more than being sorry for what you have done. It means a genuine sorrow for the ways of the old Billy Bob, a complete turning away from the old life. That you will from this moment on live your life as Jesus would have you live it."

"Pastor Parker," Billy Bob said, "In church last Sunday you said, – yes, for once I *was* listening – you said that Jesus Christ would change me and make my life over. That He would make me to become a new creature. Now you sound as if I have to do it. Well, *I* can't. I've tried lots of times. I'm just Billy Bob, and the way I am is the way I've always been and the way I always will be unless you were telling the truth and God can change me."

"God can change you, Billy Bob. I've heard of a few cases where God just completely overhauled a person, took away all their bad habits and made them completely new, so that those around them scarcely recognized them as the same person, but it doesn't usually happen that way. Usually you have to put forth a little effort yourself, make up your own mind to turn away from the old life. Tell Jesus you're sorry, genuinely sorry, for the wrongs you have done, ask him to take over and straighten out your life and make you a new creature. Then He does it."

"Billy Bob, have you definitely decided you are going to live for the Lord the rest of your life or is it something you decided you want to do because Pete did?"

"Oh, no, I mean yes, I mean I think maybe I talked

Uncle Pete into it, though I do know he wants to. But I mean yes, I do want to live for God the rest of my life. Does that mean I can't have any more fun?"

Now Pastor Parker did allow himself a smile. "Do your brothers and sisters have fun, Billy Bob?"

"Oh, I guess they think they do, but it wouldn't be any fun for me to live the way they do. I couldn't get any fun out of reading and playing dull games and the things they think are fun."

"What kind of things do you think are fun, Billy Bob?"

"Oh, climbing trees, walking bridge banisters, sliding down the barn roof, standing on a bicycle seat, hooking rides, and things like that."

"Well, some of those things are downright dangerous, though I can't really say any of them are sinful. If I were in your place, though, I think I would want to be sure I was saved before I tried many of those things. It does sound to me as if death could come mighty suddenly that way."

Pastor Parker turned back to Pete. "You haven't said anything, Pete. Do you feel you are ready to be baptized?"

"Pastor Parker," Pete answered, "I need to talk to you. Do you think –?"

"Billy Bob," Pete continued looking at him, "do you think it would be all right to ask Mrs. Cook if we can have refreshments since we have company? And don't come back short of a half hour."

Billy Bob's face took on a sullen look. "Oh, I know, you want to get rid of me, but it wouldn't be necessary. I don't steal anymore. Anyway, I think they have locked up and gone to bed, but I have a key and I can fix something. I've done it before."

What was said in Pete's Palace after Billy Bob left no one ever found out, but the next morning as soon as the chores were done, Pete and Billy Bob walked to the church to be baptized. Pastor Parker had tried to convince Billy Bob he should wait until David and Rachel returned, but Billy Bob would have none of it. He pointed out that Rachel and David both would be happy that he had done it. Pastor Parker, knowing this was true, finally agreed.

Billy Bob was baptized first. When he came out of the water, Sister Parker was there with a towel to help him dry off. Pete came up out of the water speaking in an unknown tongue. "It isn't fair," Billy Bob thought. "Why did he get the Holy Ghost and I didn't?"

Too late, Billy Bob realized he hadn't listened to see if Pastor Parker spoke Uncle Pete's name when he baptized him.

XVIII

"David, I need to talk to you a minute." Rachel said one night in early March as the family was preparing for bed.

"Now what have I done?" Billy Bob asked.

David shrugged his shoulders, "You should know better than anyone," he said.

"Maybe it's something you haven't done." suggested Nathan.

"Like your homework," put in Glenda.

"Didn't have any," Billy Bob answered. "It can't be that. And I did feed the pigs and I tended the chickens, and I scraped the ice off the back step and – I really can't think of anything."

Rachel laughed. "Oh, go on to bed, all of you. Can't David and I have a little chat without all the curiosity?"

When the two older ones were left alone, Rachel said, "David, Glenda's sixteenth birthday is next week. What are we going to do about it?"

"Well, I didn't know we had to do anything more than the usual cake and special dinner we fix for every child's birthday. She got her sixteenth birthday present early, you know."

"Yes, but David, remember Mother had a party for you on your sixteenth birthday, and one for me on mine. She invited everyone in the youth group and a few of our friends from school. Don't you think we should do that for the others? We agreed to go on doing things as nearly as we could the way Mother would."

David sighed. He knew Rachel was right. He had no right to withhold the little pleasures Mother had planned, yet a gathering of the youth group was the last thing he wanted right now. For the past few weeks, ever since the youth retreat in fact, Rachel had been receiving far too much attention from the young men to David's way of thinking. If he had his way, he would forbid any of them to step a foot on the place, certainly not invite them.

"I think it would be too much work for you," he finally answered. "Besides, there isn't time. If I remember right, Mother spent about six weeks getting ready for your party."

"Yes, I know, but there really isn't that much to do. Darlene works like an adult, and the triplets are getting to be a right big help also. We'll manage. The question is, can we afford it?"

"Oh, I think we can manage that part all right. Those peach trees took a big bite out of the finances, but I think we still have enough left."

"David, did you put your money back?"

"No," David answered. "I don't really see the use in having two savings accounts. I'm saving as much as I can and when we can afford to buy a car, we'll get one. I have to handle all the money anyway. Why have it in two accounts?"

"I guess that's right, but I just hate to see you not have your sixteenth birthday present when we girls have ours."

"Seems to me the family plays your piano and while Glenda may be the only one using her sewing machine, she certainly uses it for the family. When we get a car, if we do, it will be a family car anyway."

"Nathan is next. Has he made any mention of what he'd like to have?"

"He says if we can afford it he'd like to have his $300 in money to add to mine to save for a car. $600 should buy us a pretty good car, but I had hoped to get one before then. I have to have a pretty good one, because I know less than nothing about fixing one and we can't constantly be paying repair bills."

"Well, Nathan is taking that mechanics course."

"Yes, but he's not doing too well with it. He told me it is his worst subject. I'm afraid he's too much like me."

"Well," Rachel said, "let's get to bed. I'll go ahead with the party, then, if you don't object."

"I suppose I have no right to object," David answered as he led the way upstairs."

"Now what did he mean by that?" Rachel asked herself. "Why would he want to object?"

The preparations were made for the party, the invitations slipped to the different members of the youth group by Darlene and Billy Bob and the ones to Glenda's two girlfriends at school delivered by Nathan. The night of the party came and went without mishap. Everyone had a grand time except David. Pearl Carson, one of Glenda's school friends, said it was the "funnest" party she ever went to. Dorothy Havens, the other one, said she never heard of a sixteenth birthday party without dancing, but they were so busy doing other things they wouldn't have had time to dance anyway.

Dancy Parker said she wanted Rachel to plan her sixteenth birthday party and Paul Dobison said Rachel had missed her calling. She should have become a professional entertainer. David made a sound behind his back that Rachel could only describe as a snarl.

When the door closed behind the last guest, Rachel turned to David. "What's wrong, Big Brother? You didn't enjoy it a bit."

"Oh, nothing's wrong. I'm just glad it's over, that's

all. Glad we don't have to have another one for eighteen months." He turned and took the steps two at a time, then shut the door to his room a little harder than was his usual want.

Rachel sighed. She had had her bad days with each of the younger ones in the year she and David had been overseeing the family, but this was the first that anything had come between the two of them, and the really hard part was that she didn't even know what was the matter.

Two evenings later, David sat on a stool in the barn milking Rosey, while Pete finished feeding and watering the other livestock. Presently he heard voices and looked up just as Paul Dobison stepped to the door. "Need any help there?" he asked.

David couldn't help but laugh in spite of his irritation. "What good would it do if I did," he returned pleasantly. "A city slicker like you wouldn't know which end of the cow gives the milk, much less how to get it."

"Now, I like that," retorted Paul hotly. "I'll have you know I learned to milk a cow on my uncle's farm ten years ago. Get off that stool and I'll show you I can milk just as good as you can."

David obediently slid off the stool and stood up while Paul slipped into his place, but as he reached his hand to start milking, Rosey seemed to explode. Her whole back end rose high in the air. She lashed out with one foot at

Paul with a vicious kick just missing his nose, and making an ugly bruise on his arm. The other foot came down in the milk bucket. Paul rolled off the stool backward right into a pile of something not very clean left by Scarlet, the cow in the next stall.

"Oops! Sorry Farmer Boy," David apologized. "I forgot to mention Rosey doesn't take too kindly to strangers. Maybe you'd better try Scarlet."

"Thank ya' kindly, no, Kind Sir," Paul answered haughtily. "Maybe another time. Right now I believe I'll have to cut this visit short and go back home for a bath and clean clothes." Then he laughed. "Guess you'd better go back to your original title for me. City slicker! It seems to fit somewhat better than Farmer Boy. Sorry about the milk. I know you probably needed it. Want I should bring you a gallon from town to replace it?"

"No, that's all right. Right now we're getting more than we can use."

David watched Paul amble off. He washed his bucket at the pump, then went back to finish milking Rosey, deep in thought. "Well," he told himself, "if he came to see Rachel, he missed it this time, but something tells me he'll be back. I wish he'd move to Alaska, but what good would that do? There would still be Martin and Donnie; Steven and Carl; Greg, Cory, and *Franklin*."

XIX

David couldn't sleep. He looked at the clock again. 3:15 A.M. Five whole minutes had passed since he had looked at it the last time. He turned over on to his stomach, closed his eyes and breathed deeply. He turned on to his side. He kicked the blanket off; then he pulled it back on. "Oh, what's the use?" he muttered. "I might as well get up and study. I've not been spending enough time on my school work anyway." He sat up on the edge of the bed, switched on the light, pulled on his robe over his pajamas, slipped his feet into his well-worn slippers, and crossed the room to his desk.

Darlene came awake from a dream about a cat that was as big as a cow and was trying to climb the house to sleep in the attic. At first she was scared; then as wakefulness became more dominant, she laughed. "What a dream!" she thought. "Can anyone think up anything more silly than that?" She turned over and closed her eyes, intending to go right back to sleep, but then she realized she was thirsty. She hated having to go all the way downstairs in the middle of the night to get a drink. She decided she would endure it until morning. Again she turned over and tried to sleep, but the thirst became more vivid. Finally after an exasperating fifteen minutes she could stand it no longer.

Without turning on the light, Darlene quietly felt for robe and slippers, hoping she could slip down and back up without arousing anyone. David, it seemed, was always awake with the slightest noise. Darlene knew David worked hard and needed his rest. She tiptoed to the door and opened it carefully, but the first thing she noticed was a crack of light under David's door. Maybe it was later than she thought.

Darlene hadn't gone more than three steps down the hall before she heard David's quiet voice, "Who's up?"

"Darlene. I'm just going down for a drink of water," Darlene whispered.

"Well, turn on the light so you don't fall and break your neck. I'm a little thirsty myself. Maybe I should go with you."

"I'll bring you a drink if you are not ready to come down."

When Darlene entered David's room with a tall glass of ice cold water, the first thing she noticed was the clock. It said 3:40. She handed David the water and stood waiting while he drank it.

"Thanks, Little Sister," he said, handing the glass back to her. "That was good, but you really don't need to take the glass down until morning."

"David," Darlene said hesitantly, "What's wrong? Why are you up?"

"Couldn't sleep."

"But why, David? Something is wrong. You've been worrying about something ever since you came back from the youth retreat. Is it Billy Bob?"

"Billy Bob? What's wrong with Billy Bob?"

"He got baptized while you were gone and he didn't get the Holy Ghost yet. It really doesn't seem as if he has changed much, does it?"

"I've noticed that, Little Sister, but it is just a matter for prayer. I think Billy Bob is going to come out all right."

"Then, what is wrong?" Darlene persisted. "Is it Rachel? Are you afraid Rachel will get married and leave us?"

The minute she had spoken of Rachel, Darlene could see that she had hit the problem straight on end. David's head went down on his arms on the desk. Darlene stepped over to him and put her hand on his head, smoothing down his hair. "David," she said, "didn't Mother talk to you about this before she died?"

Slowly David's head came up. He looked hard at

Darlene and finally nodded slightly.

"We've got to let Rachel grow up," Darlene continued. "Mother talked to me about it. I rather supposed she did to you, too. She said the time might come when Rachel would fall in love and want to marry. She said we shouldn't try to keep her tied here being a mother to us. She should be allowed to break loose and have a life of her own. And David, promise you won't say anything to Glenda about this. I wouldn't want to hurt her feelings."

"All right, I won't," David promised.

"Well," Darlene went on, "Mother said that Glenda is a scatterbrain; that she's a real good girl, but that you won't likely be able to depend on her to 'mother' the little ones in case Rachel marries. She said I would have to be prepared to step in and take Rachel's place."

"But you are just a child, Darlene," David argued. "You can't possibly handle Rachel's job. You're eleven, right?"

"I'm twelve! I had my birthday before Glenda. Remember? I'm working hard, trying to learn, David. I know I'm not ready yet, but Rachel is only seventeen. The boys are just starting to pay attention to her. She likely won't marry for two or three years yet. By that time, I will be ready. In the meantime, the little ones are getting older. Already Gregory can dress himself and Sue Ellen needs very little help. Don't worry, David," she pleaded, "we'll make it. The Lord is on our side. Let Him work it out.

I think you are forgetting the 'be happy' part of Mother's instructions."

David sat for a few minutes deep in thought. "You're right, Little Sister," he admitted. "I guess I've been trying to take over God's job. I'll pray about it. Then I think I can go to sleep."

David was his usual cheerful self when morning came. He tossed Gregory up and caught him. He joked with the triplets, calling them his thirds. He hugged Rachel and actually laughed when Billy Bob tied Glenda's apron strings to her chair.

"What's eating him?" Billy Bob whispered to Nathan. "He must have something up his sleeve."

"I'm just thankful he is happy," Nathan replied. "It has been dreadful around here with him in the mullygrubs. I'm sure glad whatever burden he was carrying has been lifted."

The next evening Paul came again. He came straight to the house just as the family was finishing the evening meal. He greeted everyone, and then turned to David. "I thought I would get here a little later tonight so I wouldn't have to help with the milking."

David laughed. "I think it was your idea," he said.

"It was, and I do want to try again sometime, maybe on Scarlet, but when I try again I will try to remember to bring along a change of clothes."

It was an enjoyable evening with popcorn and games. Billy Bob challenged Paul to a game of checkers. Now Billy Bob considered himself to be a pretty good checker player, but Paul took the game, as David put it, like taking candy away from a baby.

Next, Paul played Nathan, Glenda, Rachel, and finally David, winning every time.

"I didn't know you were a checker whiz," David commented after Paul had taken David's last checker.

"A guy has to be good at something," Paul retorted. "Can't even milk a cow! Besides, there are lots of things about me that you don't know. Want to take a walk with me? I'd like to tell you about one of them."

David arose and followed Paul from the house. "Where are we going?" he asked.

"Oh, maybe all the way out to those two lawn chairs. I just want to talk."

When they were seated, Paul came right to the point. "I just want you to know, David, that I am interested in your sister. As head of the house, I thought I should level with you as to the reason that I am coming here."

David nodded. "I suspected that," he said.

"You suspected that?" Paul half rose from his chair in alarm. "I thought I was being rather discreet. I didn't want anyone to know, not even her. What gave you the idea I was interested in her?"

"Well, I'm not conceited enough to suppose you would waste your valuable time coming to see me. You never seemed to care anything about me in the past."

"You got me wrong, David. I have always liked you. Maybe admired would be a better word. I know we haven't exactly been friends, but we sure haven't been enemies. It just always seemed you never had time to make friends with anyone, but I'd really like to be friends."

"All right. I can use all the friends I can get, but I happen to remember that not five minutes ago you told me you were coming here to see my sister."

"David, I'd like to be able to come here as your friend. I don't want your sister to know, yet. I realize she's too young to think of marriage and for the matter of that, so am I. I am not asking for her hand in marriage. I just want to get better acquainted with her. Then in another year or two, if I like her then as much as I think I do now —" Paul stopped and let his sentence hang.

"OK, OK! I getcha!" David said, getting up. "It's all right with me. You wait two years and if I don't see any bigger flaws in you than that you can't milk a cow, I'll give my consent."

XX

David set his two grocery bags on the table. "I've got news!" He announced.

"News?" Rachel enthused, turning from the stove. "I hope it is good news. You seem to have a habit of bringing bad news when you come from town."

"This time it is good news," David said. "At least I hope it is. They are going to fix up the old Ford house across the road and we are going to have neighbors."

"Who is going to live there?" Darlene asked. "Do they have any children?"

"It is a son of the old Mrs. Ford who lived there when I was a little kid, or maybe it is a grandson. Anyway the place is still in the family and it is a Mr. And Mrs. Ford and their two children that will be living there."

"Boys or girls?" questioned Billy Bob.

"How old?" Glenda wanted to know.

"I don't really know the answer to either question," David answered. "Some say two girls and some say a girl and a boy. My informers didn't seem to be very well informed."

"Oh, I do hope there is a girl my age," Darlene bubbled, excitedly. "It would be so nice to have a friend."

"With all the girls you have around here?" David asked. "What is wrong with the thirds, aren't they your friends?"

"No, they are my sisters," Darlene replied.

When David and Rachel were alone, Rachel returned to the subject. "You know, David," she said, "Darlene is right. She does need a friend. Glenda fancies herself to be too grown-up to pal with Darlene. The triplets are all for each other and Darlene stands rather alone. I hope the Fords do have a girl her age."

"Which isn't saying she would be the kind of girl we would want Darlene to companion with if they do," remarked David.

"You are right, of course, but if she is anything like her grandmother or great-grandmother, she'll be sweet. Do you remember her, David?"

"Of course! I believe I am still older than you even if you are old enough to have all the guys a-teech-en."

Rachel laughed. "I do notice a few being more friendly than they used to be, but look who's talking! I have been seeing Stacy Crowlman giving you rather sweet smiles at every opportunity."

"Poor Stacey," David returned. "It has been over a year

since she first decided to have a crush on me. She has gone the rounds of almost every boy in the church and now she is back to me. Know what I wish?"

David continued without giving Rachel time to answer. "I wish Stacey would get married and maybe the rest of us could have some peace. But back to the subject of the Fords, I used to think Mrs. Ford was the nicest old lady on earth. I used to wish she were my Grandmother."

"I remember she always had a cookie jar full of cookies, but I don't remember her ever having any children or grandchildren, do you?"

David thought a moment before he answered. "Seems to me she had a son come to visit once from somewhere far away, but I don't remember him having any family. If I remember correctly he was rather old himself."

"He would have been. Mrs. Ford was in her nineties when she died and that must have been ten or twelve years ago."

"Dad was still here. I remember hearing him tell Mother she had slipped on the ice on her back steps and had broken her hip. They took her to the hospital and she never came back."

"Yes, and the house has been empty since then. It is run down some. It will probably take quite a bit of time to fix it. Do you know when this is supposed to happen?"

"Mr. Ford was there yesterday with a contractor,

making the plans for what is to be done. He has gone back to wherever he came from. They are supposed to start the remodeling immediately and be done in time for the family to move in before school starts."

"That means," Rachel mused, "that they have at least one school aged child. Well, I guess we will find out when the time comes."

XXI

Bing, bong, bing, bong, bing, bing, bing, bong.

Rachel stopped peeling potatoes and listened.

Bing, bing, bing, bing, bing, bing, bong.

"I wonder whom that is playing the piano," she pondered. "Darlene is much more advanced than that."

"Oh, maybe she is just reviewing her old pieces," Glenda answered as she washed some lettuce. "She does that sometimes."

"No, when she reviews, she plays with confidence. Whoever is playing is hesitating. There he made another mistake."

Just then David stepped into the room. "David," Rachel pleaded, "would you please look in the living room and see who is playing the piano?"

David was gone only a minute. He came back wearing a broad grin. "One third is playing the piano," he informed them. "It seems Darlene is giving the instructions and two thirds are looking on, apparently awaiting their turns."

"Well, did you ever!" Rachel said, stunned.

"Oh, I'm not surprised," Glenda announced. "Last week I found them all in the sewing room. Darlene was teaching them to sew."

"And did you drive them out with your cat-a-nine-tails?" asked David.

"No!" Glenda responded. "Why should I? They weren't bothering anything of mine. They were using material that I had given Darlene. As Darlene said, if she teaches them, it will save me the time and trouble. I had wondered why they had quit pestering me to start teaching them."

"Come to think of it," Rachel mused, "Alicia asked me several times if I was going to start them on piano lessons, but I have been putting her off."

"Poor Darlene!" David chuckled. "She sure is having a busy schedule growing up. First she wants to learn everything herself and now she has taken on teaching the thirds."

Rachel finished slicing the potatoes to fry and sat them on the stove. "She's doing a pretty good job of learning it all. I believe she could run this kitchen by herself if she didn't have anything else to do."

"The same goes for sewing," Glenda added. "Oh, she can't do everything yet, but she's doing really well. I – I wonder if you think I should let her use my machine."

Rachel looked at David and David looked at Rachel. Finally David spoke. "I think that is for you to decide, Glenda. The machine is yours. I understand Mother's machine is still alive and well. She has been using that, hasn't she?"

Glenda nodded.

"Yes, Rachel put in, "but maybe Glenda feels it is time for Darlene to learn some things that Mother's machine won't do." Then to Glenda she went on, "I think it would be real nice if you would let her use it occasionally, but only when you are with her, not when she is in the room alone."

"Sounds fair to me!"

"And *never*," David emphasized, "Should she let the thirds touch it."

Suddenly Rachel turned to David. "David," she asked, "why do you always speak of the triplets as 'the thirds?'"

"Aren't they the thirds?"

"Well, they *do* have names. It wouldn't seem so funny for you to say 'the thirds' instead of 'the triplets' as the rest of us say, but I notice when you speak to any one of them you call her 'One Third.'"

"It's because he can't tell them apart," giggled Glenda.

Rachel whirled and looked at her, then back at David. By the guilty look on David's face she knew Glenda was right. "After all these years," she sighed, "you still can't tell them apart? I guess maybe we *had* better start dressing them differently."

Glenda laughed. "That wouldn't do any good. David would never remember which one was wearing which dress."

"If you two are going to continue to discuss my shortcomings, I guess I'd better go see if I can help Uncle Pete with whatever he is doing. That *was* my secret. I didn't think anyone, except Mother, had ever found that out. I thought I was doing very well," and David strode from the room.

Rachel shook her head. "Really!" she said. "That's unbelievable! Why those triplets are as different as –"

"As three peas in a pod," finished Glenda.

"Don't tell me you can't tell them apart," accused Rachel.

"Oh, yes, I can tell them apart if I look closely, but I don't find it easy."

"I don't remember ever not being able to tell them apart," declared Rachel. "I could see a difference in them when they were babies."

"That's probably because you helped Mother take care of them. I distinctly remember she hardly let me touch them."

"And I distinctly remember that was because you picked Darlene up and dropped her when she was a baby."

"Oh, well, I was just four then. I was much older when the triplets were born. I should have been allowed to help."

"Well, let's not quarrel over something that happened or didn't happen so many years ago. Let's get this food on the table."

XXII

Paul continued to visit once or twice a week. A couple of times Rachel asked David to invite him for a meal. He seemed to enjoy visiting the family, but never paid any special attention to Rachel more than any of the others. One evening as they sat together talking, Paul spoke to Nathan, asking him how he was doing in school.

"I'm glad it is out," Nathan replied.

"Why? Don't you like it?

Nathan shrugged. "Oh, some of it is all right. Nothing worth advertising."

"What is your worst subject?" inquired Paul.

"Mechanics," Nathan admitted without hesitating. "I hate it!"

"Why are you taking it?"

"Simple! Somebody in this family needs to know some-thing about how to fix the tractor and the car when something goes wrong."

"But you don't even have a car."

187

"No, but we are saving for one."

Paul studied the weave of the carpet for a few minutes, then he spoke again. "I have just had the most fabulous idea. Why don't we go to the junkyard and get the fixings and put a car together? It will be a lot of fun, won't cost too much, and by the time we finish you will be making A's in mechanics. As an added bonus, the family will have a car."

"How could you do that?" inquired David.

"Oh, it is really simple. Lots of folks do it. You find a good body that the motor is burned up, then you get a good motor out of a wrecked car, sometimes you have to get a transmission from a third car."

"But do you know how to do that?" Nathan asked.

"Sure! I've helped change the motors in several cars. You do realize, don't you, that I am working in Phil's garage this summer? This fall I go back to Tech for my final year. When I get out I am supposed to be a heavy equipment mechanic. Putting a car together is rather elementary."

"Can we, David?" asked Nathan.

"How much will it cost?" David wanted to know.

"That depends on what kind of car you want. I would say if you just want something that will take you there and bring you back, and you don't care anything about comfort or looks, you might get by with seventy-five or a hundred dollars. If you want a nicer car, you'll have to pay more."

"We will need a big car for this family," David said, thoughtfully.

"Or maybe a school bus," ventured Billy Bob.

"What about a station wagon?" asked Paul. "I know where there is one that the owner let freeze and busted the block."

"What's the block?" asked Billy Bob in an aside to Nathan.

"The motor."

"What do you think, Rachel?" David asked. "Should we have a family conference concerning this?"

"I don't think so," Rachel answered. "You boys just work it out between yourselves. We girls know less than nothing about it anyway, only just be sure you get something that we can all get in."

"Do you have a preference of makes?" asked Paul.

"Makes?"

"You know – Chevy, Ford, Dodge?"

"Oh, it doesn't matter. I hear people arguing about which is best, but I don't know. Get whatever you think best."

"I don't believe the make is that important. There are good cars and 'lemons' of every kind. Now this station wagon I was speaking of – I know the guy that owns it. It was a good car, a Pontiac. Uses a little more gas than the smaller cars, of course, but you can't all fit in a small car. It won't be too bad though. I'll just have to see what he wants for it and see if I can get a motor to fit. In the meantime, you figure how much expense you can handle."

"I sure hope this works," worried David.

"I'll tell you what, Friend," Paul said, "if you're worried, I'll give you double your money for it when the car is done. Of course Nathan won't get paid for his work, but that will be just doing his homework, lots of it!"

"How long will it take?"

"That depends on how much we have to do to it and how much time we spend. If we just have to change the motor, we can have it done in a couple of weeks, but if we have to put it together part by part, it could run into six months or so."

"Well, all right, Paul. Find out what you can do and we will go on from there."

Two evenings later, Paul was back. The station wagon he had had in mind had been too expensive, but he had found another that he could get at a reasonable price. He said it was in bad shape, but fixable and would take less money and give Nathan more experience. Of course it would be a much longer time before they had a car.

"We don't need to get panicky about that," David mused. "We haven't had a car in ten years and we will likely get it quicker this way than if we had to save for it."

So the car was bought and work on it began. Nathan

rearranged his schedule so as to have his evenings free whenever possible. Pete and David took over some of Nathan's chores so he would have more free time.

For the first week, Billy Bob and Brad spent every spare minute watching; then they lost interest. Billy Bob went back to spending his time with Pete.

One sunny afternoon, David brought the news that the Ford family was moving in.

"Did you see any children?" asked Darlene.

"I saw only one girl somewhat larger than Sue Ellen," answered David, winking at Rachel.

"Oh," Darlene, crestfallen, uttered only the one syllable.

Rachel wondered audibly how soon she should call on them. The others all lost interest.

Working together later in the kitchen, Darlene voiced her disappointment to Rachel. "I had so hoped – yes, and prayed, too, that there would be a girl my age, but I guess it isn't God's plan for us to be totally happy on this earth."

"Why do you say that?"

"Well, I've dreamed of having a friend – a real close friend. I just have wanted it so much for years and years, well, ever since the day when I was about six and, well, I guess I was following Glenda around. Anyway she said, 'I wish you'd go tag someone your own age.' I went out to where the triplets were playing and Patricia said, 'You can't play with us. You're not a triplet.'"

"You poor kid! I've often thought you were lonely, but I didn't know it was that bad."

Darlene laughed. "Lonely? How can a person be lonely in a family of twelve children?"

"I've always heard there is no worse feeling of loneliness than being lonely in a crowd."

Darlene straightened up from the oven where she was watching the pies and smiled. "It's not so bad, really, Sis. I'm almost perfectly happy. I suppose if everything was perfect in life we wouldn't be thinking of Heaven. We would just be enjoying life so much here that we would be content, but in Heaven I'll have a friend. I think about that, too, and I do love all my brothers and sisters. Life really is very good."

Rachel said no more for a time. Her mind went to a survey of Darlene's life. Lost her father when she was too young to remember; got triplet sisters when she was still a baby herself; had no attention to speak of in her young childhood; lost her mother while still a little girl; had to learn to work like an adult with very little time to play; was sandwiched in the family between two boys that didn't really want her around and triplets that were all for each other; and yet at twelve years old, she could say, "Life really is very good."

Rachel set the pan of potatoes she was holding on the

stove and with tears in her eyes, turned around and took Darlene in her arms. "I'm sorry, Little Sister," she said. "I'm really very, very sorry."

"For what? Because I said I love all my brothers and sisters? I think that's the last thing I said."

"Oh, forget it. I guess you wouldn't understand, but I want you to know that I love you, too."

A mischievous look came into Darlene's eyes. "Better than Paul?" she asked.

"Paul? What do you mean? I don't love Paul."

"You don't? Well, I guess you'd better be telling Paul that then, so he won't waste the winter coming to see you like he did the summer."

"Paul isn't coming here to see me!"

"No? Well, he sure enough isn't coming to see me!"

For about a week Rachel was strangely quiet, but Darlene noticed an alertness about her when Paul was around that she hadn't noticed before. Then one day when Rachel and Darlene had a minute alone, Rachel again brought up the subject. "I believe you are wrong about Paul, Darlene. I really believe you are, but however, *please* don't say anything like that to anyone else."

"Of course not! I'm not stupid!" Darlene answered.

XXIII

Rachel placed the last loaf of freshly baked bread on the cooling rack and stepped back with a sigh. She was finally done. Being chief cook for a family of thirteen was quite a task and it didn't seem to be getting any easier. It seemed the more the children grew, the more they ate. She looked at her rows of baking, however, with a pleased smile. Then a thought flitted through her mind. She had not yet called on the Ford family.

"I think I'll tidy up a bit, take a loaf of that fresh bread, and go call on Mrs. Ford. Would *one* of you like to go along?

"I would!"

"Take me!"

"May I go?"

"I want to."

Rachel sat down in a chair laughing. "On second thought, I think I'll stay home."

"No, go on," David spoke, coming into the room from

the office. "Take Darlene and go. You have put it off for so long I have thought of going over myself, but I know the proper way is for you to call on Mrs. Ford first. Say! That bread sure looks good. I don't believe you have ever done better. In fact, I don't believe Moth – well, anyone ever baked any better bread."

Glenda giggled. "Perhaps you had better taste it before you pass judgment. It might be like the pumpkin pie that looked so good until we tasted it and found she had left out the sugar."

"That's not fair!" retorted Rachel. "That was over a year ago. Besides, where is the pumpkin pie you ever made? You're as old now as I was then."

"I never made any.

"Aha!" said David, getting in to the good-natured bickering. "I believe it is time for little Miss Glenda to make some pumpkin pies."

Presently, Rachel and Darlene made their way to the Ford home. As they came in sight of the house, they could see a lady and a young girl in the front yard, apparently making a flowerbed.

"Look!" Darlene whispered. "That must be the other girl. I think she is about my age."

At that moment the neighbors apparently heard the girls' footsteps and turned toward them. "Oh, good afternoon!" the lady said.

"Good afternoon," returned Rachel. You must be Mrs. Ford. I am Rachel Bradcox and this is my sister, Darlene."

"Yes, I am Ann Ford and this is my daughter, Annabelle."

Darlene and Annabelle looked at each other, and then Annabelle said, "Want to come see my new kittens?"

Rachel and Mrs. Ford sat on the porch and talked a full hour. They didn't see Darlene and Annabelle again until time to go home, at which time they appeared from around the house with their arms around each other.

"We're really good friends already," Darlene confided to Rachel as they walked home. "We are going to walk to school together and be best friends always. I told her about church and she asked if she could go with me. I really like her. She's such a comfortable person to have for a friend."

"I didn't see any other child. Did you find out if she has a brother or sister? I really didn't want to just ask Mrs. Ford and she never mentioned another child."

"She has a sister. She is seventeen and her name is Susan. She is staying with a friend where they did live and going to school. They have summer school there. Annabelle said she just needed a little bit to be able to get her diploma, so she took summer school, because she didn't want to have to go to school here. Annabelle said she's a mess. She doesn't do anything much but stand before the mirror and fix her face and hair. She wants to be a movie star and Annabelle said she acts as if she is one already."

"I don't approve of your best friend criticizing her sister, Darlene. I hope you don't pick up any such thing from her. You know we have to be really careful when we have friends of the world."

"I know, Sister, but I really like Annabelle. I guess she just wanted us to know what kind of sister she has. I am sure if she gets like that, I won't be best friends with her, but I don't think she will. She says she wants to be the right kind of person. Is it all right if she goes to church with us Sunday?"

"Of course, if her parents don't mind her walking that far. I'll be glad for her to go."

Little did Rachel realize it, but that day a friendship was born that would last the rest of Darlene's earthly life and much farther, if natural friendships extend into eternity.

XXIV

"Dear Heavenly Father, we thank you for all your many blessings throughout this day. Thank you for keeping us all safe. Thank you for the food that you have provided for us, and for all your richest blessings. In Jesus name we pray. Amen."

David lifted his head and looked around the table. All the faces showed peace and contentment. "All right," he said, "now which one of you saw the most interesting thing today?"

"I think I did," Bradley answered. "There was a girl here from the circus."

Rachel gasped and Billy Bob snickered.

"From the circus? I didn't know there was a circus around close."

"Oh, I guess she wasn't really from a real circus," Bradley continued, "but she sure looked a lot like some of those clowns in that circus book I've got. She had thick bright red lips and green eyelids and her face was real white except for a spot on each side of bright red —"

"Yes," Billy Bob interrupted, "and log chains in her ears that hung to her shoulders."

"I wondered, David," Bradley again took over the conversation, "if that is what Pastor Parker meant the other night when he was preaching about the chains of sin."

"Hush, Brad!" Darlene admonished, "You're making Rachel sad."

David looked at Rachel and saw her eyes were dewy with tears. "Who was here, Rachel?" he asked.

"Susan Ford."

"Susan Ford? What's she like – really? I mean underneath the paint and log chains."

Rachel sniffed and tried to smile. "Underneath the paint and log chains is really a very nice person, one I could really like. There is just something about her – I'd like to be friends."

"'To each his own taste,' said the man whose wife had kissed the pet pig. Be friends all you like, just be sure she's gone before I come in. I don't need another Stacey Crowlman and of the world besides."

"Oh, you don't have to worry about Susan. She is *very* devoted to her boyfriend. His name is Tony and he is off in college somewhere. She won't get to see him again until Thanksgiving and she just doesn't see how she can live until then." Rachel smiled then. "I'll admit I did get a little tired of 'Tony' every other sentence. He must really be *some guy!*"

"I notice her sister, Annabelle, is under foot quite a lot lately. She's not so bad. She really seems to be interested in God. I suppose if this Susan is anything like her sister, I could put up with her being around some, seeing as romantically speaking, she is already attached."

"Oh, no!" Darlene exclaimed, "Susan isn't a bit like Annabelle. Annabelle really is interested in God. She wants to be saved – to be baptized, but her mother said for her to wait until she could check in to it some. I don't suppose you could drag Susan to church."

"I've already asked her," Rachel replied, "and she said she would like to go."

"I saw Mr. Ford yesterday," David said. "He asked if it would be all right if the whole family goes Sunday. He said he needs to see what kind of thing Annabelle wants to join. I felt bad that I hadn't invited him."

The Ford family attended church for the next three Sundays. Then Mr. Ford gave permission for Annabelle to be baptized. His comment was, "I'm not saying I believe this is the right church. It seems a little far out to me, but Ann and I talked it over. We feel Annabelle is old enough to make her own decision about religion. If this is the route she wants to take we will give her our support."

The family was all there the next Sunday when Pastor

Parker baptized Annabelle in Jesus Name. She came out of the water speaking in an unknown tongue. She had a glow on her face the likes of which her parents had never seen before. Tears ran down Mrs. Ford's face and Mr. Ford took out his handkerchief and blew his nose. As soon as Annabelle could speak, she went to her parents and hugged them. Then she went to Susan and hugged her and told her she loved her. David noticed blue streaks running down Susan's face from her eye shadow. "Oh my," he thought, "she must have spent a good half hour putting that stuff on and now just look at her. If she could see herself in the mirror right now she would be shocked, but she looks better to me than she ever did."

As the Bradcox family walked home, Bradley commented. "That circus girl had hubcaps on her ears this morning, but she doesn't use very good paint because it washed off."

The next day, Susan had a long talk with Rachel. She mentioned that Annabelle hadn't hugged her like that since she was 6 years old. "We're so different," she said. "We've never been close. We've never even ever liked each other, but I am getting to where I like Annabelle better than I like myself. Do you suppose, Rachel," she asked, "that I could ever change and be like Annabelle?"

Rachel shook her head. "God didn't make you alike. He doesn't want you to be alike. He wants Annabelle to be Annabelle, and you to be you, but He does want you both to be the best you can for Him."

"I don't know, Rachel," Susan replied. "I think I'm hopeless as a Christian. What is there in it anyway? I like my jewelry and my make-up. I like to go to shows and to dances. I think being a Christian would be so boring. Take you, for instance, you never have any fun. Don't you ever wish you weren't so tied down? Wouldn't you like to date? Have you ever tried smoking? Do you know what a thrill you feel when you're drunk?"

Rachel shook her head. "I don't know and I don't want to find out. I wouldn't want the kind of thrill Sam Woodbury felt last year when he got over his drunk and found out he had killed a man and his wife and left three little children orphans. That's not my idea of a thrill."

"Well, I've never actually been drunk but once and if my Dad knew that he'd have a heart attack. He thinks his little Susan is the model of perfection. I just wish I could be the kind of girl he thinks I am. Sometimes I think a lot about trying to change, but really, Rachel, don't you find life awfully boring?"

Rachel sighed. "Boring? I don't really see how anyone could be bored trying to 'mother' a bunch of kids. To be really truthful, the only part of life I find boring is the cooking. I hate the cooking!"

Susan was amazed. She had found Rachel in the

kitchen each time she came and had just assumed she enjoyed being there. Susan herself enjoyed cooking. It was about the only thing called work that she did enjoy. Oh, Susan wasn't lazy. She dutifully did whatever task her mother assigned her, but she thought it all boring except cooking. Suddenly she laughed.

Rachel whirled around from the stove where she had just placed a pan of potatoes. "What's so funny?" she asked.

"Oh, I was just thinking how different people are. You say the only thing in life you find boring is cooking and cooking is the only work I don't find boring. I would just love to be able to cook the meals at our house, but unfortunately Mother likes to cook. All the cooking Annabelle and I are allowed to do is just enough to assure Mother that we know how. Why is life so complicated? I wouldn't want to be you. I'd hate trying to 'mother' a bunch of kids. I'd hate the endless round of duties that keep you always tied. I'd hate not going to parties and not being allowed to wear the kind of clothes I want to wear or wear make-up and cut my hair. I'd hate it all, your whole life, except the cooking. I really envy you that."

"You would hate that too if you had to do it three times a day, seven days a week for years and years, probably the rest of your life. Not one of the other girls wants to cook. When we have work assignment time, Darlene is the only one who chooses to cook and she admitted that she doesn't really like it, that she just wants to be able to do everything. Oh, it gets so boring! The girls take turns helping, but none of them are willing to do it for even one meal. I'm sure you would hate it too."

"Try me!" Susan replied. "Just try me!"

"What do you mean?"

"Just what I said. Just let me do the cooking for this family. I promise I won't get bored and even if I do, at least you will have had a rest."

"Oh, David would not allow that. He doesn't know how much I hate it and I would not want him to know. He certainly would never approve of letting you do it."

"Would he have to know?"

"Of course! We don't keep secrets from each other. Besides, you would be here. He would see you doing it."

"Now, Rachel, you know David never comes in the house when I'm here. He avoids me as if I had leprosy. I would just get the meals and leave before he comes in. Please, Rachel, I want so much to do it. Isn't there something you would like very much to do if you had the time, like maybe write a book or something?"

"Me? Write a book? I would never get the first page written." Rachel cupped her chin in her hands with a dreamy, far-away look in her eyes. There is one thing I would do if I had enough spare time, though. I'd like to knit myself a dress. I've had the pattern for two years, but there has been no time for it. You would have to cook a lot of meals to give me enough spare time to do that."

"Oh, that would be perfect," Susan exclaimed. "You could sit in here and knit while I cook. That way if David happened to come in I could hide in the pantry and you could pretend to be doing the cooking."

They talked for an hour. Rachel showed Susan the pattern and Susan took notice of how much and what kind of yarn it called for. The next day she arrived with a big package of yarn and a new pair of knitting needles, which she presented to Rachel. She could see the longing in Rachel's eyes as she looked at the yarn and admitted it was the perfect color choice, but Rachel declared she could never accept such a gift.

"Oh, it isn't a gift," Susan explained. "I'm just paying you for the privilege of cooking, one skein for each day you let me cook until your dress is finished. Then I'll have to find some other way to pay."

"Oh, you would never last that long," laughed Rachel.

It was finally decided that Susan could cook the evening meal. Rachel, with her knitting sat where she could watch to see if David came. It slowed her knitting a bit, but still she had made quite a nice beginning by the time the meal was ready.

When David came in, Rachel was dishing up the

food and there was no sign of her knitting or of Susan. "Something sure smells good in here tonight," he said. "It has been a mighty long time since this kitchen has smelled this good. I hope it tastes as good as it smells."

At the table, everyone complimented Rachel on the cooking. She felt a little embarrassed, but as she was used to such compliments, she took it all in stride. "Something is different about the food tonight, Rachel," David commented. "Did you hire a cook while I was out?"

"Oh, I think it is some different spices," Rachel answered.

"It sure is better food than usual," David went on. "If you keep on cooking like this we are likely to lose you to some Prince Charming."

Darlene, who was in on the secret, spoke up. "Now David, you know you always liked Rachel's cooking. You have said many times that Rachel was a good cook, almost as good as Mother."

"Sure, sure, but if Rachel cooked this meal, then good just got better," David answered. "If I was looking for a wife and she wasn't my sister, I'd sure like to marry the cook." David couldn't understand why Rachel got choked and Darlene and Glenda both giggled.

"Well," spoke up Brad at the supper table a few nights later. "What about the dog?"

"What about it?" David asked.

"At a family conference, 'bout a dozen years ago, we talked about we needed a car and a dog. Looks like we're getting the car. What about the dog? We need that, too."

"Oh, you think so, huh? Well, maybe we do. Do you happen to know where we can get one?"

"Sure I do! Marilyn Ellis has a gob of them she wants to give away. She says they're really good dogs."

"If they are such good dogs, why does she want to give them away?" queried Letitia.

Bradley gave her a scornful look. "She don't," he said.

"Doesn't," corrected Rachel.

"You said she did," replied Letitia.

"Oh, her mom won't let her keep forty dogs. She said she can just keep the mother dog and has to give the puppies away, or she can keep a puppy and give the mother dog away. But she said Old Missy is the bestest dog in the whole big world and she won't never part with her, and so I thought if Missy is the bestest dog, her puppies should ought to be second bestest."

Rachel shook her head in despair. She just didn't know what she should do about Bradley's grammar.

"How old are they?" David asked.

"Oh, she just got them yesterday night, but I thought if we was going to get one we ought to tell her today before they are all gone."

"If there are thirty nine of them, I wouldn't suppose

there would be any hurry," David assured him.

Presently, David took a small notebook from his pocket, tore out a sheet, and wrote a few words on it. He folded it and handed it to Bradley saying, "As soon as you have finished eating, I would like you to take this note to Uncle Pete. Wait until he writes an answer and bring it back to me."

"Can I go, too?" asked Gregory.

"May I," corrected Rachel.

"Yes," David answered.

The two little boys hurriedly shoveled in the last bits of food from their plates and scooted for the door. As soon as the door closed behind them, David said, "Darlene, please take Sue Ellen into the playroom and keep her there five minutes. I promise to repeat to you every word that is spoken while you are gone."

After Darlene and Sue Ellen had left the room, David explained, "As Bradley seems to be the one most interested in a dog, and as he has a birthday coming at about the right time, I am wondering if all of you would agree to letting the puppy be his birthday present."

"Could we still pet it?" asked Alicia.

"I don't believe Brad would be stingy with it."

"I've always wanted a dog," said Billy Bob, "but as you said I don't believe Brad would be stingy. I suppose it is all right."

"Everyone agreed?" David asked. "I know Darlene will. We only have five minutes."

Everyone agreed.

The next day, David went to the Ellis' and got his pick of the litter of six beautiful puppies. Two others had been spoken for, but not picked out.

XXV

It was Friday night and Paul had stayed for supper. "If all goes well," he said, "we should have the car running in one more day. We still have to buy a battery, but I think that will be the last of the expense. We will give it a trial run tomorrow evening and then unless you want me to take it and give you double your money back like I said, you can go to church in it on Sunday."

"There is only one problem, Paul," David answered. "No one here has a driver's license."

"No one has a driver's license?" Paul exclaimed. "You mean – not even *you*? *You* don't have a driver's license? Why not?"

"For one thing," David answered, "I have never had need of one until now and for another there might be some difficulty in obtaining a driver's license without a car."

Paul looked around the table. "Do any of you know how to drive?" he asked.

"We all know how to drive the tractor," David answered.

Once when Aunt Gladys Cook, Mother's best friend, was here a few years back, Mother had her teach me to drive a little. She said I should know. Of course that was just here at home. It wouldn't be quite the same as driving on the highway, but I think I could pick it up if I had someone to teach me."

"I would suggest that everyone who is 15 or older go to town early Monday morning and get beginner's permits," Paul suggested. "This new car is going to need some drivers. What about Pete? Do you suppose he knows how to drive?"

"He likely knows how," David answered, "but I am fairly certain he doesn't have a license. I'm equally certain that he wouldn't be willing to get one."

"Do you want me to teach you, David, or is there someone else you'd rather have?"

"Oh, you are probably as good as any and better than most," David assured him. "We will take the two girls and take turns. Take turns laughing at each other, that is."

"I'm not sure I want to," put in Rachel. "I'd rather just let David do the driving until Nathan is old enough to help. Besides, who would stay with the children?"

"Oh, come on, Rachel," Glenda begged. "I want to learn. You know you ought to. You might need to go to town when David is busy and I'm in school."

So early Monday morning Paul came and took David

and Glenda to town for beginner's permits. They spent the afternoon taking turns driving. David was quick to catch on, having already had some lessons, but Glenda did well enough. The next day Rachel and Nathan had their turns. Nathan was still too young for his permit, but the first lessons were in the cow pasture where he could have his turn. When they progressed to the county roads, he went along for the ride. Then the evening was spent studying the book. They took turns reading it aloud, then asking questions of the other three and seeing who could be the first to answer correctly. Nine times out of ten it was Billy Bob who answered.

David, because he was over eighteen could take his driving test any time he felt he could pass it, but the others were required to wait thirty days.

XXVI

Patricia came bounding into the kitchen where Letitia was watching Susan prepare supper, or rather dinner, as Susan preferred to call the evening meal. "Come on, Letitia," she said. "Darlene said she has a little time to help us in the sewing room."

"Aw, you and Alicia go on without me," Letitia answered. "I'm learning to cook. I'd much rather do that than sew."

Alicia is practicing the piano and she doesn't want to leave it, but she said she would if you will. Darlene won't take us unless we all go," Patricia replied.

Rachel looked up from her knitting. "Don't you enjoy sewing, Letitia?" she asked.

"Oh, yes, I like it well enough, but not like Patricia does," Letitia answered, she wants to sew all the time. I'd much rather cook."

"Patricia sighed, "And Alicia wants to spend all her spare time practicing the piano. Honestly, I can't get my sisters to agree with me at all anymore."

"Nor can I get mine to agree with me," laughed Letitia as she slowly dragged herself out of the kitchen.

Rachel resumed her knitting. "Well, that is another milestone behind us," she said.

"How so?" asked Susan.

"Mother worried because the triplets were so much alike, always wanting to dress exactly alike and be always together. She worried that they were not developing individuality."

Susan sprinkled cinnamon over the concoction she had just finished putting together and placed it in the oven. Then she turned to Rachel. "You know, Rachel," she said, "that is the first time you have ever mentioned either of your parents to me. I have wanted to ask about them so many times, but I didn't want to intrude where I might not be wanted. I have wondered a lot."

"What do you want to know?" Rachel asked. "I hold no secrets concerning them. When Mother first left us, we talked about her all the time, but it has been well over a year now. She is still mentioned by one or another almost daily though. It is different with Dad. He has been gone eleven years. Billy Bob and the ones younger don't remember him at all and Nathan not more than a few little incidents. We rarely speak of him, but we are not hiding anything."

"But where did they go?" Susan asked. "Did they just leave you or are they – a – dead?"

"Oh, I'm sorry! I just took it for granted everyone knew. Mother passed away a year ago last April. She had cared for the family and managed the little farm for ten years. Dad left us before the triplets were born. He went out West and we heard later that he was dead."

"Then your mother married the little ones father?"

"Oh, my, no!" Rachel exclaimed. "Mother never married again. The little ones belonged to her cousin. She and her husband were both killed in a plane crash. She had left it in her will that she wanted Mother to raise the children."

Susan sat for some minutes slicing apples into a pan. Hesitantly she spoke again. "Do you know why your father left, Rachel?" she asked.

"Yes, we older children know, but the triplets don't know yet. We will tell them if they ever ask, but if not, we don't want them to feel they are to blame. Dad never wanted any children. Mother had us all so close together and with every one, Dad got a little more upset, until Billy Bob. Dad's name was William Robert. When Mother named Billy Bob, Robert William, Dad said that one was his and she could have the rest. He started right off calling him Billy Bob, and wouldn't let Mother discipline him at all. They got into more arguments over Billy Bob than anything else. Then Darlene came along and Dad was so mad he said he never wanted to see her. He wouldn't even look at her until she was three months old. Then when the doctor said Mother was going to have twins, Dad said if she was going to start having her babies in litters, he was leaving permanently. He tried to take Billy Bob with him. Mother objected and they got into a real fight. That is the only time he ever beat her up. I guess he would have killed her if David hadn't called the police.

"David felt awfully bad for a long time for calling the police on his own father, but one day Mother talked to him. She pointed out that he had probably saved her life and the life of her babies. After that it didn't bother him anymore.

"Mother was pretty well battered and bruised, but she said if Dad would just go and not bother her anymore that she would not press charges against him. So he went. The next day he sent her a dozen roses with a little card that said, 'You were the one love of my life. I'm sorry for what I did, but I won't be back. Take care of my little boy and raise him to be a man, not a sissy like your other boys.' We never heard from him directly anymore. As far as we know, he never did find out the twins turned out to be triplets.

"Billy Bob was two and a half years old and spoiled rotten. He's never been the same as the others. It just proves how important it is to bring babies up right."

"I wouldn't have believed the first two and a half years would make that much difference," Susan said.

"It does! Billy Bob is living proof of that. He was a real problem when we were first left alone, but last December when we were gone to youth retreat, he and Uncle Pete both got baptized. Things have been much better since."

"He's still different," Susan mused.

"Yes, he is. I suppose he will always be different, but if he can be saved that is what is important."

Susan turned off the oven and sat down across from Rachel. "Exactly what does it mean to be saved?" she asked.

"Well," Rachel began, "it can mean several things. We use it mostly to mean when a person turns from the world and becomes a Christian, but the Bible says, (Matthew 24:13) *But he that shall endure unto the end, the same shall be saved.* So none of us are permanently saved until we have endured unto the end."

"They taught me in the church where I came from that to be saved means to accept Christ as your saviour. After you do that you are a child of God. You are permanently saved; God won't give you up no matter what you do. Isn't that right, Rachel? Isn't it true that if you had a son that turned out to be an outlaw, that he would still be your son?"

"Saved is a process, not an act," Rachel explained. "Although we use the word for when we turn from our old ways, be baptized in Jesus name and get the Holy Ghost, that is not exactly proper speaking. That is properly called 'being converted'. Let's look at it this way. In the summer before Nina's Fabric Store has its annual sale, Glenda cleans the sewing room. She throws away everything that she doesn't feel will be any good to her. Actually, she gives her scraps to Granny McCodder for quilts, but as far as Glenda is concerned, they are discarded. Let's say she picks up a little bundle of pink and white checked gingham scraps. She says, 'I think I'll save that.' Another year goes by and she is again sorting. She comes across the same bundle of pink and white scraps. She looks at it and says to herself, 'I've had that a year and it hasn't done me any good. I'll toss it.' So it goes in the box for Granny McCodder. Although it was saved last year, it was not permanently saved."

"Isn't there any way to be permanently saved?" Susan asked.

"As I see it, it is as I said – to endure to the end. If we repent of our sins, be baptized in Jesus name, and are filled with the Holy Ghost as it says in Acts 2:38, we are saved, then! If we continue on to follow Jesus we can stay saved, permanently."

"I would like to be saved, but I'm not sure I could keep

it up, permanently. A party would happen along and I would want to go."

"Your problem, Susan, is that you are not ready to give yourself totally to Jesus. When you are ready to be totally committed, and you repent, turn away from the old life, get baptized in Jesus name, and He gives you the Holy Ghost; that is Jesus living in you. You commit your body to Him to live in. Jesus living in you wouldn't want to go to any party that was not the right kind of party."

"That's another thing I don't – Oh, my goodness! There's David!"

Rachel jumped up and crammed her knitting into the bag as Susan disappeared through the pantry door, and David entered from outside.

Rachel, with flushed face, stammered, "I'm sorry I'm late. I just let time get away. It's all ready though. I'll have it on the table in a few minutes. Patricia, isn't it your turn to set the table?" as the triplets came through the door.

"I thought someone was here with you." David wrinkled his forehead. "I was sure I heard voices as I came to the door. Was someone here, Rachel?"

"Well, you don't see anyone, do you? No one went out past you did they? And I don't see anyone hiding under the table."

"Well, you don't have to get so snappy," David returned. "If you don't want to tell me who visits you, I guess it isn't required, but what did you do with him?"

"*Him?* What do you mean *him?*" Rachel's voice rose higher. "There's no *him* been visiting me. What do you think I am anyway, a sneak?" Rachel was crying now.

"Rachel, Rachel, calm down," David soothed. "I didn't mean that. I – Oh, I don't know. I just thought someone was here. I'm sorry Rachel."

Rachel ran from the room, up the stairs, into her room and locked the door. The children were all gathered in the kitchen now. They looked from one to the other. "I think," said Darlene to David, "that you have hurt Rachel's feelings."

David said nothing but sat with his head in his hands.

"Well, aren't you going after her?" Billy Bob asked.

"I don't know what is best. Should I let her cry it out or should I go and see if I can make up? I've never had that experience with her before. I've never known her to act like that."

"Well, you were rather hard on her, accusing her of having a man in here," Glenda commented.

"Did I say that? I don't remember saying that."

Just at that inopportune time, the wind blew the pantry door open. David stepped over to close it and noticed the open window in the pantry. "Now who opened the pantry window?" he asked as he stepped to close it. Before the words were more than out of his mouth he noticed the crushed vines below the window. "Something is really wrong here," he said to himself. "I think we've got real problems."

David stepped back into the kitchen. "You kids go ahead and eat," he said. "Don't wait for me. I'm going up to talk to Rachel and I have no idea how long this will take."

By the time David knocked on Rachel's door she had already cried herself out. She sat up and blew her nose. "Come on in," she said.

"It's a little hard to do that with the door locked," David replied.

Rachel unlocked the door and the brother and sister stood looking at one another. Finally David spoke. "We need to talk this over, Rachel. You and I have never had secrets from each other except birthday secrets and it's hardly time for my birthday."

Rachel's reaction to that was a fresh burst of tears. David let her cry a few minutes, then put his arm around her and wiped her tears. "All right," he said, "tell big brother all about it."

"I'm so ashamed!" Rachel blurted. Then between sobs she told David the whole story.

David's desire was to laugh, but with difficulty he kept a straight face. "I don't see as you have done anything so dreadful, Rachel," he said. "While it is true, I don't really like the idea of someone outside the family doing the cooking when we can't afford to pay them, I don't see as it is a sin for you to dislike cooking, and the food *has* been really good lately."

"But can't you see, David? It's the deceit. All of the children know. I've been a bad example to them. I've actually been teaching them to be sneaks. Now they will think they can do whatever they please as long as they can keep it from you. Oh, I'm so ashamed!"

"Well, Rachel, do you suppose the children all think you are perfect? Infallible? As I see it the only thing to do is to go down and tell them you were wrong, that you have made a mistake. We'll all make it a matter of prayer in devotions tonight, then it will be behind us, not to be mentioned again. Then tomorrow you can tell Susan the secret is out and she doesn't need to go out the pantry window anymore."

"You mean she can keep on cooking here?" Rachel threw her arms around her brother and gave him a bear hug. "Oh, you marvelous, adorable, darling, lovely, considerate brother. No one else ever had such a good brother!"

XXVII

Rachel was putting the finishing touches on the birthday cake. It was a beautiful cake. Rachel had taken great pains to get it just right. She had made it in the form of a train with candles in the smokestack. She was thinking how they could get a picture just after the candles were blown out and the smoke would show in the picture.

Bradley came through the door, threw his lunchbox on the table and plopped down in a chair. "It's not fair!" he said.

Rachel sighed. "No, I suppose it isn't, whatever it is," she mused. "I've never heard that life was supposed to be fair, but what new obstacle has been placed in your pathway now, Little Brother?"

"Well, he said we would get a dog!"

"Did he ever say we wouldn't?" Rachel asked.

"No, but I told him about Marilyn Ellis' puppies and I thought he was gonna get one, but today Marilyn said about half of them were already gone and all the rest had been spoken for. I'm so mad I could just cry! Hey! That's a neat cake! Whose birthday is it?"

"Now Bradley, why don't you see if you can figure that out? Who usually has a birthday on September tenth?"

"September tenth? Is it September tenth today? Wow! You mean my birthday sneaked up on me and I didn't even hear it coming? Hey, it's my birthday!" as the other children came in from school. "What do you 'spose I'm gonna get?"

"Oh, maybe a corncob wrapped up in a box with a pretty pink ribbon tied on it," suggested Billy Bob.

"Or a new shirt to take the place of the one you tore at school today," offered Nathan.

"I think we will see when the time comes, won't we?" Rachel put in. "Now all of you change your clothes and get your work done so we can have the evening after supper to enjoy Bradley's birthday. Bradley, you give that shirt to Glenda so she can see if it is mendable. What happened anyway?"

"Oh, I can mend it," Glenda spoke up, "but I'm not sure but it will be too little. I'll have to take a bigger seam. Maybe it will have to go to Greg."

"I'm sorry about the shirt, Rachel," Bradley hesitated. "I guess I got in a fight."

"A fight? Bradley! You know you aren't supposed to fight."

"Yes, I know – but – but – Andy called me a bad name and said I was a coward if I didn't fight him. I told him names couldn't hurt me so he said our family was a pesilence to the community. I don't know what a pesilence is, but I know it's bad 'cause of the way he said it. I told him he better shut up or I'd be c'pelled to hold up the diggity of the family and he said our family didn't have any diggity. I guess I could have took that, too, if he hadn't said what he did about our Mother. He said her husband left 'cause she bossed him all the time and then after he left she was too lazy to wash the lice off of her and they ate her 'til she died. Did our Mother ever have a husband, Rachel?"

"Yes, Bradley, Mother had a husband, but he was gone before Andy was born. Mother may have worked herself to death, but she certainly didn't die from laziness. You shouldn't let kids rile you up so, Bradley."

Bradley hung his head. Then he grinned. "I didn't tear his shirt, but he's sure got a pretty black eye. I don't think he'll be makin' 'marks about my family again soon."

Happy Birthday to you, Happy Birthday to you,
Happy Birthday, Dear Bradley, Happy Birthday to you.

Letitia looked all around. "Don't we get birthday presents anymore?" she asked. "I see a cake and I see some ice cream, but I don't see any present."

Bradley looked up and spoke confidently, "It's all right,

Letitia. Remember last year I only got a new shirt that Glenda made and a slingshot that David made 'cause we had to pay the taxes. David said nice birthday presents don't have to be something you buy, and I guess he's right 'cause I really like my slingshot, but I guess we had to pay the taxes again this year and maybe he didn't have time to make me anything. Anyway, I didn't get anything. I really like my train, though, but we're gonna eat that so I can't keep it."

"Yes, we are going to eat the train right now," declared Rachel. "Then we will see if David has some kind of present. We can't have a birthday without a present. Didn't you get anything for Bradley, David?"

David scratched his head. "Well, I didn't make him anything and I can't remember buying him anything, but there must be something around here that he would like. I'll have to look after I am finished here."

When the last crumb of cake and the last bit of ice cream were gone, David left the table. He was soon back with a shoe box, tied with a red ribbon which he handed to Bradley. "Here," he said, "maybe you will like this."

"It moves!" exclaimed Bradley. He lost no time in untying the ribbon and bringing forth a fuzzy brown puppy with a white collar. "Oh, he is so cute! Did you get him from Marilyn Ellis?"

The puppy washed Bradley's hands and then

immediately started on his face. Gregory reached over to stroke him. The puppy gave one lick to Greg's hand and then resumed his job of washing Bradley's face.

"It looks like he already knows his master," declared David. "What will you name him, Bradley?"

"Mister!" announced Bradley. "His mommy's name is Missie so shouldn't he be Mister?"

The remainder of the evening was spent with the other children trying to get Mister's attention, but he had eyes for only Bradley."

When Rachel went in to check on the boys before going to bed, she noticed an odd bump under the blanket of Bradley's bed, which turned out to be Mister. She called David.

"What shall we do, David?" she asked. "We really shouldn't let him sleep with Mister."

"I'll make a bed for him in the basement," David replied.

Rachel awoke suddenly from a sound sleep with the feeling that someone was in her room. She opened her mouth to scream just as Gregory spoke. "I can't find Brad, Rachel. I think he must have runned away."

"Oh, I don't think Bradley would run away," Rachel replied. "He's around somewhere. I'll get up and look."

As she came out of her room, she met David. "What's

up?" he asked.

"Oh, Gregory says Bradley is gone. I just got up to find him."

A search of the bedroom revealed no Bradley. Nathan and Darlene heard the commotion and got up to help. They broadened the search to all the other bedrooms. No Bradley!

"Maybe he went downstairs," suggested Nathan, but a search of the downstairs went unrewarded. Rachel started to cry.

"Now wait, Sis," David said. "He's got to be here somewhere. I've checked all the outside doors and they still have the night locks on. He couldn't have gone outside, so he has to be inside. You and Darlene go back upstairs. Check every window and look in every place big enough to hold an eight-year-old boy. Nate and I will do the downstairs. He's got to be here somewhere."

Fifteen minutes later, David and Nathan met in the kitchen. "I don't understand it," David said. "There's no way he could have gotten out. We've checked all the windows and –"

"David, do you see what I see?" Nathan interrupted. "The basement door is unlocked." David switched on the light and took the basement stairs two at a time. There on the floor asleep on an old rug and covered with a coat, was Bradley with a furry brown bundle in his arms.

"One, two, three, four, five, six, seven, eight, nine, ten." David sighed and sat down on the basement stairs.

"What's that supposed to mean?" Nathan asked.

"Mother used to say at moments of crisis when you are afraid of saying or doing the wrong thing, to count to ten. I don't see as it helped me any. I don't know how to handle this. What would you do, Nate? You're pretty level-headed."

"Well, I won't be the man of the house here until after you and Stacey get married, but I —"

"Then you will never be the man of the house here. But go on. What would you do?"

"Why, I think I'd carry him back to his bed and take Mister's bed along and put it in his room."

"I don't think I should approve the dog sleeping in his room, but bring him along." David picked up the sleeping Bradley who awoke instantly.

"Mister was crying," he said. "He was afraid down here by himself. I just came down here to keep him from being afraid."

XXVIII

The snow started in the early afternoon; great big lazy looking flakes floating slowly down to earth to settle on the green grass. Rachel, standing at the kitchen window watching, devoured the beauty while thinking that November tenth was a little early for snow. She watched as the snow settled on the pansies, the chrysanthemums, and the shrubs. She swallowed. Oh, how it hurt! The snow was coming faster now. If it kept on at this rate, the ground would soon be covered. Rachel did hope it wouldn't last. A snowstorm always made more work. Dirty floors, wet clothes, and she was so tired. She sat down in a chair, leaned back and closed her eyes. Rachel was almost alone in the house. Sue Ellen was taking one of her rare afternoon naps. Gregory was out somewhere with David and Uncle Pete, and all the others were in school. Rachel knew she should be baking Billy Bob's birthday cake, but her head hurt.

A knock on the door roused Rachel from her lethargy.

She opened it to admit Susan Ford, wearing a wide smile underneath a mop of freshly cut blond curls. "Oh, I've got the most fabulous idea!" she gushed.

With difficulty, Rachel managed an answering smile. "Come on in, sit down and tell me about it," she said.

As she made her way back to her chair, Rachel had the sensation of riding in a boat. She wondered if the earth had gone crazy and was really rocking, but Susan didn't seem to be noticing it.

"Oh, this is a jim-dandy idea!" Susan bubbled. "Melvin Campbell called me a while ago."

"Who is Melvin Campbell?" Rachel asked.

"Oh, you know! Melvin and Marvin Campbell, twin sons of *the* Campbell's, Campbell's Drug Store. I met them at Felicia Jordan's birthday party and Melvin and I got real chummy."

"I've heard of them, but I have never met them. Go on."

"Well, Melvin wanted me to get another girl and the four of us could go out together."

"Nothing doing!"

"Why?"

"Lots of reasons. First of all I don't date, but if I did I wouldn't blind date."

"Oh, come on, Rachel. Be a good sport. It isn't exactly a blind date. I know both the boys, that is I've met Marvin,

231

or anyway, I've seen him."

"Susan, you know one of the first things my mother ever taught me was the meaning of 'No.' If she said 'No' she meant 'No.' If she said 'maybe' or 'I don't know' or 'I'll think about it' then we could beg, but 'No' was indisputably final, a closed subject and not even open for discussion. Now I am saying, 'No!'"

"Well, that is that! I tried. Now, I can't go either."

"Why?"

"Well, I was going to tell Dad you were going and wanted me to go with you."

"Susan! You wouldn't!"

"Why not? It wouldn't exactly be a lie. If you were going you would want me to go, wouldn't you?"

Rachel pondered this a few minutes before answering. Her head ached so much thinking was difficult. She actually wished Susan would go home. Finally she spoke. "I just don't understand you, Susan. Since I've known you, you have dated at least seven boys. What does Tony think of you dating all these guys?"

"Tony?"

"Yes, Tony! The day I met you, you led me to believe you were madly in love with Tony. I've been hearing of Tony's virtues and his manly beauty every time we've been together from that time until now. I *thought* you were probably planning to marry Tony. He really must be *some guy* if he is willing to put up with this."

"Rachel, Tony is –" Susan stopped and a slow smile spread over her face. "I just had never realized you expected me to marry Tony. Now that you mention him, that is one of the things I came over to talk about. Tony will be here in a couple of weeks. You'll get to see what a really fabulous guy he is. We are going after him. We will be leaving as soon as Annabelle gets out of school tomorrow and we will be gone two weeks. We are going to visit some aunts, uncles, and cousins, then bring Tony back here for a week. Do you think you can manage the cooking after tonight until I get back?"

"I managed it before you came."

"Rachel, really, is something wrong? I never knew you to be so disagreeable."

"Sorry! I'm just feeling disagreeable, I suppose."

At that moment the telephone rang. It was Mrs. Ford. The snow, she said, was predicted to get deep. They had decided to get Annabelle from school and leave immediately as going west they would soon drive out of the storm. If they waited another day they might become snowbound at home.

Susan left in a whirl of excitement, apologizing for having to leave the supper to Rachel. Rachel leaned her head back and closed her eyes. She really felt sick. "Supper!" she thought. "How can I get supper? And I have to bake

Billy Bob a birthday cake. How can I? Vegetable soup. Mother often made vegetable soup in stormy weather."

Rachel pushed herself up from her chair and by holding to things, managed to go to the freezer for a package of boiling beef. She put it in a kettle and put it on the stove. "Plenty of water," she told herself. "Remember, plenty of water." After she had added the water, Rachel made her way back to her chair. "I'll just lean back and rest awhile. Then when the beef gets to boiling, I will get up and put in the vegetables and bake the cake."

It seemed the house was getting dark. Rachel closed her eyes. The world was still rocking and she was cold – so cold!

Sue Ellen awoke. "Wachel!" she called. But Rachel didn't answer. She crawled over the side of her crib, dropped to the floor and ran downstairs.

David leaned on his pitchfork and listened. "What is it, David?" Pete asked.

"I thought I heard the gate. The kids can't be home from school yet."

"I'll see," Pete answered as he stepped through the barn door. He was soon back holding Sue Ellen by the hand. She wore no hat and her hair was sprinkled with snow. Her light jacket was unbuttoned and on upside down.

"Sue Ellen!" David exploded. "What are you doing

out here? Does Rachel know you are out here?"

"Wachel won't wake up. Her's asweep," the little girl replied, "Her's awful hot."

David dropped his pitchfork and his face went white. Rachel might be – but no! If "her's awful hot" she wouldn't be dead. He picked up Sue Ellen and ran toward the house calling over his shoulder. "Uncle Pete, look after Greg. He's out somewhere playing with Mister."

Rachel opened her eyes and looked directly into the kind eyes of Dr. Gillard. "What's wrong?" she asked.

"You're sick," the Doctor answered, taking Rachel's wrist to feel her pulse.

"Oh, sick," Rachel said, and closed her eyes again.

The doctor straightened up and looked at David. "That's a relief!" he said. "The last three days there have been many moments when I have wondered if we would win this battle. With this strain of flu, there are many who just don't make it. Good clean living and a healthy diet always helps, though. She may sleep another long time before she wakes again, but I feel confident now that she is going to be all right. Just keep on taking good care of her and I'll see you again tomorrow. You sure you don't need me to send a nurse?"

"No nurse!" David answered. "My sister is taking good care of her. Glenda has taken a leave of absence from school. Her grades will allow it. She really has surprised me with her abilities. She can run this house just as well as Rachel. She is doing it and taking care of Rachel, besides. Of course the others help after school, but Glenda won't let one of them miss a day of school, nor will she let any of them in Rachel's room except me. I just wouldn't have believed Glenda could do it. We have always depended on Rachel."

"I'll tell you, David," the doctor said. "I think sometimes these things have to happen to give someone else a chance."

"Glenda never seemed to want a chance before."

"Did anyone ever ask her?"

Dr. Gillard heard a movement behind him and turned to see Rachel turning her head from side to side and mumbling something. He bent his head to listen. "Got to put vegetables in the soup and make Billy Bob's birthday cake," She muttered.

"It's all right, Rachel," Dr. Gillard said. "Glenda will take care of that."

"Got to put the vegetables in the soup and make Billy Bob's birthday cake."

"When is Billy Bob's birthday?" the doctor asked.

"It was Thursday, the day Rachel took sick. Glenda put the vegetables in the soup, but I am afraid Billy Bob's birthday was totally forgotten."

"For three days now, I have wanted her to wake up. Now I hope she will sleep. I may have to give her a shot to calm her."

"Got to put the vegetables in the soup and make Billy Bob's birthday cake."

XXIX

Rachel opened her eyes and looked about the room. The sun was shining and Rachel knew it was well past time to get up and fix breakfast. She was well. Why should they keep her in bed any longer? She sat up and slipped her feet out of bed and to the floor. The room seemed to be turning around. She closed her eyes a moment. Why did she still feel so weak? Presently she lay down again. "Just for a minute," she told herself.

Darlene tiptoed into the room and seeing Rachel awake said, "Good morning, Big Sister. How are you feeling today?"

"Oh, I'm feeling fine except I'm so weak and the room seems to move when I sit up. I do want to get up though. Will you help me, Darlene?"

"I don't think I should; not until the doctor says you can."

"Darlene, I'm well now. I've been well for a week. I'm just weak and I can't get stronger lying in bed. Why won't they let me get up?"

"Rachel, you have been awfully sick. We thought you were going to die. Pastor Parker called for volunteers to fast and pray. Enough people volunteered that he formed a prayer chain. For five days there was someone in the church all the time, day and night, praying for you. Almost the whole church fasted one or two or three days."

"How long have I been sick?" Rachel asked.

"Almost three weeks. You took sick on Thursday, two weeks before Thanksgiving."

"I don't remember anything except the last few days. I've wanted to get up and bake Billy Bob's birthday cake and it just felt like something heavy was holding me down. Tell me all about it."

"For the first two weeks you slept almost all the time. If you woke up you just mumbled, 'Got to put the vegetables in the soup and make Billy Bob's birthday cake.' Glenda wouldn't let anyone in the room except Pastor Parker, David, and the doctor. She's awfully bossy when she's in charge, but she did the best she could. She didn't want any of the rest of us to get sick, so she took all the care of you herself."

"All I remember of that time is I wanted to sleep and Glenda came in every fifteen minutes or so to change the sheets on the bed. Did she really do that or did I dream it?"

"She did have to change the sheets often because you perspired so much you would have them wet in a couple of hours, but it wasn't every fifteen minutes."

"Well, go on. Tell the rest."

"After the fever left, she let us come in sometimes one at a time, but you never wanted to talk much until today. Some of the church ladies have been here, but Glenda hasn't let anyone in except Sis. Parker. She is afraid too much company will tire you and I had better get out before she realizes how long I have been in here."

Darlene met Dr. Gillard at the door of Rachel's room. She stayed to hear what he had to say.

"Well, good-morning! I see you are awake and alert. How do you feel?"

"I feel like I have been in this bed about six months. I have been pampered and petted and babied and coddled far too long. I want to get up!"

"You don't need to push yourself, Rachel. As sick as you have been, you will need to take it pretty easy for a while. A backset could easily put you right back where you were."

"Well, I won't take a backset. When can I get up?"

"Rachel, you know how you feel better than anyone else. Sit up as much as you want, but if the room seems to be moving, then lie down again. When you feel like you can stand, try it, but don't push yourself."

The next afternoon Rachel was sitting up when Susan came to visit. "Oh, I'm so happy you are better," she squealed. "When we got home and Glenda said you were so sick, I felt really bad because I had left you that day. I realize now that you were sick then. I should have stayed with you, but we really had a marvelous trip. It's been awful since we got home and I couldn't bring Tony over to show him off. Are you possibly well enough to see him? He has to leave the day after tomorrow."

"Why, I guess so. Suppose you bring him over after supper tomorrow evening. I think I can be up and going by then."

Susan smiled. "Glenda and I have been talking. She said you folks hadn't had Thanksgiving dinner yet. We thought maybe we could fix it together tomorrow. David said it was all right if she invited Tony and me to come."

"David actually agreed to let you eat a meal here?"

"Yes, I suppose he thinks it is safe with Tony along. He still doesn't realize that Tony is my brother."

"Tony is – your brother?"

"Yes, of course. You didn't suppose that if I had a fabulous guy like Tony for a boyfriend that I would look twice at any of these other guys, did you?"

"I just thought –"

"Oh, of course I know what you thought and it was lots of fun letting you think it, but I decided I had better tell you the truth."

David and Tony were immediate friends. The dinner and visiting time afterward were a complete success. Tony talked much of the difference in Annabelle and David explained to him the plan of salvation. Tony went back to college unconvinced, but with lots of things to think about.

By the middle of December, Rachel was back in the kitchen and Glenda was back in school. It was just after family devotions on Thursday evening that David brought up the subject of Glenda.

"I guess I really haven't expressed my feelings to you, Glenda," he said, "about the superb job you did of managing the house while Rachel was so sick. I want you to know that I am very pleased with you."

"Does that mean that I'm grown-up?" Glenda asked.

"I don't know as it has aged you any. You're still only sixteen, right?"

"I'll be seventeen in March. You know Mother always said being grown-up wasn't a matter of years. Wasn't the food as good as Rachel cooks?"

"Yes."

"I even made a pumpkin pie and didn't leave the sugar out."

"You would bring that up," Rachel put in.

"And didn't I keep the house clean?" Glenda continued

her conversation with David.

"Yes, but —"

"And did you ever see Sue Ellen running around dirty or with her hair not combed?"

"No. I realize, Glenda, that you did a very good job. What are you asking anyway?"

"I think," Darlene spoke up, "that she might be wondering if you consider her old enough to have a boyfriend."

"Is that it, Glenda?" David asked.

Glenda nodded.

"Got anyone in mind?"

Glenda smiled then, a really sweet smile. "Oh, yes," she said. "I've had somebody in mind for years and years."

"I didn't know it."

"You weren't supposed to know it. I was just asking if I was grown-up enough to let you know it."

"Well, who is he?"

Glenda hesitated a while before she raised her eyes and looked directly at David. "Don't you think it might be a little awkward to let that be known before he is ready to let it be known? What if word got to him that I had mentioned it?"

"I suppose you are right. I will just have to be a little more observant, but please, Glenda, promise you won't elope or anything."

"I have no intention of doing anything so stupid and even if I was that crazy, I'm sure he isn't. You will have plenty of time to adjust to the idea. After all, as you say, I'm only sixteen, but thanks a lot, Big Brother, for your permission."

"I really wasn't aware that I had given any permission," David said.

"Well, David," spoke up Rachel, "of course you are the head of the house, but you know that *is* what Mother said. Glenda is a good girl and won't let us down."

"I suppose you are right, as usual, Rachel. All right, Glenda, you have my permission. Just let me know who he is before it gets too serious."

XXX

The rest of the winter passed without mishap. It was a cold winter with lots of snow. The boys were kept busy shoveling snow and keeping the stock fed and watered. Sue Ellen fussed continually about being cooped up in the house, but the weather was too nasty to let her out.

David and Rachel thanked God daily for a car, as without one they knew they would be staying home from church week after week. As it was, David had to take the children to school and get them. Times when the snow fell in the night and the snowplow didn't go by early they simply had to stay home.

David worried about Pete alone in his palace, as his cough seemed to be getting worse; but the palace was well insulated and Pete said he was snug as a bug in a rug.

It was late March before the warm south wind blew the cold back up north where it belongs and little patches of earth began to show. Rachel bundled Sue Ellen up and took her outside to show her the crocus blooms.

"Come and see Scarlett's new calves," David called to her.

"Calves?"

"Yes, I said calves, with an 's' on the end. Plural form of calf, you know. Ever hear of the word? Maybe you would understand better if I said twins."

"Twins! I can't believe it! Twin calves? I never heard of it before."

"Oh, it happens once in every several thousand births or maybe it is once in several hundred thousand. I don't know the exact statistics, but I know it is rare. You know, Rachel, God really is very good to us."

"Of course!" Rachel answered. "He knows we are here doing our best without Father or Mother to guide us so he is just being extra specially good to us."

"I just hope he continues to be extra specially good to us as the children grow up to marriageable age," David said. "That part really worries me. Marriage is so final and it is so easy to make a lifelong mistake. Do you have any idea whom Glenda has her eye on?"

"Of course! Do you mean you don't know?"

"I haven't the faintest idea. Want to tell me?"

"No, but I'll tell you he is all right. You don't have to worry."

"Please pass the potatoes, Glenda – Glenda, I'd like

some potatoes – Glenda! Glenda! *Glenda*! Would you *please* pass the potatoes?"

"Oh, I'm sorry. I guess I wasn't listening."

"What can be on your mind to keep you in such deep concentration?"

"Maybe she was thinking about him."

"She probably flunked her math test!"

"Glenda never flunked a test in her life!"

"She has a history test tomorrow. Maybe she is worried about this being a first."

"No, you are all wrong," Glenda contended. "I do have a history test tomorrow, but I'm not worried about it. I was just wondering if it would be all right with God for me to go to the senior class party. I don't want to do anything wrong, but I just can't see that it would be wrong."

"Isn't there drinking and dancing?" Rachel asked.

"No drinking. It isn't allowed. There will be dancing, but it will be in a separate room from the rest of the party. I wouldn't need to go in there at all."

"What will the rest of the party be?" David wanted to know.

"Oh, eating and some speeches and the class prophecy. You know – what they think will happen to all the seniors. Maybe those of us who don't dance will play some games. There really are quite a lot of kids who don't dance."

"Who is taking you?" David asked.

"I thought maybe you would, since you don't like me to have the car out alone at night."

"Me? I'm not a senior in that school. To go to the senior class party you have to go with a senior in that school."

"Not if you *are* a senior!"

"But you are not a senior. According to my calculations, you won't be a senior until next term."

"Your calculations are faulty, Big Brother," Glenda said. "I have worked hard for three years to be able to graduate this year instead of having to go another year and just today I found out I am going to make it."

"Well, congratulations! Of course you can go to the party if you think it is an all right place for a Christian to be," David assured her.

"But I will need a new dress," Glenda said.

"You can have it. You certainly deserve it. Three of them if you want them. After all you are this family's first graduate. Let's see, you'll need a new dress for the party, one for the graduation, one for – what else is there, anyway?"

"The prom, but I'm not going to that, and I don't need a new dress for graduation. I will be wearing a gown that will cover whatever dress I wear anyway."

David shook his head. "I just can't believe it! Glenda graduating at seventeen! What do you plan to do afterward? Do you plan to get a job or just stay home?"

"What do you think I should do, David?"

"Of course the decision is yours, but unless you feel you are missing important things by not having more money, I'd rather you would just stay home, especially if you plan to marry. I never liked the idea of wives and mothers working, but those girls who don't plan to marry should, of course, be prepared to support themselves in case it becomes necessary. Would you like more schooling? If there is something more you would especially like to study we might be able to afford to give you a year or two of Tech."

"Absolutely not! No more schooling. I'd really like to just stay home, but I'll be needing money for – things a little later, perhaps."

"I understand. We are doing well now and I don't think you need worry about that. We will take care of that when the time comes."

XXXI

Rachel opened her eyes, yawned and stretched. Suddenly she realized that the alarm clock hadn't awakened her. She turned to see her bedside clock just as the old grandfather clock downstairs started to strike. One, two, three, four, five, six. "Oh my!" she thought, "the boys will soon be in from doing chores and I don't have the breakfast even started. She jumped up and reached for her slippers before she remembered.

At the work assignment time last night, it had been agreed that Glenda and Darlene would each fix breakfast two mornings a week. Except for when she was sick, it was the first time in over two years that Rachel had not set her alarm before going to bed. Never one to be able to awaken from habit, she had dutifully wound the clock and set the alarm every night until last night. Now she lay back again and closed her eyes. How nice to have time to awaken slowly. She lay a few more minutes and then got up.

After a quick shower, Rachel chose one of her better

dresses. "If I am going to be a lady of leisure, I might as well look the part," she said to herself. "I can always change when breakfast is over and my real workday starts." She arranged her hair more carefully than usual and applied just a mite of perfume. Then she thought ahead to what must be accomplished today.

Glenda's graduation would be at 1:00, with a party afterward, at 4:00. The party had been David's idea. Actually, it was an open house. All the church folks would be stopping by as well as most of Glenda's classmates. Of course there would be other parties, so her classmates wouldn't stay long here, but she expected the church youth group to be here all the evening. Rachel shook her head. David was proud of Glenda. That was easy to see. She remembered back to Glenda's sixteenth birthday and how David had hated the whole thing. Now just over a year later he had suggested a party, taken Glenda to town and paid a fabulous price for material for her dress, and even offered to hire someone to come in and help for the day if Rachel thought the work would be more than she and the other girls could handle. Of course Rachel had declined the hired help, saying that Darlene and the triplets would be getting out of school at noon and Susan was coming over to help for the whole day.

Thinking back over the past two years, Rachel smiled to herself. They sure had had some stormy moments, but as of today, the first one of her younger siblings would be officially grown-up. Oh, of course she wouldn't be of age until next March, but it was generally considered anyone who had graduated was an adult. Well, if that was what it took, she, Rachel, would probably never be an adult. David had suggested several times that she try to finish her schooling, saying she knew it was Mother's desire for all of them to graduate, but she felt if folks know what happens on earth after they are gone, that Mother would agree with her.

David himself had finished his high school course and taken the final exams. He was now awaiting the results of those exams. Neither he nor Rachel had any doubt that he had passed and Rachel had suggested that the party be for both Glenda and him, but David had replied that he didn't wish to make a public announcement of the fact that he was nineteen years old before he graduated from high school.

Rachel descended the stairs and entered the kitchen just as her brothers came in from doing chores.

"Good morning, Beautiful Sister," David greeted her. Glenda continued to dish up the breakfast.

"I think your brother is speaking to you, Glenda," Rachel said.

"And I think he was speaking to you," Glenda retorted.

"Well, everyone knows you are more beautiful than I, so I still think he was speaking to you."

"And I think he was speaking to you!" said a masculine voice from the doorway. Rachel turned to see Tony Ford framed in the doorway with Susan's laughing brown eyes looking over his shoulder.

"Come in, come in! You're just in time for breakfast," was David's hearty welcome.

"No, thank you. We've had breakfast," Susan replied. "We can't stay. Tony got in late last night. Dad is taking him off to Springfield this morning, but we wanted to surprise you."

"It is a surprise. We thought you wouldn't be home until next week." David answered.

"I rushed things a bit. I'll have to go back for graduation, but I couldn't miss the party. I thought it wasn't until 4:00. Am I wrong? Rachel looks as if she is ready for it now."

Rachel blushed and tried to explain, but Tony interrupted. "That's all right, Rachel. You don't need to explain. In a scrub dress you would still be the most beautiful girl on earth, but we've got to run if we make it back in time for the party. See you –"

"I'll be back before an hour is up," Susan called as they turned to go.

"Careful with the flowery speech, Tony," David called after him. "Rachel is almost spoken for."

Rachel put her hands on her hips. "Now what do you mean by *that?*" she demanded.

"Oh, nothing," David said. "Let's eat."

XXXII

V'room, put, put, put. V'room! Put, put, put.

"Isn't it a beautiful day?" Susan mused as she arranged flowers on the dining room table.

"Just perfect!" Rachel answered. "I hate to be proud, but didn't you think Glenda was the prettiest girl in the class?"

"Of course! Everyone knows Glenda is beautiful, but I still like you best. You're beautiful, too, and also nice."

"Are you saying Glenda isn't nice?" Rachel asked.

"No, but you are my friend."

V'room! Put, put, put. V'room! Put, put, put.

"What's that I keep hearing?" Rachel cocked her head to one side and listened.

"It sounds like a motorcycle and I think it is coming here," Susan answered. "Do any of your friends own a motorcycle?"

"Not that I am aware of," answered Rachel as she went to the window and pushed back the curtain. "Yes," she said, "it is coming here and the family is forming a welcoming committee."

"Let's join them and see who it is," Susan suggested.

"No way!" Rachel answered, "I'm not that bold."

"Oh, come on. It's likely someone you know, maybe one of the boys in your church youth group. Come on! I want to see who it is."

Just at that moment the motorcyclist stepped off his machine and pulled off his helmet.

"It looks like – it IS. It's Paul!" Rachel couldn't keep the excitement from her voice. I wonder if he'd let David give me a ride. I've always wanted to ride one of those things. Come on!"

"Not me! I'm scared to death of those things," Susan said, but she let Rachel pull her outside.

"Hi, Paul," Rachel greeted him. "Is it yours?"

"All mine!" Paul answered. "I thought I'd come out and show it off. Anybody want a ride?"

"I do!" "I do!" "Take me!" I want to!" "Let me ride!" A chorus of voices answered Paul's question.

"I'll tell you what," Paul decided. "Let me give you all a ride, starting with the youngest first. Want a ride, Sue Ellen?"

Sue Ellen stepped back a couple of steps and shook her head.

"How about you?" Paul asked Gregory.

"Can I, David?" Gregory asked.

"May I," Rachel corrected.

"May I, David?"

"I guess so," David answered. "I'm a little afraid of those things myself, but I guess Paul knows how to handle it."

Paul lifted Gregory to the seat behind him and said, "Put your arms tight around me and hang on. Here we go!"

"May we ride it?" asked Alicia.

"What do you think, David?" Rachel asked. "Are you going to let the girls ride?"

"I don't see why not." David answered. "Paul is trusty and he is almost family. Are you going to ride, Rachel?"

"Not unless he lets you take me," Rachel said.

"I wouldn't feel qualified to handle it," David replied. "It would be all right, you know, if you want to ride with Paul."

Paul returned with Gregory and picked up Bradley. "I want a long ride," Bradley demanded.

"No, don't take a long ride," Billy Bob said. "Then it would be too long before my turn."

"I'll have to change," Glenda mumbled.

"What!" David replied, shocked. "You weren't thinking of riding it, were you?"

"Yes," Glenda answered, "I had intended to when my

257

turn comes. Why shouldn't I?"

"Because you can't! That's why! I thought you had better sense! Don't you have any scruples at all?"

Glenda faced him with an angry countenance. "Yes, I have scruples. You said Rachel could. You said it was all right. Now *why* is it all right for *her*, but if *I* want to do it *I* have no scruples. Isn't it important for Rachel to have scruples?" Glenda was shouting now.

David lowered his voice, a sure sign that he was angry. "That's different and you know it is."

"Sure it's different! I know it's different. That's Rachel and I'm Glenda! You said I could have a 'friend.' Is it so wrong for me to take a little motorcycle ride with a friend? Why can't I have Paul for a friend?"

"Glenda! I didn't think you could stoop so low. You'd do that to your sister? You little – a – a – BRAT! You SNEAK! Go to your room!"

"But –"

"I said GO! NOW!"

Glenda turned and ran toward the house, tears streaming down her face and falling on her beautiful dress. Rachel and Susan turned to follow her just as Paul arrived back with Bradley to pick up a triplet.

"I think I had best disappear," Susan suggested.

Rachel nodded.

"What's the problem?" Paul asked.

"Oh, just a little family misunderstanding," David replied. "Nothing you need bother your head about."

"But aren't the others going to ride?" Paul asked. "I had especially wanted to take Glenda. Rachel and Susan can ride too, if they want."

"You especially wanted to take Glenda?"

"Yes, I like her. Isn't that all right?"

"No, that is certainly NOT all right! You are as bad as Glenda. Now you take your motorcycle and GO before you do any more damage."

"But, David," Paul protested, "what has happened? Why are you doing this to me? You told me I could come. What have I done wrong?"

"Done wrong? Plenty, if you are a party to Glenda's attitude and feelings. You are a dirty double-crosser! Now I said 'GO,' and I mean 'GO,' and *don't come back!*"

Paul straddled his motorcycle and went slowly down the driveway. Halfway to the road he stopped and shut off his engine. Turning his head toward David he called. "David,"

"Yes," David answered.

"When you realize you need to apologize, it won't be necessary. I've already forgiven you. All you need to do is call me and say, 'You can come back now.'" Paul restarted his engine and went on toward home.

Rachel, in Glenda's room was trying to console her,

but Glenda's sobs overcame everything Rachel attempted to say. "Don't cry, Sister. It's going to be all right. David doesn't understand. Don't cry. You're ruining your dress. Everything will be all right when David understands."

"He t-t-t-told me I could! He called me a s-s-s-sneak! I'm n-n-not a s-s-s-sneak, Rachel. He t-t-t-told me I could."

"Yes, I know. It will be all right. David doesn't understand."

"W-w-why? H-h-how can I m-m-make him understand? D-d-d-doesn't he l-l-l-like Paul?"

Rachel got a washcloth from the bathroom and wiped Glenda's face. "Now sit up and listen to me," she commanded. "I want to talk to you. You wouldn't tell David whom you liked. Remember?"

Glenda nodded. "Yes, but it's Paul. It's always been Paul, ever since we first went to that church when I was six years old. Every time I looked around, Paul was looking at me. Then after church he walked by me and untied my hair ribbon. We've liked each other ever since — at least I've liked him and I think he likes me."

"But David thinks Paul likes *me*." Rachel tried to drop her bombshell gently.

"*You*! Oh, no! He doesn't. I know he doesn't. Oh, Rachel! You're not in love with Paul, are you? Please tell me you're not. I'd just die! There just wouldn't be anything left for me to do but die. This has got to be the worst day of my life." Her sobs brought a fresh torrent of tears.

"Now come on, Glenda, Don't cry. This is your graduation day. This truly can be the best day of your life. You've just got to make David understand. No, I'm not in love with Paul. I truly like Paul a lot. I think he is a great guy, but only as a brother in the Lord and a future brother in the family."

"Oh, thank you, Rachel!" Glenda jumped up and threw her arms around Rachel. "Will you talk to David?" she pleaded. "Will you try to make him understand?"

"Yes," Rachel assured her. "I will talk to him, but you've got to get rid of those tears and change your dress. You've ruined your beautiful dress. Now you will have to wear something else for the party."

"Oh, I will wash this out. It will dry on a nice day like this in half an hour and be good as new. It is that kind of material. That is why I let David pay such a price for it."

Rachel found David with his head on his arms at the kitchen table. "David," she said, "we need to talk."

David raised his head and Rachel saw there were tears in his eyes. "Oh, Rachel," he said, "Why does life have to be so complicated? Why couldn't Glenda have had a father and a mother to bring her up right? Big brothers and big sisters are all right in their places, but it is not their place to bring up children. We've made a mess of it, Rachel. I knew we had made mistakes, but I didn't realize we were doing so bad as to have the oldest one turn out like that."

"What is wrong with Glenda, David?" Rachel asked.

"What's wrong with her!" David exploded. "Everything's wrong with her! She's a lying, deceiving, sneak. Any girl that would stoop so low as —"

"Whoa! Wait a minute! Let's go at this one thing at a time before you say a lot of things you will be sorry for afterward. She's a lying, deceiving, sneak? Just what has she lied about, how and who has she deceived and what has she done that makes you call her a sneak?"

"Well, she deceived me! She let me think she had a friend I would approve of. She said —"

"And just why don't you approve of Paul?"

"Paul? He's as bad as she is. He told me he was interested in you. He never said one word about Glenda. Any girl that would do that to her sister isn't fit to be called a sister."

"David," Rachel said, pulling out a chair to sit beside him. "I think this is all a big misunderstanding. I don't believe Paul is, ever was, or ever will be interested in me."

"He said he was."

"Well, he has never in any way let me get any idea of it and even if he is, I'm not interested in him."

"You said you were!"

"I'm sorry, Big Brother, to have to say it this way, but

I did not!"

"A long time ago, when I found out Franklin was interested in you —"

"Franklin! Oh, no!" Rachel groaned. "I thought he was going with Stacey Crowlman."

"He is now, but a year or two ago it was you."

"I'm glad I didn't know that, but go on. What about Paul?"

"I asked you whom you liked, to see if you liked Franklin and you said you liked Paul."

Rachel thought back. She vaguely remembered David questioning her, but she knew she had never said anything about liking Paul. "David," she said, "my memory isn't that good. I don't remember exactly what I said, but I do know I never said I liked Paul that way. I have always admired Paul. I may have said I liked him as a person, may even have said he was the nicest guy in our youth group. Isn't that what we want for Glenda? David, I've told you numerous times I do not intend to marry — ever! At least not until Sue Ellen is grown and by that time I will be an old maid so set in my ways no one will want me.

"Now, it is getting late," Rachel went on. "We've got a party. Get on the phone and call Paul and get this thing settled. It's ruining Glenda's graduation day. She's a good girl, David. She is not a liar, a deceiver, or a sneak. She's just a young girl in love. She's too young, yes, I know that, but Mother told me she expected her to marry young. She may have known about Paul. Mothers usually do."

"But Paul said –"

"Shhh!" Rachel admonished. "You'd better talk to Paul and see what he said. You're likely as mixed up on that as you were on what I said. Now call Paul and talk to him, but first let me call Susan and get some help. I'm running late."

"I think I will talk to Glenda, first," David decided, turning toward the stairs.

Ten minutes later, David re-appeared accompanied by Glenda. She wore a smile and the traces of her recent tears were almost gone. "David wants me to go with him to talk to Paul," She said. Then she whispered to Rachel, "I've got a really, really nice big brother."

XXXIII

"Is there any of that delicious fruit drink left from the party?" David asked as he pushed his chair back from the table after winning his fourth game of checkers with Paul. "I seem to have eaten too many chips and this guy has suddenly forgotten how to play checkers. He used to be a challenge, but tonight he is no fun at all."

"I would think just getting engaged would put a lot on your mind," Tony interjected. "That was a surprise! I had no idea. How long have you been in love, anyway?"

"Oh, about ten years," Paul answered. "I noticed her the first time I saw her, those big blue eyes staring at me under that mop of brown curls. I couldn't help but watch her, but I didn't exactly fall in love with her until the next time I saw her. I had planned to chase her with a little frog I had found, but she said, 'Oh, how cute! May I hold it?' I fell in love right then and I've never considered another girl since."

"I knew you and Glenda liked each other, but I didn't

suppose it would happen so soon," Susan remarked.

"Actually, I hadn't planned it to happen so soon. It was just that circumstances warranted it. Glenda can't marry until she is eighteen next March, and I hate long engagements. Besides I have agreed to go to work for Darver Aviation in Chicago to get the experience I need to be top mechanic at the airport here. I feel that will take me about eight months. An eight month separation when you've just gotten engaged isn't my idea of perfect happiness."

David slapped him on the back. "Oh, that will be good for you," he said. "Absence makes the heart grow fonder, you know."

"I've always heard, 'out of sight, out of mind,'" interjected Tony. "'There are lots of pretty girls in Chicago. What do you think about it, Glenda?"

Glenda smiled. "I'll miss Paul of course, but I'm not worried. Paul will be true. He's a real Christian. There are a lot of things I need to do yet before I'm ready to get married. The time will pass quickly and we will be married on my birthday."

"Just what does being a Christian have to do with it?" Tony asked. "Is that supposed to make you trustworthy? I don't get it. Now just take Susan and me. Neither of us is what the rest of you would call a Christian. Yet, if I was engaged and a separation was necessary, I know that I would be true blue. Just as well, I know Susan, if separated from her fiancé, would be flirting with the first handsome guy she met."

"I'm not that bad," Susan pouted. "If you don't take that back, I'll take my toys and go home where somebody loves me."

"You can't! I'm not ready to go yet and it's dark out there. You're afraid of the dark. Anyway, the parents wouldn't like it. You'll have to stay until I'm ready to go unless David wants to walk you home."

"Nothing doing!" David retorted. "Just as sure as I would do that, Sis. Stevenson would drive by just as we crossed the road and she can make a mountain out of any molehill."

"Glenda and I could walk her home," Paul suggested.

"Again I must say 'nothing doing!'" David answered. "Mother raised me the old-fashioned way when couples didn't go off in the dark alone. You would have to come back alone. I thought you understood that."

"Of course I do. That was the whole idea. It's a beautiful night for a walk. We'd walk Susan home and then she would have to walk back with us. By that time she would be over her pout and we could come in and finish the evening."

"It is a beautiful night for a walk. Let's all take a walk," Glenda suggested. "We could walk over to Carson's and see if Pearl's party is still going on. Hers didn't start until seven."

"I don't believe Susan and I were invited to that," Tony replied.

"Paul wasn't invited either, but the invitations all said, 'bring a friend.' Paul can be my friend, you can be David's and Susan can be Rachel's."

"All right," David answered. "Come on, Rachel. It's Glenda's day and her suggestion. She only gets one graduation party in a lifetime."

"And one engagement party in a lifetime," Glenda added. "It just happened to be the same party."

David posted a note on the bulletin board in case any of the younger children would happen to awaken and find them gone and they stepped out into the night. Glenda linked her arm through Paul's and they walked ahead. Susan and Rachel came next, followed by Tony and David.

"I'd still like to know about this Christian thing," Tony started up the conversation. "Take our family. Annabelle is the only Christian. Yet, the rest of us are all honest and trustworthy, even Susan. Dad would not cheat his worst enemy out of a wooden nickel, yet I know some so called Christians who would skin their best friend out of his only shirt."

"I know there are lots of honest, trustworthy, people

who are not Christians," David replied, "and much as I'd like to, I can't say that all Christians are honest and trustworthy, but they should be."

Rachel paused to let the boys catch up. "I believe Tony answered his own question," she said. "He said he knew some 'so-called Christians,' not all 'so-called Christians' are real Christians. Real Christians are followers of Christ. A follower of Christ couldn't be anything except honest and trustworthy."

"Who is to say what makes a Christian?" Susan questioned. "Almost everyone I know claims to be a Christian, yet they don't believe like your church. What makes a real Christian anyway?"

David stepped up beside her. "The spirit of God is what makes people real Christians," David answered. "The Bible says – *if any man have not the Spirit of Christ, he is none of his.*" (Romans 8:9)

"Without His spirit dwelling in us, we are just living out our lives. With His spirit, He is living in us and directing our way."

Susan pondered the thought. "Well," she said, "if Christ were living in me, he might direct my way in a different direction from what I want to go."

"If Christ were really living in you and you were totally dedicated to him, you would want to go wherever he directed," David replied.

"I think it would be great to have Christ living in me, directing my way," Tony stated. "That way I would always be on the right track."

"Oh, it is great!" Rachel answered.

A car zoomed by, then slowed. At the next driveway, it turned around and crept slowly back by. The moment Rachel recognized Sis. Stevenson at the wheel was the first she had realized she was walking with Tony, and David was walking with Susan.

"Did you see that?" David asked, aghast.

"I sure did!" Rachel answered. "Can't you just hear her?" Rachel mimicked Sis. Stevenson's high-pitched voice. "'I saw the three oldest Bradcox kids out walking in the middle of the night. Both the girls were walking with their fellows and David had a girrrl!' It will be all over the county by 9 a.m. tomorrow."

"Is *that* what you call a real Christian?" Tony asked.

XXXIV

"Why don't you make somebody's birfday cake, Rachel?" Gregory questioned, as he watched Rachel hulling peas.

"Because none of us are having a birthday," Rachel answered.

"Why don't none of us have a birfday? It's been a long time since we had a birfday cake."

"It hasn't been so long since we had a cake. Susan helped Letitia bake one just the other day. Didn't you like that?"

"Yeah, it was good, but I like it better when dere's candles on it and presents. Can't somebody have a birfday?"

"The next birthday isn't until Nathan has his in September," Rachel replied. "It just happened that none of us were born during the summer."

"Well, I imagine Uncle Pete would have a birfday if we'd ask him. We never have Uncle Pete a birfday. Why don't we have Uncle Pete a birfday?"

Rachel stopped hulling peas and looked at Gregory. "Yes, why don't we?" she asked herself silently. She and David had often pondered what they could do special for Uncle Pete to show their appreciation for all he did for them. "Maybe we could have a birthday for him," she thought.

"Well, why don't we?" Gregory demanded.

"First of all, we would have to find out when his birthday is," Rachel replied.

"Oh, Billy Bob probly knows. He knows all about Uncle Pete." He left the house on a run to find Billy Bob.

A thorough questioning of Billy Bob revealed no such knowledge. He had asked Uncle Pete about his birthday and received the reply that folks by the time they were as old as he, had quit having birthdays.

Billy Bob had kept pestering him until Uncle Pete had said, "If you insist on me having a birthday, then just make me one."

"When?" Billy Bob had wanted to know.

"Oh, anytime," Uncle Pete had answered. "One date is as good as another."

"Okay, then, let's make him a birfday. It can be today." Gregory ran back to the house. "It's today! It's today! You gotta bake his birfday cake today."

"Did he say his birthday is today, Greg?"

"No, he said make up a day so I made up today."

"I'm sorry, Gregory, but I can't do it today. I've got to get these peas in the freezer. Why don't you go find all the girls except Glenda and tell them I want them to come and help me."

"Why 'cept Glenda? Is it 'cause she's gonna get married, she don't have to work anymore?"

"Doesn't, Gregory."

"She doesn't have to work anymore. But won't she have to do work after she is married?"

"She does have to work now."

"You said she don't."

"She doesn't, Gregory."

"But you just said she does!"

"Oh, go on and find the girls. Glenda has so much to do to get ready to make a home for Paul and her, that I don't want to ask her to help."

Gregory took off in search of the girls while Rachel tried to analyze the conversation to find out what she had actually said.

Alicia arrived first, followed closely by the other triplets. "Greg said Uncle Pete is having a birthday tomorrow and you're gonna make a cake with 89 candles. Uncle Pete isn't that old, is he?" she asked.

"And he said Glenda doesn't have to work anymore because she's going to get married," added Patricia. "Is that true?"

"No, of course not. Where is Darlene?"

"You let her go over to Annabelle's house, remember? Why do you let her go over there so much? You never let us go anywhere, except to school unless you go."

"Annabelle is Darlene's friend," Rachel answered. "The Fords are nice people and I know Darlene will be all right over there. She is helping Annabelle make herself a new dress. Go call her, Alicia, and tell her I need her at home."

"Why doesn't Glenda have to help?" Patricia wanted to know.

"Glenda will help!" assured Glenda as she came into the room. "I'm still part of the family and I will still try to do my fair share."

"You don't need to, Glenda," Rachel said. "You have so much to do. We may as well get used to doing without you."

Tears came into Glenda's eyes. "Oh how can I leave you with so much work? Sometimes, I think I can't, but I love Paul so much I just have to, but I'll miss you all so much! I wouldn't want my family to be unhappy, but I do hope you miss me. Do you think you will?"

"Course not – you're bossy!" Bradley stood in the doorway, backed by Nathan, Billy Bob and David.

"Greg said you needed some help hulling peas," David said, "so you would have time to bake Uncle Pete a birthday cake. Did you really find out when Uncle Pete's birthday is?"

"No, that is just Gregory's idea. He thinks we should make a birthday for him. Really I think it is a good idea."

Darlene, Annabelle and Susan appeared at the door. "Oh," Susan said. "Annabelle said Darlene had to come home to hull peas so she begged me to come along and help so you could get done sooner. She wants Darlene to have some more free time to help her on her dress. She wants to wear it Sunday. I didn't know the boys were helping or I'd have stayed at home – or maybe I could have gotten Tony to come."

"You couldn't!" Annabelle interrupted her. "He left for a job interview an hour ago. He said he has lain around for too long now."

"I didn't hear him go," Susan said.

"Of course not!" Annabelle answered. "You were far too deeply engrossed in your novel."

"Come on in if you want to help," David said. "I know you used to avoid me as if I had the plague and vise versa, but you're not so bad without all your artificial decorations – rather easy on the eyes, I'd say. Your eyes are real pretty, but they look scary when they are trimmed with black and green."

Susan stuck her nose in the air. "How should you know?" she demanded. "You never looked at me."

"I tried to," David answered, "but I couldn't see you through all the powder and paint."

"Twit yer twarlin," Sue Ellen spoke up. "It not nice to twarl."

Everyone laughed and Sue Ellen hid her face in Darlene's skirt.

"Are we really going to have Uncle Pete a birthday party?" Nathan asked. "I hope so."

"What do you think, David?" Rachel asked. "Gregory suggested it and I just thought it would be a way we could show a little of our appreciation."

"It's a good idea, but it would have to be a surprise or he would never stand for it."

"A surprise, of course, but it will take a lot of planning. Anyone have any ideas?"

"Maybe we could get some nice color paint and cover up that horrible gray he's had to live with for two years," Billy Bob suggested.

"And paint the outside, too," Nathan added.

"I could make him some curtains," Glenda put in.

"And I will make him a cushion for his chair," Darlene decided.

"Well, it sounds as if it is pretty well decided," David said. "Now when are we going to have it and how are we going to get him away for a day so we can fix up his palace?"

"For a few minutes, all was quiet except for the sound of pea pods breaking. Then Billy Bob slowly lifted his head. "I know a way," he said, "but I would hate to miss helping."

"What is your suggestion?" David asked.

"I have been pestering Uncle Pete to go fishing with me down at Hidden Cove. I thought you'd let me go if he went with me. He said as soon as you could spare us for a day he would go, if it was all right with you."

"I think that would be all right," David decided. "Of course we could use your help painting, but if you can keep him away for a day I suppose you would be doing your part."

"I'll buy him a parakeet, since I can't help with the work. He said he would like to have one to talk to when I'm not there." Billy Bob paused, then continued. "I really do like to paint, but I don't know any other way. Just please, let me pick the color."

"*You?*" Nathan put in. "I think you are responsible for that paint that is on there now."

"It was all I had and no money to buy any. If we can buy some, I know what he wants."

"What?" David asked.

"Yellow and not yellar."

"What's the difference?" asked Nathan.

"Lots of difference. Yellar is ugly and yellow is pretty."

"I wish Uncle Pete was really our uncle," Alicia said.

"So do I," added Letitia. "I like him."

"Can't you pretend he is really your uncle?" asked Rachel.

"No, it's not the same. He can't live here and eat with us and be a real uncle. I wish we had a Dad."

"I wish we had a Mother," Patricia put in. "Rachel said when she first died that we would get over missing her so much, but I haven't. I miss her just as much as I did. I still don't understand why God took her."

"Rachel makes a good mother." Alicia commented.

"And David makes a good dad," Rachel added.

"Not for me!" Glenda remarked. "I just can't make *parents* out of a brother and sister so near my own age."

"Did you ever think that you are getting new parents, Glenda?" David asked. "When you marry Paul, you aren't getting just a husband, you are getting a whole new family. His parents are your parents, his brother and sister, your brother and sister, his aunts, uncles, and cousins, your aunts, uncles and cousins."

"I don't like to think about it," Glenda answered. I'd rather think of Paul as part of this family. I like his parents well enough. They are really nice, but I don't want to leave this family. Sometimes I think I can't. I just wish Paul could just move in here with us. Why can't he?"

"No way!" David answered. "You and Paul need your

own home. No house is big enough for two families. You and Paul will be the beginning of a new family."

"Maybe I am just too young to get married," Glenda stated.

"Yes, maybe you are." David answered.

Rachel stood up. "That's the last of them," she said. "Thanks a bunch for all your help. As Mother always said, 'many hands make light work.'"

"So are you gonna make Uncle Pete's birfday cake now?" Gregory asked.

Rachel turned to David. "I do believe Gregory has a one-track mind. When would be the best time to do it?"

"How about one week from today? That will give us time to get ready," David answered.

"All right, Kids," Rachel admonished, "one week from today, but you are all going to have to be extra careful not to let the cat out of the bag."

"Where is Kitty in a bag?" asked Sue Ellen. "I want to see the Kitty."

XXXV

Rachel critically studied the cake she had just finished decorating. It was beautiful, yes, but was it appropriate? A man's cake wasn't usually decorated with roses, yet it seemed right. Uncle Pete loved flowers. He had planted them all around his palace. He was especially fond of yellow roses. Yes, the cake must be all right.

Rachel crossed to the window and looked out. Nathan and Bradley were painting the outside of the Palace. She knew David was inside. He was hurrying to get done so the paint would be dry in time to put up the curtains Glenda was finishing. Everything seemed to be going according to schedule.

A strange car drove into the yard. A well-dressed lady got out with a sheaf of papers, which she placed under her arm. Rachel gave a start. "That looks like – Oh Dear God, it is! It's Mrs. O'Conner! Dear God! Help us! What is going to happen now?"

Mrs. O'Conner opened the back door and helped two

children out of the car; a little boy about four years old and a little girl, probably five. She took them each by the hand and walked toward the house.

Rachel met them at the door. "Won't you come in, Mrs. O'Conner?" she said graciously.

"I was passing by and decided to check on how you were doing," Mrs. O'Conner said. "It has been a while since I've seen you."

Rachel took Mrs. O'Conner into the parlor and offered her the most comfortable chair, but instead she took a seat on the sofa with a young child on either side of her.

"Everything looks very nice," Mrs. O'Conner said. "I see the shed is getting a coat of paint. Is that where the hired man lives?"

"He can hardly be called a hired man as he won't accept any pay, but, yes that is where he lives. He works for just his living."

"That's odd. Are you sure he is all right? Perfectly trustworthy?"

"He has been here over two years now, and yes, we have found him to be perfectly trustworthy."

Mrs. O'Conner stayed for an hour. She asked every imaginable question from the children's school grades to plans for Glenda's wedding.

Sue Ellen came in and asked if the children could go see the new kittens.

Mrs. O'Conner answered. "Rose may go, but Dennis had better stay with me." Rachel noticed that Mrs. O'Conner still held the little boy firmly by the hand.

"Well, Rachel," she finally said, "you seem to be doing very well. I'm very proud of you. I –" she seemed to choke, swallowed, and her face turned red. "I really hate to do it, but I would like to ask a favor of you."

"Yes," answered Rachel, "and what can I do for you?"

"I was wondering," Mrs. O'Conner went on, "if you could keep Rose and Dennis for a few days. Their father beat up their mother. She is in the hospital and he is in jail. I have no place to put the children. All of my foster homes are full to capacity and you are doing such a wonderful job of bringing up your brothers and sisters –"

"I thought foster homes had to be licensed and the foster parents had to go through training. I really think I have enough children."

"Oh, you would hardly notice two more. I'm just asking it for a few days. There is a clause in the rules that allows for emergencies if the home is known to be all right and of course I know there isn't a better place for children in the county than this one. I'll just have to look around and see that there are groceries in the house and no poisons where the children would have access to them." Mrs. O'Conner arose and still holding Dennis by the hand, began a hurried inspection of the house.

"Really, I don't think –" Rachel began.

"That's all right. It won't take long," Mrs. O'Conner said.

"I think I'd better call David."

"No, don't bother David. You know he won't care. He wouldn't want to leave the two little darlings without a place to stay all night." Mrs. O'Conner continued her inspection with Rachel following. "It shouldn't be more than a few days until I find a home that will take them. A home for Rose would be easy, but I have to place them together and I haven't found a place that will take them both." Mrs. O'Conner spoke hurriedly. "If you will just sign this paper, I'll get their clothes and –"

"Really I can't sign anything. David wouldn't like it. I'll just call him and –"

"Oh, that's all right. I'll just leave the papers and pick them up later." She laid the papers on the table and hurried out the door. Rachel reluctantly followed.

At the car, Mrs. O'Conner set out two suitcases. Only then did she give the hand she was holding to Rachel and hurried into her car. She started the engine and just before driving away leaned out her window to say, "Remember, no corporal punishment."

David stepped up beside Rachel. "What's going on here?" he asked.

Rachel released her hold on Dennis' hand and wiped

her brow. "It seems we have had two children temporarily added to our family," she said.

"Really, Rachel, how could that be?"

"She said she had no place for them."

"Well, she can't leave them here!"

"She already has!"

"Why did you let her?"

"I didn't. She just left them!"

"Why didn't you call me?"

"She wouldn't give me time."

"Wouldn't give you time? She was here over an hour. I kept wondering what was going on, but I thought you would send one of the kids if you needed me."

"Oh, David, please don't scold." Rachel started to cry. "It wasn't my fault, really. I told her we couldn't keep them and she just left them anyway."

David put his arm around his sister. "I'm sorry, Rachel," he said. "Please, don't cry! Come, let's go in and you tell me all about it, but first, where are the children?"

"Sue Ellen took Rose to see the kittens and Dennis is – Oh, where is Dennis? He was here a minute ago."

A quick survey of the yard revealed no small boy. David made a beeline for the barn while Rachel went to check the house. She found Dennis seated atop the kitchen table, a very badly mangled birthday cake before him, his face covered with icing.

"Dennis!" she cried. "You can't do that!"

"I am!" he answered, stuffing another handful of cake in his mouth.

Rachel picked up the small boy and headed for the bathroom. She held him firmly while she washed his face and hands. "Now Dennis," she said, "that was a very bad thing to do."

"What you gonna do about it? You can't spank me. Can't nobody spank me. My daddy said so. My Momma was gonna spank me and Daddy beat her up good. I've never been spanked. I do what I want to do," and with that announcement, Dennis pulled loose from Rachel and ran for the door. He met David just coming in.

David scooped up the boy and said. "Oh, here you are." Then to Rachel, "You found him, I see."

"Yes, I found him," said Rachel angrily. "Would you please look on the table?"

"Oh, no!" David moaned. "Oh, Rachel! That is awful! All your work! And what are we going to do. We can hardly have a birthday party without a cake. I know you don't have time to bake another one. Do you suppose I could go to town and get one?"

"Martha's bakery does them, but they are very expensive." Rachel looked at the clock. "Yes, I can make another one if you can assign somebody to take charge of that child."

"I'll take charge of him!"

"I want down!" Dennis demanded. "I want down, I said!"

"No, you don't get down until you decide to behave yourself."

"I will too get down!" Dennis said as he doubled his fist and planted it firmly in David's nose.

Dennis got down, fast! Rachel grabbed a towel and gave it to David to soak up the blood. By the time his nose had stopped bleeding and he had changed his shirt, Dennis was nowhere to be found.

Sue Ellen and Rose came in.

"Rose, we can't find Dennis," Rachel said. "Can you find him?"

"Probably not," Rose answered. "He always hides. Mother usually doesn't look for him. She says when she can't see him she doesn't have to worry about what he is in to."

"Well, I do!" answered Rachel. "We will have to find him."

Dennis was found in the office. Every desk drawer had been emptied in the floor. Dennis had a pen and as fast as possible was scribbling on every paper.

David picked him up and pried the pen loose from his fingers. Then he took both his hands. "Now listen to me, Boy," he said. "You can't act like that here. You have to be good in this house."

"Who said so?" Dennis asked. "I do what I want to do and you can't spank me. Can't nobody spank me. My daddy said so."

"We'll see about that, Buddy!" David said angrily.

Rachel touched him on the arm. "Mrs. O'Conner," she reminded. "We've got to be careful."

"We didn't ask for the brats, did we? If she doesn't like it, let her come and get them!"

"But we don't want any more trouble with her. The last words she said as she drove away were 'remember, no corporal punishment.' We have to find another way."

David nodded. "Just leave this mess," he said. "I'll see to it later. I'll take this chap out with Nathan and Bradley. Maybe together we can keep an eye on him. Go ahead with the cake if you can."

David carried Dennis out to Uncle Pete's palace. Sue Ellen and Rose followed. "What are you going to do to him?" Rose asked. "Are you going to spank him?"

"I don't know, Rose," David answered, looking at Rose for the first time. "Oh, she's beautiful," he thought. "Say, are you bad, too?" he asked.

"No, I try to be good, but Dennis won't try," the little girl said. "He's always bad. Momma always spanked me when I was bad, but Dennis has never been spanked. I don't know what you can do with him."

"Well, don't worry, Honey. We will think of something."

"I want down!" Dennis announced.

"Will you stay here with us and not do anything bad?" David asked.

"Oh, sure! Anything you say."

"All right," David said. "I'll let you down, but you stay here and behave yourself."

"I want to paint!" announced Dennis, running toward the stepladder where Nathan was spreading green paint on the trim of the palace.

"No, Dennis," screamed David, just as the little boy started scrambling up the backside of the ladder. Rose darted under the ladder to stop him just as his head came in contact with the paint shelf upending the quart can of paint on top of her head.

David grabbed a rag and started wiping green paint from the child's mahogany curls. Nathan climbed down and caught up with Dennis just as he was climbing over the gate of the pigpen. "Now listen, Boy, you can get killed in there." He said as he took him down. "I don't know who you are or why you are here, but if you are going to stay any length of time, you've got to do better than this. Only nice boys are allowed around here."

"You let me down!" Dennis screamed.

"*No!*"

"I said let me *down*!"

"Not until I know you will try to be nice. Only nice boys here, Remember?"

"You're not nice!" Dennis screamed. "You're a *#~* and I hate you. You hear me? I *hate* you! You're a *~`*"

Nathan put a hand over Dennis' mouth just as Dennis' fist came in contact with Nathan's eye. Nathan held on. He managed to get both the little boy's hands in one of his and held the other over his mouth. Dennis started kicking. Nathan let go of the mouth and pulled Dennis into his arms, squeezing him tightly against his chest. Dennis took a bite of Nathan's shoulder.

At that moment Nathan spied a small lead chain that someone had left attached to the fence. It had a hard to undo snap fastener on each end. He tucked Dennis under one arm and with the other got the chain. He fastened one end to the belt loop on the back of Dennis' pants and the other to a post.

"Oh, boy!" Dennis said excitedly. "I'm in jail, just like my daddy!"

Nathan went back to the disaster scene. There stood Rose, a dejected looking little girl with green hair, tears running down her face. Green paint was splattered over the white siding on the shed.

"Want me to get Rachel?" Nathan asked.

"Where is Dennis?" was David's reply.

"I tied him up?"

"You *tied him up*?"

"Yes, if I'd held on much longer I'd have spanked him and not knowing who he is or where he came from, I decided I'd better not do that."

"He seems to be a product Mrs. O'Conner has dumped on us for a few days. No, don't get Rachel. She has had enough already. Where are all the other girls? Sue Ellen, do you know where all the girls are?"

"In the sewing room with Glenda."

"Go get them. Nate, you see if you can get enough paint from this can to finish the trim. You're almost done, I see. We'll have to re-do the siding. Don't cry, Honey," he said to Rose. "Somebody will help you in a minute."

"We can't repaint the siding over that wet green paint and it will take it hours to dry." Nathan said.

David took a rag and began to wash the green paint off with turpentine, taking most of the fresh white paint with it. "It's a good thing this is the backside of the 'Palace.' I'm afraid it won't be finished tonight."

Glenda, with Darlene, came around the corner followed by the triplets. "Oh, no!" she cried, aghast. "Who is that and what happened?"

"That seems to be your new temporary sister," David answered. "Disaster has struck. Her brother dumped the paint on her head. Do you suppose you could some way clean her up?"

"I wouldn't know how to begin. Can't we get Rachel?"

"No, don't bother Rachel. Just take rags and some paint thinner and wipe it out the best you can. Oh, I don't know what to do. You can't really wash her head in turpentine. It might kill her."

"I'll clean her up," Darlene decided. "I know what to do. Glenda you go back and finish the curtains. I'll just run and change my dress. I am afraid I might get paint on me. I wouldn't want to ruin this dress. David, can I just throw her clothes away? Does she have more?"

"I don't know, but yes, throw them away. You can dig up something to put on her, something you have outgrown."

Darlene hurried away to change and soon returned, wearing her oldest dress and carrying a bottle of olive oil. "You girls go see if Glenda can find something to put on her," she said.

"I've got clothes," Rose said, speaking for the first time. "My suitcase is still out where Mrs. O'Conner set it out of her car."

Alicia ran for the suitcase and Darlene led the little girl toward the barn. Suddenly she stopped short. There in front of her lay a pair of little boy's pants attached to a chain. "David!" she yelled.

David came running. "What's wrong?" he asked.

"What's that?" Darlene asked, pointing to the pants.

Dennis had broken jail.

David, Gregory, and Bradley searched the farm. Nathan joined them as soon as he had finished the painting. The triplets searched the house. They looked in every spot large enough to hold a small boy, but it was a full two hours before Nathan found him asleep in the barn loft, his naked body covered with hay.

Meanwhile, Darlene took Rose into the barn and stripped off her dress. She used turpentine on a rag to wipe the worst of the paint off, being careful as much as possible not to touch her scalp. Then she applied a generous amount of olive oil, wiping it out with clean rags. After three applications of oil and two shampoos, her hair still looked slightly green.

"That seems to be about the best I can do," Darlene said.

"Thank you!" the little girl replied. "It would have been less work to have just cut it off."

"Oh, I wouldn't want to cut off your beautiful hair!" Darlene exclaimed. "You wouldn't be so pretty, then. Besides, Jesus wouldn't like it."

"Jesus? Does Jesus live here?"

"He certainly does! We couldn't get along at all without Jesus."

"Jesus doesn't live at our house. Mommy said so. She

said he can't live there as long as Daddy lives there."

"How awful!"

"Yes, it is awful!" Rose agreed. "Mrs. O'Conner said I might not ever go back to that home. She said we might get new parents because we can't live in the place my daddy lives anymore and they took my mommy to a hospital where crazy people are. I think my daddy drove her crazy. I hope if we get new parents, that they let Jesus live with us, but I don't guess Jesus would want to live with Dennis either."

"What happened to lunch?" Bradley asked.

"I don't believe anyone had time to think of lunch," David remarked. "Billy Bob and Uncle Pete will be home in a couple hours. We'd better skip lunch and concentrate on supper."

"I thought we were going to have a cook-out," Nathan said.

"We are. We have to get a fire going to roast wieners. I think Rachel and Susan have made some salads and things. We want to have it all set up when they get back. Nathan, do you want to build the fire and get everything ready or do you want to look after Dennis?"

"I'll just build the fire if you please. I've had enough Dennis."

For the next couple of hours everything went well.

After Rachel had finished the cake, she served sandwiches and lemonade to all the children.

The cake was very pretty, although Rachel said it wasn't as pretty as the first one.

Pete's Palace, except for the one side, which would be repainted later, was as well done as the children knew how to do it. The inside was painted lemon yellow. White curtains at the one window, were bordered with bands of yellow, orange and brown. A new brown blanket covered Pete's cot. Around the rack David made to hold Pete's clothes was a drapery of flowered chintz, which matched the chair cushion. Several packages lay on his cot, containing a new shirt, some socks, and other items. One large box with many air holes, contained a bird cage with a little green bird which Pete later named Pollianne. The birthday cake sat in the middle of his small table.

XXXVI

Coming home from Hidden Cove with a goodly amount of fish, the first thing Pete saw was his Palace. "Oh, Billy Bob," he exclaimed, "they've painted my Palace!" Then he saw the fire, which had burned down to a bed of coals.

"Come on!" David shouted. "We're having a party."

"Oh, I thought we would have fish for supper," Pete answered. "They're all clean. What is the party for, anyway?"

"Your birfday!" Gregory answered. "We made you a birfday!"

"Why this isn't my birthday, Gregory."

"Yes, it is. You said make you a birfday, so we made you one. Your cake has got ninety-seven candles on it!"

Pete threw up his hands. "Oh, my," he said, "I think I'm my own Grandpa!"

Sitting around the fire roasting wieners and marshmallows, eating their fill of potato salad and baked beans, the family really enjoyed the evening. Billy Bob teased Nathan about his black eye and he and Pete laughed until their sides hurt over the escapades of Dennis. David, however, told them that if they had been there, they wouldn't have been able to see anything funny. David and Nathan took turns holding Dennis' hand.

They did not allow Pete to enter the Palace until they were ready for dessert. When at last they could eat no more, they followed Pete to his Palace. Pete stopped in the doorway and his eyes filled with tears. Then he turned and threw his arms around the person closest behind him, who happened to be David. "Oh, I just love you kids so much!" he said.

"And we love you!" they all answered.

Pete opened his gifts and adequately admired each one. Then Rachel lit the candles, which were arranged in a circle around the base of the cake. As they sang Happy Birthday, Dennis carefully slipped his hand from David's. All eyes were on Pete, as the happy tears ran down his face. No one thought of Dennis until suddenly David smelled smoke. He whirled around to see Dennis on Pete's cot holding a lighted candle to the corner of the curtain. With a leap he grabbed both the candle and the curtain and dropped them into Pete's wash basin. Miraculously, nothing but the curtain was burned, but David had broken the curtain rod and torn the brackets from the wall. He also had burned his hand, though not seriously.

Billy Bob picked Dennis up. "I'll take care of this little boy for a while," he said, "so he won't do any more damage. You all just go ahead with the party, but save us some cake and ice cream."

Billy Bob and Dennis were gone about fifteen minutes. When they returned, the younger children were all sitting on the floor eating cake and ice cream. Dennis walked in and sat down on the floor in the corner. "I'm sorry I've been bad," he said. "I won't be bad anymore. May I please have my cake now?"

Billy Bob sat down by Nathan on the other side of the room. "Hadn't you better sit by him?" David asked.

"No." Billy Bob answered. "It won't be necessary. He'll be all right now."

"What did you do?" David asked.

"I spanked him. That's what you should have done hours ago."

Later as the family walked back to the house, Rachel asked David. "Where shall we have them sleep?"

"I better take Dennis in with me," he said. "You can tuck Rose in somewhere."

"I want to sleep by Billy Bob, David." Dennis said. "May I please sleep by Billy Bob? I *like* Billy Bob!"

A week went by and nothing was heard from Mrs. O'Conner. Rachel called and was told she was 'out.' She left a message for her to call back, but no call came. She tried again a few days later with the same results. It was three weeks before she finally contacted her only to be told that the Mother had had a complete nervous breakdown and likely wouldn't be able to take charge of the children for a year. There was no way they could be released to their father. Would Rachel *please* just keep them a few more days until she could find a home that would take them?

Dennis followed Billy Bob everywhere and was very obedient to him. He didn't like David or Nathan so they just left him to Billy Bob.

When Mrs. O'Conner finally came for the children, Billy Bob protested that they should just stay and be a part of the family.

Mrs. O'Conner had found a home that wanted both the children. The father and mother had both agreed to adoption, stating that the children caused all of their problems and without them they thought they could make their marriage work.

Neither of the children wanted to leave, but when Rachel explained to them that they were going to a home where the parents wanted them and they would be a part of that family always, they agreed to go. Dennis stated flatly that if he didn't like it, he still remembered how to be bad, but Billy Bob told him if he ever heard of him being bad again, he would pay him a visit.

David entered the kitchen and dropped two bags of groceries on the kitchen table. "Have I ever got news!" he said. "You're not going to believe this!"

"Good news or bad?" asked Rachel.

"Actually, I have two pieces of news and I can't decide for either one of them if it is good news or bad."

"Well, don't keep me so long in suspense."

:Franklin Parker is going to Bible School. He is preparing to be a missionary and he and Stacey are planning to get married."

"No!"

"I believe you heard me correctly."

"I'm in shock! Anyway that's one you won't have to worry about anymore and one I won't have to worry about. What is the other news?"

"You had better sit down for this one. It is more shocking than the other."

"Oh, come on!"

"Our temporary children have gone to live at the home of Bro. and Sis. Stevenson. From henceforth they will be known as Carolyn and Samuel Stevenson.

"Oh, the poor children!"

"We maybe don't need to take it that way. Pastor Parker said the Stevenson's have always wanted children.

He said as the years went by, Sis. Stevenson began to get bitter because they couldn't have children. He thinks that is what has made her the way she is. He said they are perfectly delighted with the children and the children seem happy. She did tell him Dennis or rather Samuel keeps asking for Billy Bob, and she wonders if we would let him visit them."

XXXVII

It was a Saturday evening in July and Paul had been gone six weeks when Glenda brought up the subject of her wedding. "Do you think it is too early to start getting ready?" she asked. "I don't want to have to hurry at the last. I'd like to get our dresses made as soon as possible."

"Do you have your plans made, Glenda?" Rachel asked.

"Most of them. Paul said whatever I want is fine with him. I would like a church wedding with two attendants. Do you think we can afford that, David? I really don't think it will cost so much if we do it all ourselves."

"You know, Glenda, most of the weddings – church weddings – have five or six bridesmaids these days. I think we can manage it if you want it."

"No, I'd rather not have so much. I thought just you, Rachel, for my maid and Sue Ellen for flower girl, but then I got to thinking about what David said about having a new family and I decided I'd better ask Paul's sister, too."

"Paul wanted David for best man, but I want David to give me away, so Paul said he would have his brother and Donnie Nichols. I'd like to have the wedding in the church and come back here for the reception. Are those plans all right?"

"Whatever you want, Glenda," David assured her. "You're pretty sensible. I can trust you not to overspend the budget."

"Can we get the pattern and material for my dress now? I'd like to get it made first."

"Go Monday and pick out whatever you want."

"Oh, I know just what I want. It's a new material that has just come out. I don't know what it is called, but it is very beautiful and doesn't cost much. However, it doesn't wear well. I just don't see paying a big price for something I'll only wear once."

"You might want to keep it for your daughter to wear," Rachel suggested.

Glenda shook her head. "If I ever have a daughter, she'll want to pick her own. The style would be all wrong by then."

A knock sounded on the door. David arose to answer it. "Who comes more often than we do?" Tony asked as he and Susan came into the room.

"No one, unless it's Annabelle," David answered.

Tony shook his head. "We've got her beat. She only

302

comes here half the time. The other half Darlene goes over there. You and Rachel never come to our house, so we come here all the time."

"It's a little hard to get away," David answered.

Tony nodded. "We understand. Well, did we interrupt a serious discussion?"

"We were just making wedding plans."

"Are they all made? If they are not, we can come back later."

"That's all right. You stay. We have settled the important issues and the rest will fall in line later."

"I thought the only important issue was settled back in May," Tony said. "Anyway, if there is nothing more of importance to be discussed tonight, why not let me introduce an important subject?"

"What?" David asked.

"God!"

"*God?*"

"You do get right to the point don't you, Tony," Susan mused. "Couldn't you have just led up to it?"

"Why waste time? For my part, I think it's time to get this matter settled. I want God in my life. I've come here to find out all the requirements."

"Maybe you should talk to Pastor Parker."

"No, if your religion is worth a nickel you ought to be able to sell it to me."

"Sorry! My religion isn't for sale."

"Oh, you know what I mean. Let's get serious. Rachel, this brother of yours doesn't seem to want to share his religion with me. Are you willing to share yours?"

"I don't have religion – I have salvation."

"And just what is the difference between religion and salvation?" Tony asked.

Rachel considered a moment before she answered. "Religion is learned," she said, "salvation is experienced!"

"That's what I want!" Tony declared. "Salvation! Will you share yours?"

"Sure! Salvation doesn't divide, it multiplies!"

"Do you mean, if you share your salvation with me that I can have as much as you have and you will still have as much as you have now?"

"I'll probably have more, because God expects us to share our salvation with others and if we obey Him, that's how we get more. But, Tony, I can't give you any of mine. I can just share my knowledge and you have to ask God for what you want."

"I know," Tony answered. "I'm really serious about this. I've watched Annabelle all summer. She's different! I really didn't realize how different until last night when we had that terrible storm. Annabelle used to be just petrified of storms."

"Well, the storm got really bad," Tony continued. "The

house was shaking, Dad was walking the floor, Mother was crying and Susan was on the couch with a pillow over her head. I walked over to where Annabelle was looking out the window and she said, 'Isn't the lightning beautiful, Tony?' I asked her if she wasn't scared and she shook her head. '*The Lord rideth upon a swift cloud*, you know. The Bible says so. (Isaiah 19:1). As long as he is on the cloud, he will be directing the storm, and nothing will happen to us that isn't his will.' This morning at the breakfast table I told Mom, Dad, and Susan that I thought the whole family needed to get a good dose of Annabelle's religion. They all agreed and we talked until nearly noon, but Annabelle just can't explain to us why Pastor Parker believes in One God and baptizes in Jesus name, and every other church in town believes in the trinity and baptizes in the name of the Father, Son, and Holy Ghost."

"That's easy," David explained. "You can find that in the Bible." (Matthew 7:13-14) He reached for his Bible and read, *Enter ye in at the strait gate; for wide is the gate, and broad is the way, that leadeth to destruction, and many there be which go in thereat: Because strait is the gate, and narrow is the way, which leadeth unto life, and few there be that find it.*

"Now that says the road that many are going leads to the wrong place," David continued. "We are going the road that few people take. We're following Jesus so we take his name."

"But the Bible says – Tony read it to me – that we are supposed to be baptized in the trinity, the Father, Son, and Holy Ghost," Susan stated.

"Does it really say that?" Rachel asked. "I thought I had read the whole Bible and I don't remember reading that. I didn't know the word trinity is in the Bible."

Tony took the Bible. "See, right here it is," he said. "Matthew 28:19. *Go ye therefore, and teach all nations, baptizing them in the name of the Father, and of the Son, and of the Holy Ghost.*"

"I guess you better back up a verse, Tony," David said. "Matthew 28:18 says *And Jesus came and spake unto them, saying, All power is given unto me in heaven and in earth.* If there is any such thing as a trinity, then two of them don't have any power because Jesus has all the power. Rachel is right. The word 'trinity' is not in the Bible."

"Well, why did Jesus say to baptize that way?"

"Oh, come on, Tony, you've graduated from college. You've got lots more education than I have. You ought to be able to understand that verse. Are any of those three words names? Is 'father' a name? Is 'son' a name? When you were in college and wrote home to your dad, did you address it to 'father' and when he wrote back did he address it to 'son'?"

"I never thought of that." Tony scratched his head. "It's

confusing," he said. "Can you explain it to me."

"It is not confusing, Tony, except as so-called intelligent men have confused it," David answered. "There is only one true God. His name is Jesus. He is the Father. He is the Son. He is the Holy Ghost. That verse says the NAME; it doesn't say 'names'. If the Father, Son, and Holy Ghost were three separate persons, then the verse would say names, with an 'S', plural form, you know."

Tony pondered a while, then asked. "Didn't Jesus have a father?"

"Who was his father?"

"Well, God! The Father."

"Matthew 1:18 says the Holy Ghost was his Father."

"You're getting me more confused than before."

"Tony, who died for you?"

"Jesus died. The Son!"

"1 John 3:16 says God died. Did two of the three die?"

Tony shook his head.

"Tony, God is a spirit. He is the Holy Spirit. Yet, He is the Father. A spirit cannot die. God had to prepare a body to dwell in so that he could die. The spirit didn't die. The flesh died."

"I think I'm beginning to see."

"All the Apostles baptized in Jesus name. All through the book of Acts, no one was baptized any other way.

It was over three hundred years after the death of Jesus before a people decided they wanted to do it differently. If you don't believe that, when you get home from work Monday, I'll take you to the library and prove it to you. Any good set of encyclopedia will confirm that."

"Oh, we've got a good set at home. I don't doubt your word, but I'll look it up and show it to the parents." Tony stood up. "OK Susan, let's go home. I've got something to think about."

Rachel jumped up. "Oh, as long as you are here, can't you stay for a snack?" she asked.

"Hmmm, I thought you'd never ask," Tony grumbled.

Rachel headed for the kitchen. Tony followed. "I'll help you," he said.

Susan turned to Glenda. "When have you heard from Paul?" she asked.

"Oh, I had a letter today."

"Yes," David interrupted, "she had a letter today, one yesterday, one the day before yesterday, and so on as far back as you want to go."

"No," Glenda disagreed, "I don't get one every day. The mail isn't that dependable, but he does write every day, and he calls every Sunday afternoon."

Rachel and Tony returned with cookies, ice cream, and colas. "I've been trying to convince Rachel that she ought to be my girlfriend," Tony stated, "but she's a confirmed old maid and doesn't want friends."

"That's only half true," Rachel objected. "I *am* a confirmed old maid, but I do want friends. I'd like having you for a friend, but if you want a girlfriend, you need to look somewhere else."

"All right, let's just be friends," Tony said, but David heard his barely audible "for now," though Rachel didn't.

The next night when the invitation was given the four older Fords left their seats and walked down the aisle to the altar. All were later baptized in the name of the Lord Jesus Christ.

Annabelle said she thought she couldn't be any happier than she was the night she got saved, but she found she could. She *was* happier.

XXXVIII

It was a rainy Saturday in late August, one of those days when the world seems out of sorts, with everyone snapping at everyone else. The children couldn't go out to play, so they were running all over the house. Glenda was trying to make school clothes, but was spending more time looking out the window than sewing. She hadn't received her usual letter that day. David was doing paperwork in the office, but every fifteen minutes or so he would open the door to say, "Rachel, can't you do *something* to quiet those kids?"

Rachel made a pot of potato soup and a big batch of grilled cheese sandwiches and called the family to lunch. "What are you so glum about?" Nathan asked Glenda.

"Oh, she didn't get a letter from Paul," Patricia answered.

"Is something wrong, Glenda?" David asked. "You heard from him yesterday, didn't you?"

Glenda nodded.

"Well, there is no cause to worry. Cheer up! You'll likely get two Monday."

Glenda didn't cheer up.

"Is something else wrong, Glenda," David continued. "It isn't like you to worry over missing one day."

Glenda wiped away a tear that was threatening to leave her eye. "It's just that the letter I got yesterday wasn't – oh, I don't know. It just wasn't like he usually writes. I couldn't help but feel something was wrong, even before I didn't get a letter today."

"Maybe he found somebody else," Billy Bob suggested.

"He did *not* find somebody else. I'm not a bit worried about that!"

"Then what are you worried about?" Rachel asked.

"I don't know. He – "Glenda pulled a letter from her pocket. "This is the letter I got yesterday." She handed the letter to David. "Here, you can read it."

"We don't need to read your letters, Glenda," David said.

"It's all right. I don't care." Then she smiled. "I guess I've got some I wouldn't want you to read, but I really want you to read that one. Tell me if you think there is something wrong."

My Dearest Glenda,

I'm missing you as usual. The weather

has turned chilly. It looks like rain. The boss hit me with a hard question. I don't know what I should do. I wish we were closer, but we may soon be farther apart. I wish I could think straight. I'm in a hurry. Sorry about the short note. I will try to do better tomorrow. Remember, no matter what happens, I still love you.

Yours forever,
(signed) Paul

David passed the letter over to Rachel and said, "Yes, I do see what you mean, but I don't suppose there is cause to worry. Paul depends on God and I'm sure with God's help, he will make the right decision."

Rachel read the letter and passed it back to Glenda. "It's that sentence about being farther apart. What do you suppose he could mean?"

"Maybe they are going to send him to California," Nathan suggested.

"Or Alaska," Billy Bob added.

"I've thought of that. It's bad enough having him in Chicago, but —"

"Oh, Glenda, the mail comes all the way from California," Darlene said. "It might just take your letters a little longer to get here, but they would still come and there are telephone lines."

"I know, but in Chicago he does get to come home for a weekend once in a while," Glenda reminded them.

Mister set up a joyous barking and David jumped up to investigate. "Well, Glenda," he said, "your once in a while has just happened again. Here comes Paul."

Paul entered and after his usual greetings, turned immediately to David. "David, I need to talk with you – alone!"

"Let's go to the parlor," David answered. "It's raining outside and I've been working in the office all morning. You couldn't get in."

Seated in the parlor, Paul came right to the point. "David, I made you a promise when you let Glenda and me get engaged."

David nodded.

"Now I need some advice from you," Paul continued. "What would *you* do if you had made a promise like that and you found out you positively *had* to go to Europe for a year?"

David whistled. "Say, that does complicate matters, doesn't it. I know you don't want to wait a year to get married. Likewise you know that I won't allow Glenda to come to you to be married when she is eighteen."

"I wouldn't want that."

"Is it absolutely imperative that you go?"

"It is either I go or face the ruination of all my lifetime career plans. The company wants me to go. I'm not saying I wouldn't have a job if I refuse, but you can understand what it would be to refuse an assignment like that right at the beginning this way. They think the training I can get there is what I need and they have work I can do while I train."

David nodded and sat pondering. Finally he spoke. "Do you object if I call Rachel? We agreed not to let any of the children marry before they are eighteen."

Paul agreed and paced the floor while Rachel came. David related the problem to her and asked, "What do you think I should do?"

"David, you are the head of the house, of course, but since you asked, I don't see as there is anything you can do but give Paul back his promise. Do you realize what it would be like to have to live with Glenda for a year if Paul were in Europe? Today wasn't even a small sample. And don't you think it is what Mother would do? Besides, what other chance will she ever have to see the world? I do think, though, that we ought to consult Glenda. She has probably chewed off all her fingernails by now and her hands will look a fright for the wedding."

The three returned to the kitchen and found Glenda, not chewing her fingernails, but walking the floor and wringing her hands. "Sit down, Glenda," David commanded. "We need to talk to you." Glenda sat, but a small tear emerged from one eye.

"Don't cry, Glenda," David consoled her. "Paul still loves you and he still intends to marry you. It's just that he can't marry you on your birthday. He will be in Europe then."

Glenda nodded, "I expected something like that," she said as the tears ran down her face.

David continued. "Are you willing to wait for him a year or would you rather skip the big wedding and marry him now?"

"Of course I'll wait for him. I'd wait – What! What did you say? Marry him *now?* Did you really say that? Oh, could I?" She jumped up and threw her arms around David.

David pushed her back to where he could look into her eyes. "If you are sure that is what you want, but what about the wedding?"

"I don't care about the wedding. I can get married without a wedding."

"How much time do we have?" Rachel asked.

"Two weeks," Paul answered. "The boat sails two weeks from tomorrow. We would have to be married on Friday to get to New York in time."

"Oh, that will give me time enough!" Glenda said. "I

didn't plan a big wedding and my dress is already made, but – oh dear! The school clothes aren't all made."

"Don't worry about that, Glenda," Rachel answered. "It isn't your job anymore."

"But I had intended to keep on doing it," Glenda said. "I wanted to feel I'm still helping. Isn't that what Mother would expect of me? Darlene isn't ready yet. Oh, she knows how, well enough, but she is still slow."

"I'll help, Glenda," Rachel assured her, "and Patricia is doing quite well. She can help. We'll get by. The family might not be as well dressed as you have dressed us, but we will be all right. Right now we will all have to work together for the wedding."

"Oh, Donnie Nichols has a broken foot, Paul. What will you do for a best man?" David wanted to know.

"I wanted you, David. Isn't there some way you can be my best man? Let Nathan give away the bride."

"No way!" Nathan answered. "I wouldn't give her away. I'd keep her. She's pretty nice to have around."

"Why can't Uncle Pete give her away?" Billy Bob asked.

"Uncle Pete isn't even related!" Glenda retorted.

"He is so!" Alicia stated. "David said we could pretend he is our real uncle so he is our real uncle."

"Pretending isn't real, Alicia."

"Well, he loves us and we love him, so he's family."

"Anyway, he wouldn't do it," Glenda reasoned.

"I think he would be honored to do it if you would ask him," Billy Bob put in. "He's always saying how much he loves us and wants to feel we accept him as part of the family. Everyone is always wishing they knew something they could do for him. Well, that is something you can do for him."

Glenda shrugged. "I don't care. I just want to get married, but what will everyone think?"

"Like whom do you mean by everyone?" David asked.

"Oh, the church people and the neighbors."

"Glenda, the church people all know how much Uncle Pete has done for us and how we feel about him. As for the neighbors – I couldn't care less! What is most important is what does God think and what do you want? If you want me to give you away, Paul can find someone else for best man."

"No, Paul let me plan everything. He at least ought to have the best man he wants. Go ahead and ask Uncle Pete, but you do it. I don't want to."

"Is it all right with you, Paul?" David asked.

"Sure!" Paul answered. "It has always been hard for me not to think of Pete as part of the family."

When David approached Pete with the question that evening, tears ran down his face. "I'd love to do it, David," he said. "I would be greatly honored, but I can not do it without Glenda knowing something of my past that she doesn't know now. If you will have Glenda and Paul come together to my palace, I will talk with them, then if she still wants me, I'll do it."

Glenda emerged from Pete's Palace sobbing as if her heart was broken. Paul tried to comfort her. "Oh, Paul," she cried. "If he just hadn't made me promise!"

"It's all right, Glenda," Paul soothed her. "It's his right! This has to be done his way."

David stepped up to her. "If you don't want him to do it, you don't have to let him; promise or no promise. I will interfere and it won't be you breaking your promise."

"There is no way that I would want anyone else," Glenda answered.

XXXIX

Dum dum de dum dum dum.

The wedding guests stood and turned to watch the bride as she came down the aisle on Pete's arm, wearing the beautiful white dress she had made for herself and carrying a sheaf of white roses.

She was preceded by little Sue Ellen, lovely in her new pink dress with pink roses in her black hair, scattering rose petals in the path of the bride.

Pete stood handsome in the new blue suit Paul had bought him for a surprise, his only comment being, "You deserve it."

"Who giveth this woman in marriage?" Pastor Parker asked.

"Her brother and I do," Pete answered in a firm voice. Then he placed her hand in Paul's and with erect head, walked back to where Nathan and Darlene were seated with the younger children.

On through the wedding ceremony and soon Glenda

Bradcox had become Mrs. Paul Dobison.

At the reception in the Bradcox home, Pearl Carson commented on the church decorations. "The church was so beautiful. Your attendants had roses and it isn't even the season for roses."

"Oh, Bro. and Sis. Stevenson had the church decorated and bought all the flowers for the attendants. Of course Paul bought mine, but they did the rest. They said it was my wedding present and the family's reward for taking such good care of their children before they got them."

"Nathan's birthday is only two weeks away, Rachel," said David at the breakfast table the next morning.

"I know," Rachel answered. "We got so busy with Glenda's wedding I haven't given it much thought. What do you want for your birthday, Nathan?" Rachel asked.

"Oh, I put mine on the car," Nathan answered. "I guess if I get my driver's license that will be present enough. There is one thing that I can tell you I don't want."

"What is that?" David asked.

"A party."

"What! No sixteenth birthday party?" David exclaimed. "Why not? Don't you enjoy parties?"

"Yes," Nathan answered. "I enjoy parties – usually. What I'm looking at is what happens after the party. You had your sixteenth and the next Sunday after church, I was looking for you and when I found you there were so many girls around you I couldn't get to you. After Rachel's sixteenth birthday party, I thought I was going to have to carry a baseball bat to beat off the guys, there were so many. Everybody seems to think once you have a sixteenth birthday, it's time for you to be grown-up. I'm not grown-up and I don't want to be grown-up for another five years or so. When I am old enough to think about girls I want to be able to look them over and pick my own, not have them packed around me so tightly I can't see straight."

"Good Ole Nate!" David said, slapping him on the shoulder. "I always did think you had more sense than any other kid in the whole United States."

"Thanks, Big Brother," Nathan returned. "I just try to copy you."

Two days later Darlene approached Rachel with a request. "Rachel, wouldn't you like to have a room all to yourself?" she asked.

"Why?" Rachel asked.

"Because it is lonesome in my room without Glenda. I've got twin beds and I thought Sue Ellen is too big for a crib. She could move in with me."

So Sue Ellen moved in with Darlene. Her comment was, "I'm a big girl now."

XL

Something was wrong with David. Rachel could see it in his eyes, hear it in his voice, notice it in his every movement. "Do we need to talk, Brother?" she asked.

David shook his head. "There isn't anything to say." He continued his pacing of the kitchen where Rachel was baking cookies.

"Why don't you go to bed, then? I'm almost done."

Again David shook his head. "I couldn't sleep."

"I know," Rachel comforted. "That is why I am baking cookies. I know I couldn't sleep either. I think we had best talk it out."

"You have the same problem?" David asked.

Rachel nodded. "Oh, David! How did we let this happen and what are we going to do?"

"I never meant to let it happen, Rachel. I know you didn't either. I don't know what you are going to do, but I know what I've got to do. I promised Mother I would see to these kids being brought up. Sue Ellen is just four. I couldn't ask any girl to wait for me for fourteen years. I'll just have to make Susan understand."

"I've told Tony and told him, but he just says, 'I'll wait.' But David, you could marry, you know. Uncle Pete and the boys can take care of everything and you could live close where you could keep an eye on us."

"No, I promised Mother I would stick. I hate to tell you this, but Uncle Pete is coughing up blood again. He doesn't expect to live through the winter. The boys couldn't handle everything alone."

"Oh, no!" Rachel replied.

"But Rachel," David went on, "don't you think Darlene and the girls could manage without you? I don't want to keep you tied down here being a mother when you want to marry and have a home of your own."

"Like you, I promised Mother. Now with Glenda gone there is even more to do. We will just have to make Tony and Susan understand."

"I hate to lose their friendship, but I guess there is no other way. We can't go on like this."

The next evening after the younger children were all in bed, the two couples were seated in the living room listening to a new record Tony had brought. Rachel jumped up. "I think I will pop some corn," she announced.

"Sounds good!" David agreed.

Tony followed Rachel to the kitchen. "Rachel," he

began, "there is a gospel sing over at Springfield Friday night. The Gospel Harmonies quartet is singing and the Smithson Family. They are two of my favorites. Can't you go with me? I know you would enjoy it."

Rachel shook her head.

"Rachel," Tony continued, coming a step closer to her, "don't you like me at all? I love you so much."

Rachel backed away. "Please sit down, Tony," she said. "We need to talk."

Tony sat down and Rachel took the chair across the table from him.

"Tony," Rachel began, "I never meant this to happen. I told you when we first got acquainted that I could not be your girlfriend. Mother left me to bring up my brothers and sisters. I can't think of having a boyfriend."

"Having a boyfriend isn't getting married, Rachel. Why can't we be just friends for now?"

"Having a boyfriend leads to other things, Tony, as you well know. I don't like to use the word marriage, when you are speaking of just friends, but you said you loved me and I know as well as you do that that is what you have in mind. Tony, I can't get married. I just can't."

"Don't you like me, Rachel, just a little bit?"

"Tony, I like you a whole lot – too much! That is why I can't go on being friends. The longer we let it go on the worse it is going to hurt both of us."

"I'm willing to wait."

"For fourteen years?"

"I'd rather wait for you for fourteen years than to have any other girl."

They argued for fifteen minutes. Tony begged and pleaded, but Rachel was firm. There were no tears.

"I don't like to hurt you, Tony, but you've just got to understand. Just look around you. There are plenty of good Christian girls. If you would just quit looking at me, you might see another one you could like."

Tony stood up, "Well, Rachel," he said, "I have said everything I can think of to say. I'll take myself out of your life, but won't you just let me kiss you once so I'll have something to remember for fourteen years?"

"No! Oh, no! That would be the worst thing I could do. It is hard enough now. That would make it unbearable!"

Rachel totally forgot that she had come to pop some corn. She led the way back to the living room. As they entered, Tony said, "David, I'm going home. Will you see Susan home when she is ready to come?"

Susan jumped up from the chair where she was sitting facing David. "I'll go with you," she said. "I was ready to go anyway. At the door she turned back to Rachel, tears streaming down her face. "I'm going to miss you, Rachel," she said. "You were the best friend I ever had."

As the door closed behind the brother and sister,

Rachel burst into tears. David put his arm around her, but could find no words to comfort her. The ache in his own heart would not have allowed him to speak if he could have found the words.

A gloom settled over the Bradcox home. Susan came no more to cook the evening meal. David and Rachel spoke only when it was required of them. The younger children talked in a whisper, fearful of annoying David or Rachel. Annabelle and Darlene walked to school together and were still best friends, but neither asked to visit the other in her home.

Sunday came and the family went to church. When the Ford family came, both David and Rachel noticed there were only three people. After the service was over, David walked over to where the three were getting into their car. He greeted Bro. and Sis. Ford, then said, "Tony and Susan, they haven't quit church, have they?"

"Oh, no!" Bro. Ford answered. "They went to Springfield to church. They may start going there regularly. Tony said he couldn't come here right now. He said he might not be able to come back here for fourteen years, but he wasn't about to quit God. He said he needed Him now more than he ever did before. I don't know what he meant by fourteen years."

"Both the kids are very badly hurt," Sis. Ford took up the conversation. "Both John and I had hoped it wouldn't end this way. I think if we had all worked together we could have come up with a solution."

David shook his head. "I'm sorry, Sis. Ford. We didn't want to hurt Tony and Susan. Incidentally, we are hurting too. The biggest decisions of life are not always easy, but we have to do what we feel is right regardless of how much it hurts. We both promised Mother."

Bro. Ford answered. "We understand, David. We really do. We believe you are wrong, but we do respect your right to be wrong!"

XLI

Winter came to the area. Week after week the weather was clear and cold, without wind, which made skating the general sport of the community. All of the Bradcox children had skates. Mother Bradcox had been a skater in her youth and had managed skates of every size to hand down from one child to the next.

Just beyond the Bradcox land, Mr. Smith owned a small lake. Although there were signs posted "SKATE AT YOUR OWN RISK," Mr. Smith had posted the signs only for his protection. He had no objection to anyone skating on his lake at any time.

Early in March the weather warmed. "You kids all stay off the lake," David commanded.

"Aw, as thick as the ice is, we'll be able to skate until June," Billy Bob answered.

David gave him a stern look, which he answered with a sullen one. "Billy Bob," David remonstrated, "the ice is thick, yes, but it is rotten."

"Who ever heard of ice rotting? It's not made of potatoes."

David tried to suppress his rising anger. "Billy Bob, ice rots. Besides that, it will all be loose from the banks. It isn't safe. Now do as I say and stay off the ice."

"Yes, Boss," Billy Bob answered.

Billy Bob's eyes turned toward the lake as he passed going to and from school. He saw it drawing farther and farther from the bank. He saw it beginning to break up. "I guess David was right," he said to himself. "It is rotten, although it is still thick."

After several days of warm weather, the temperature took a sudden nose-dive. Overnight the lake froze over. Walking home from school that afternoon, Billy Bob said to Nathan, "Let's hurry with our chores and go skating."

"No, thanks," Nathan answered, "I wouldn't enjoy skating on that."

The lake was no longer smooth for skating. The water had frozen around the floating ice chunks, which extended up a couple of inches above the surface of the water. "I'd like to try it," Billy Bob answered.

"No fun! Anyway, it hasn't been cold long enough. It wouldn't be safe."

Billy Bob said no more. At home he hurried with his chores and then said, "C'mon, Brad, let's take a walk."

"It's too cold," Bradley answered. "I'm going inside."

Mister, as usual, followed Bradley to the door and lay down. Billy Bob whistled to him. "Mister, Old Boy, you come with me. Your company is better than Brad's anyway. You won't tell."

Pete had just come in and taken off his coat. After a spasm of coughing, he sat down to read his Bible. "I wonder where Billy Bob is," he said to Pollianne. "He's usually here by this time." Pollianne, as usual, didn't answer him. Pete returned to his reading.

A whine, then a scratching at the door interrupted Pete's reading. Pete opened the door. There was Mister, but as soon as he saw Pete, he turned away. Pete closed the door and immediately Mister whined and scratched. When Pete again opened the door, Mister turned and ran.

"Maybe he wants me to follow him," Pete thought and grabbing his coat, he left the palace. Mister ran a few steps ahead, then came back to Pete and ran ahead again. "He wants me to hurry." Pete thought. Although the pain in his chest was rather severe, Pete hurried as best he could. Mister ran straight to the lake and right out on to the ice.

"Mister, Old Boy," Pete said, "I can't go out there. The ice wouldn't hold me. I don't know what you want, but whatever it is you'll have to get it yourself." Then he saw a head bob up between the chunks of ice and a hand catch hold of the ice, but after a few seconds, it disappeared again.

"Someone is in trouble," Pete thought. He didn't hesitate. He plunged out on to the ice. His first step broke the ice and got his feet wet, but he managed to get atop a big piece of old ice. "If I can keep to the big pieces," Pete reasoned, "I can make it."

Pete carefully went from ice chunk to ice chunk, hurrying as fast as possible. Billy Bob's head was again above water and he was holding to a piece of ice, but was unable to climb on to it. When Pete finally reached the area where Billy Bob was, all the new ice was broken away. There were no big chunks left close enough for him to reach Billy Bob. "Kick your feet, Billy Bob, like you're swimming and move closer to me." Pete commanded.

Billy Bob tried, but was too cold and too exhausted to move. Finally, taking off his coat, Pete held it by one sleeve. "Now, Billy Bob, I'm going to throw you my coat. You grab it and hold on!"

"God help him!" Pete prayed. "He isn't saved. Please, God."

Billy Bob grabbed the coat and held on. Pete pulled him to his own ice chunk and helped him on to the ice. Billy Bob fell in an exhausted heap.

"Get up, Billy Bob," Pete commanded. "We've go to get home."

"Can't," Billy Bob answered. "I'm so cold!"

Pete picked up his coat and put it back on. It was more wet than dry, but did offer some protection from the wind. Then he jerked Billy Bob to his feet. "Stand up!" he commanded. "We've got to get home! You don't want to *die*, do you?"

It was slow work getting the half-conscious boy to shore. "How am I ever going to get him home?" Pete pondered.

David had just started to take off his shoes when he heard Mister whine at the door and then scratch on it. "No, Mister," he said, "you can't come in. The house is for people, not animals."

Mister whined again, then barked.

"He's cold," Bradley pleaded, "and he's probably forgotten where his house is." Bradley started to open the door.

"Don't go out again, Bradley," David said. "It's too cold. Where is Billy Bob?" No one knew.

"He asked me to take a walk with him," Bradley stated, "but I wouldn't."

David opened the door. Mister turned and ran. "That's odd," thought David. "Mister never has especially liked me, but he has never run from me before."

Mister again whined and scratched. David opened the door. Again Mister turned and ran.

"I think I had better follow him," David said. "Billy Bob may be in trouble. You better go with me, Nate. The rest of you stay inside. It's getting colder and the wind is rising. I think we are in for a real blizzard."

Mister led David and Nathan straight to the lake where they found Pete and Billy Bob on an ice chunk about fifteen feet from shore. Pete was trying unsuccessfully to keep Billy Bob on his feet. David took in the situation at a glance.

"Go quickly, Nathan. Tell Rachel to call Dr. Gillard, then you bring the car back." Nathan left running.

David took out his pocketknife and started whittling down the tallest sapling he could find. He stripped off all the branches, took one end and pushed the other toward Pete. It didn't reach. David looked around for a longer one, but finding none, he again tried to reach Pete with the one he had. The space between the end of the sapling and Pete was more than before. "They're floating farther out," David said to himself. "I'll have to get them, now!"

David walked out into the icy water. He was knee-deep before he could reach the sapling to them. When Pete had a firm hold on the sapling, David turned and walked back to shore, pulling the ice chunk with Pete and Billy Bob after him. Just after he reached the shore, he encountered another problem. The bottom of the ice chunk hit the ground and would come no farther. "Can you bring him ashore, Uncle Pete?" David asked.

"I don't know, but I will try. I think my feet are frozen."

Nathan brought the car to a stop and jumped out. "I took time to grab a couple of blankets," he said.

"Good boy," David answered. He took one blanket and wrapped it around Billy Bob, lifting him to the seat of the car while Nathan wrapped the other around Pete. They arrived home just as Dr. Gillard pulled into the yard.

"What's the problem?" Dr. Gillard asked.

"Three frozen people," Nathan answered.

Dr. Gillard carried Billy Bob into the house while Nathan assisted Pete. "I can't go in there," Pete protested. "Take me to my Palace."

"You get in here right now!" Dr. Gillard ordered. "I'm the doctor and I give the orders." Pete obeyed.

Dr. Gillard carried Billy Bob up to his room and laid him on his own bed.

"Where should I take Pete," Nathan asked. David looked at Rachel. She nodded.

"Put him in Mother's room," David said.

At the door of the room, Pete again resisted. "I can't go in here," he declared.

"Doctor's orders," Nathan replied.

The next two hours was an anxious time. Rachel persuaded David to put on dry clothing and she rubbed his feet until they were red. Sitting in front of the open oven door, David was soon warm again. Dr. Gillard administered to the now unconscious Billy Bob.

Nathan managed to get Pete into a pair of Nathan's own flannel pajamas and into bed, but he was so cold. Nathan rubbed his feet, trying to bring some life back into them.

Darlene appeared at the door with a blanket. "Rachel said to bring you this," she said, handing it to Nathan.

"The electric blanket!" Nathan exclaimed. "Just what I needed! I had forgotten we owned that."

Nathan took the blanket and spread it over Pete. It was soon warm, but Pete continued to shake. "I-I-I'm c-cold!" he stuttered. "I-I-I'm s-s-s-so c-cold!"

When Dr. Gillard felt it was safe to leave Billy Bob, he checked Pete. Then he gave his report to David and Rachel. "I gave Billy Bob something to keep him asleep for a few hours," he said. "Some of his fingers and toes were frozen and the rims of his ears. I've done all I can for him. He will be in some pain and his fingers, toes and ears will peel, but I don't anticipate any serious problems, unless he takes pneumonia. He likely won't. Billy Bob is healthy. Give him hot soup and all of anything you can get him to drink. Keep him in bed as long as possible. I won't give him anything for pain unless it is absolutely necessary. Your mother didn't approve of pain medicine. She called it dope. I rather like to carry out her wishes, even though she is not here anymore."

"Pete is another matter," the doctor continued. "He doesn't have any frostbite. I don't understand why."

"Probably because he had to get back in the water just about the time he should have started to freeze," David interrupted.

"You're likely right. Well, anyway, maybe you know Pete is in bad shape. His lungs – he should be in the hospital, but when I mentioned it, he would not hear of it. He wants to go back to his Palace. He said –" the doctor paused, looked around the room and lowered his voice. "Can you take this?" he asked.

David nodded. "We've known for over two years. The doctor that examined him just before he came here gave him six months to five years."

The doctor went on. "He said he didn't want to die in a hospital. He said he wanted to die at home where people care about him, but he thought you kids wouldn't want him to die in the house. He wants to go back to his Palace."

"Mother died at home. She wanted it that way. We can't properly care for him in the Palace," Rachel commented. "But, Doctor Gillard, does he really have to die? Can't we do something to save him?"

"We will try. If he doesn't get pneumonia he might

pull through, but if he does – there's no hope." The doctor cleared his throat and continued. There's only one chance in a thousand he won't get pneumonia." He paused, and then continued. "Pete doesn't mean that much to you kids, does he? I know you care about him, but I understand he isn't related or anything. He's just a hired man, isn't he?"

"Uncle Pete means a lot more to us than a hired man," David answered. "He isn't a hired man. He has worked for just his living going on three years now. He cares about us and we all love him. He's like – he's like the Dad we should have had, but didn't."

Billy Bob awoke about midnight and asked what happened to supper. Rachel fed him all the hot soup he could hold, then left him a pitcher of orange juice, with instructions to drink all he could if he woke during the night.

Billy Bob was up at the usual time the next morning, but when he attempted to put on his socks and shoes he couldn't stand the pain.

"Looks like you are going to get a few days school vacation," David commented.

"Hadn't I better stay home, too," Nathan wanted to know, "to help care for Uncle Pete?"

"I can take care of Uncle Pete," Billy Bob boasted. "I can do that without my shoes."

Pete was too weak to be up although he tried. Billy

Bob stayed with him every minute.

"Billy Bob, can't you help me to my Palace?" Pete asked, pleadingly.

"Noo-o," Billy Bob answered. "David and Rachel want you here. We all do."

"But I shouldn't be here!"

"Now you listen to me for once, Uncle Pete. It's cold in your Palace. If you went back, I'd have to move in with you to keep the fire going. You're not able to be up. You will be more comfortable here and it will be a lot easier to take care of you. When you are better, able to walk again, then you can move back to your palace."

"I'm not going to get better, Billy Bob. I'm going to die."

"You can't *die*!" Billy Bob exclaimed. "God wouldn't let that happen."

"Why wouldn't he, Billy Bob?" Pete asked. "I told you I've lived a bad life. I have destroyed my body. It's worn out. Gone! I'm not going to make it this time."

"B-but you are living for God now. Why can't He heal your body?"

"He could, Billy Bob, but I haven't asked him to. I asked him to let me live until I could get things made right with Him. He did! Then I asked him to give me a couple years more so I could help you kids a little. He did! Billy Bob, I won't ask for more. I'm *almost* content to go. There is only one thing more I want, then I want to see my God!"

Billy Bob started to cry. "B-but but if you *die* that means I will have killed you. I don't want to be a murderer. I never want to kill anyone, certainly not *you*!"

"You won't be a murderer, Billy Bob. That word is for folks who intentionally kill people. You didn't mean to do it. You didn't even ask me to go after you. How do you figure you are to blame?"

Billy Bob hung his head. "David told me to stay off the lake," he said in a small voice. "If I hadn't disobeyed, it wouldn't have happened."

Pete reached out and pulled Billy Bob to him. "I know, Billy Bob, but you didn't kill me. Consider that I gave my life to save yours. But Billy Bob, that wasn't such a big thing. Jesus Christ gave His life to save you eternally. The difference is I was going to die anyway. I wouldn't have made it until spring. Jesus wasn't going to die anyway. He came to earth just for that purpose – to die so you and I might live." Pete stopped, swallowed, and tears came to his eyes. "I could die happy if you had the Holy Ghost, Billy Bob. I would just like to know I'll see you again in Heaven."

Rachel stopped peeling potatoes. "What's all the yelling I'm hearing in Uncle Pete's room?" she asked.

"Oh, that's just Billy Bob getting the Holy Ghost," Greg answered. "Uncle Pete told him he's going to die and he wanted Billy Bob to get the Holy Ghost first. Is Uncle Pete really going to die, Rachel?"

"Billy Bob getting the Holy Ghost? Oh, Praise God!" Rachel dropped her paring knife and headed for Pete's room. By the time Billy Bob had finished speaking in tongues, all of the children had gathered from the four quarters of the house. It was a joyous time of rejoicing and praise.

After Billy Bob had hugged all of his brothers and sisters, he went back to Pete. "Thank you, Uncle Pete," he said. "Thank you for saving my life and for helping me to get my soul saved. I still don't want you to die, but I'm glad you can die happy."

"Billy Bob," Pete spoke softly, hesitantly. "There is one thing more I'd like you to do for me."

"What, Uncle Pete? I'll do anything I can for you," Billy Bob answered.

"Don't you feel like a new person?"

"Yes."

"You *are* a new person. The old Billy Bob is gone! Shouldn't the new person you are have a new name? From now on I think you should be called 'Robert.'"

XLII

It was Friday. Pete had been down for two weeks. He was running a low-grade fever and was gradually growing weaker. Billy Bob, or rather Robert, had put on his shoes and limped off to school. Because of Robert's feet, David had allowed Nathan to drive the car to school.

David entered Pete's room with a glass of orange juice and a straw and sat down by the bed. "How are you feeling today, Uncle Pete?" he asked cheerfully.

"Blue," was the prompt reply.

"I'm sorry," David answered. "Is there anything I can do? Won't you tell me about it?"

Pete spoke, his voice hardly above a whisper. "Robert tells me that you and Rachel have both had a falling out with the Ford kids."

David didn't answer.

"David, I know I have no right to interfere in the way you run your life, but all summer when those kids were coming here so much, I thought it meant two more weddings. They seemed like such nice kids. Then toward fall they stopped coming and you and Rachel both got the blues. I supposed it to be just a little quarrel and would soon be patched up, but I waited and waited. May I ask a question?"

David nodded.

"Is something really wrong between you or do you just feel you can't get married?"

"We promised Mother!"

"Promised your mother what?" Pete tried to raise himself up on one elbow, then fell back. "Did you promise your mother you wouldn't marry, David?"

"I promised Mother I'd raise the kids. So did Rachel. We've got to keep our promises. We can't marry."

"So you think you couldn't raise the kids if you got married? How funny! I thought that was one of the reasons *to* get married – to raise kids."

"Uncle Pete, you don't understand. How could I get married? Mother always taught me when a person gets married they have to establish a home. I don't feel I can leave Nathan in charge. If I came back every day and helped, how would I finance my own home? It takes money to set up a home."

"David, this home is already established. Use it."

"You mean bring Susan here? What about Rachel?"

"Rachel and Tony, if I am not mistaken, are just

as much in love as you and Susan. Why shouldn't they marry?"

"Rachel won't do it. She'd never leave the kids."

"David, I didn't say anything about leaving the kids. This house is big enough for all of you."

"Mother always said no house is big enough for two families."

"Then make it one family."

David had to lean down close to Pete's mouth to hear the last words. Pete had exhausted himself talking. David smoothed his sheet, fluffed his pillow and spoon-fed him some of the orange juice.

Pete mouthed the words, "Want to rest," and closed his eyes.

When Robert entered the room after school, Pete was awake and smiling. "Hi, Robert," he said feebly. "I'm glad you got home. I wanted to see you again. I'm going home tonight."

Robert reached out and rubbed Pete's head. "You are home, Uncle Pete," he said.

Pete shook his head. "This is not my real home, Robert. This is only temporary. I am going to my eternal home. Tonight will be the night."

Robert nodded. Tears ran down his cheeks. He couldn't push any words past the lump in his throat.

Pete reached out and took Robert's hand. "Don't cry,

343

Robert," he said. "We'll meet again. My time here is over, but you still have some time. Make the most of it, Robert. Don't waste it as I did mine."

Robert nodded again.

Pete rested a few minutes and then continued. "I can't talk much. Too weak. I need to talk to the Ford kids and to David – not together. Can you get them?"

Robert left on the run. He passed David coming in from outside. "Pete says tonight is the night. He wants the Ford kids. You and Rachel get out of sight."

It took some persuasion to convince Tony and Susan that they should go to Pete, but Robert was persistent. Tony and Susan were in Pete's room about ten minutes. Then they left without encountering anyone.

Next, Robert went in search of David. He found him pacing the floor of his room. "He wants to talk with you now," Robert said.

The Doctor arrived and he and David went to Pete's room together. "He says he is going tonight," David said.

The doctor agreed. "I thought when I was here last night it would be about another twenty-four hours." The doctor checked Pete's temperature and his pulse. "The heartbeat is definitely getting weaker. He won't last the night. Do you want me to come back after I've made my rounds and stay until it is over?"

"I'll call you if I do."

The doctor left and David went back to Pete's room. He drew a chair up beside Pete's bed, sat down and took his hand. "Don't you want me to call your people now?" he asked.

Pete hesitated, then shook his head. "If they won't forgive me I don't want to know it. You have the information?"

"Right here in the dresser drawer," David answered.

"Open it as soon as I am gone."

"Is there any message to them?"

"Tell them –" Pete paused. "Tell them I'm sorry for everything. Tell them God has forgiven me and I hope they will. Tell them I love them so very much and I'm oh, so sorry for what I did."

"Is there anything else I can do for you, Uncle Pete? You've done so much for us, we'd like to do something for you."

"Marry the Ford kids!"

David let the tears fall for a while, then shook his head. "It wouldn't work," he finally said.

"Make it work!" Pete snapped in a whisper. After a few minutes, he spoke again. "May I see the other kids, all of them? Would they be afraid?"

"I don't think so. I'll get them."

David assembled the family and told them Uncle Pete was dying. Most of the children started to cry. "What's dying?" Sue Ellen asked.

David took the little girl on his knee and explained as best he could how that Uncle Pete would leave his body and go to be with Jesus. Then they would bury his body in the ground in the cemetery the way Mother was buried. "Do you want to go tell Uncle Pete good-bye?" he asked.

"Yes." Sue Ellen answered.

David admonished all the younger children to be very quiet as the rest of the family joined Robert in Pete's room.

"He's getting weaker," Robert whispered.

Sue Ellen walked up to the bed. "Kiss Unca Pete bye," she said.

David picked her up and held her down where she could kiss Pete's cheek. "Good Unca Pete," she said. "Bye, now." Tears ran down the side of Pete's face and dropped on his pillow.

"You other kids want to kiss him good-bye?" David asked. One by one they came, first Gregory, then Bradley, Letitia, Alicia, Patricia, Darlene, and Nathan. Then Darlene took the younger children from the room. Robert wrapped his arms around Pete and sobbed. Then he kissed him good-bye. Pete's eyes went to David. David leaned over him. "Thanks, Uncle Pete," he said. "Thanks so much for all you have done for us. We do wish you could stay with us, but we know you are ready for your heavenly home." Then he, too, kissed him good-bye.

Pete's eyes sought Rachel's. When she saw the pleading look in his eyes, she could no longer resist. She leaned over and kissed him on the forehead. "We love you, Uncle Pete," she said.

"Thank you," Pete whispered. "Thank you all." Then he closed his eyes and lapsed into a coma.

David called Dr. Gillard. He and Robert stayed in Pete's room. The younger children all went to bed. Rachel and Nathan sat in the kitchen and waited.

Robert sat by the bed and held Pete's hand, feeling the pulse grow weaker. When at last he could feel it no longer, he nodded to Dr Gillard and ran from the room.

It was about 1:00 a.m. when David entered the kitchen. In his hand was the little packet labeled Pete's Identity. "I thought I wanted you with me when I opened this," he said.

"I'd better get Robert," Nathan said.

When the two returned to the kitchen, David took out his knife, cut the end off the packet, and let the contents slide out on to the table.

The first piece David picked up was a wallet size picture of his mother when she was young. "How did he get that?" David pondered. Then he picked up another, which proved to be a copy of his parent's marriage license, then a drivers license. William Robert Bradcox, it said.

David let out a cry. "Oh, Rachel, Nathan, Robert," he said. "He was our Father!"

Dr. Gillard entered the room. "We need to call a funeral home, David," he said. "Do you know what you want done with him?"

"Yes," David answered. "Call Steeman's! He was our Father. We will lay him beside Mother."

Rachel sighed. "I wish Glenda could know," she said.

"I believe she does," David answered. "I believe Uncle – Dad told her."

The family was slow getting up and around the next morning. It was nearly 9:00 by the time the chores were all done and breakfast over. David sat down to think, then he called the Ford residence and asked for Tony. "Tony, would you and Susan please come over?" he asked.

Tony and Susan arrived promptly. David took them, with Rachel into the parlor and seated them. "We've had quite a shock," he told Tony and Susan. "Uncle Pete is gone and we have found out that he was our Father."

"Oh!" Susan exclaimed, "Why didn't he tell you before?"

"It is a long story, Susan. I'll tell you all about it sometime, but for right now, let's just say he had done some things that he was afraid we wouldn't forgive."

"He *was* our father," David went on. "Ever since we lost Mother we have tried to live and do whatever she would have had us do if she had been here. Now that we know we had a father, I'm thinking maybe we should obey him some." David stopped speaking and looked around. No one spoke. Then he continued. "He wanted us to get married."

Rachel and Susan both started to cry.

"Sounds good to me." Tony said.

"How can we?" Rachel asked.

"I've been thinking," David answered. "We have enough room. We could all live here. Susan could be in charge of the kitchen and you could raise the kids and take Glenda's place sewing. Tony has his job and I can continue as I am. We could make it."

"But Mother always said one house isn't big enough for two families," Rachel objected.

"We will have to make it one family."

"I'm sure with God's help we can make it work," Tony agreed. "Dad has deeded me a piece of the home place to build a house. I'll put most of my wages in here, but I'll save enough so I can build a house. Then after thirteen years, seven months and eighteen days, Rachel and I can move over there. Is that all right with you, Rachel?"

I – I guess so," Rachel answered. "If you think it is all right, David. I sure wouldn't want to break my promise to Mother." She arose and went to Tony's outstretched arms.

"Susan?" David asked as he stretched out his arms to her.

"Yes! Oh, yes!" Susan replied, running to David.

"It's a nice warm day. May I walk to church this morning?" asked Robert at the breakfast table, early one April Sunday morning.

"Why, I guess so," David answered. "Why would you want to do that?"

"Oh, I like the sunshine and sometimes I just like to take a walk – alone."

"I guess that cuts me out," Nathan said. "I was just going to suggest walking with you."

"Robert ignored him and turned back to David. "And please, Big Brother," he went on, "would you please, just this once retract your rule that we can't sit in the back? I promise I won't chew gum, carve my initials in the pew, write in the songbook, fidget, or whisper. *Please*, Big Brother."

"All right," David answered. "You haven't caused me any problems in a long time now. I guess I can trust you."

"I wonder what Robert is up to now," David pondered to Rachel, after Robert had left the house.

"I have no idea," Rachel replied.

It was five minutes until ten. The Bradcox family was all seated in their usual place, but Robert had not arrived.

"What shall I do, Rachel?" David whispered. "Shall I go look for him?"

Rachel shook her head. "I believe he will come," she said.

At exactly 9:59 the door opened and fifteen boys of Robert's schoolmates filed silently into the back pews of the church, Robert among them.

"Most of them have promised to come back tonight," Robert announced at dinner.

"How did you do it?" David asked. "How did you get them all to come?"

"Oh, I just kept after them until they all agreed," Robert answered. "I decided if I was going to take Dad's place being a missionary, I should be getting some practice."

THE END

LaVergne, TN USA
31 December 2009
168685LV00001B/3/P